FRIENDS

Gary Hope

"Friends," by Gary Hope. ISBN 978-1-947532-28-1 (softcover).

Published 2017 by Virtualbookworm.com Publishing Inc., P.O. Box 9949, College Station, TX, 77842, US.

Travel leaves you speechless, then it turns you into a storyteller.

PREVIOUS WORKS OF FICTION BY THE AUTHOR:

"It's Too Late To Die Young Now"

"Abbey"

"The Girl From Tir-na-nOg"

"The Confluence"

"Niamh"

1

"HELLO."

"Bill?"

"What?

"What are you doing?"

"Nothing."

"This is Allen."

"I know who you are."

"I have a question to ask you."

"Okay."

"You're not even interested in what sort of question it might be or what it's about?"

"No."

"Sometimes I wonder why I even call you. You never call me, you never ask me anything, and you don't seem to care about anything. What's wrong with you?"

"Is that your question?"

"No, it's not my question! I've got a good mind to hang up and call one of my other friends."

"You don't have any other friends. I'm the only one left who'll talk to you."

Allen thought about that for a few seconds and tried his best to think of a friend he could call. He couldn't. So he said, "Are you going to answer my question or not?"

"Yes."

"Is that your answer?"

Bill thought about hanging up, but he knew Allen would just call him right back. "What's your question, Allen?"

"Do you want to take a trip with me?"

"Sure."

"Don't you want to know where? Or, when? Or, for how long? Can't you just ask a question for once in your life?"

"Okay," Bill answers, "driving or flying?"

Allen hung up the phone, but after a few moments of calming down and thoughtful examination of his life, he remembered that Bill is his best and oldest friend. Allen's wife died eight months ago of liver cancer and his two children have their own lives in a different part of the country. And, Bill was right. He has alienated his other so-called friends who are still living. The other friends he and Bill had have either died off or moved away. Those things happen when you're sixty-nine years old.

Bill's phone rang again and he answered, "Hello."

"Is this Bill?" Bill didn't answer because he knew Allen was just messing with him. "Are you there?"

"Yes, I'm here."

"We'll be driving. Do you still want to go?"

"Not in your car."

Allen was a little indignant at this statement. "What's wrong with my car?"

"It's an old man's car."

"Well, I am an old man, just like you, my OLD friend."

"I'm not taking a trip in an eleven year old Buick."

Allen then said, "Well, hayseed, lucky for you that I'm renting us a car to drive."

"What kind of car?" Bill asked.

"The kind of car that will pull a camper where we can sleep at night and bring stuff with us that we'll need on such an epic journey. The kind of car that we can pick up women with and have a romp in the hay. The kind of car that's called a pickup truck."

"Okay."

"Okay?" Allen nearly screamed into the phone. "That's all you can say, Okay? You're not interested in where we're going that we'll need a camper? Or how long we'll be gone that we'll need a camper? Not even interested in what sort of women we could pick up in a camper?"

"We're not going to pick up any women."

"Speak for yourself, old man. Where I come from, men never stop trying to pick up women. And, I'm not nearly as old as you are and I'm twice as good-looking."

Bill thought for a moment, then said, "We're from the same place. I'm three months younger than you, twice as smart, and have more hair than you."

"Having more hair in your ears and in your nose don't count."

"Goodbye." Bill said, "Call me the night before you're ready to leave so I can pack." He hung up the phone, thinking to himself that he hopes his friend Allen is serious about this so-called trip. Unlike Allen, Bill's wife left him nearly a dozen years ago. Just walked in the house one day and told him she didn't want to be married anymore—at least, not to him. She packed some bags and left. Their lawyers worked out the details and Bill has been alone ever since.

He dated several women from the church over the years, but most of the women were interested in conversations with more than one word answers. And he rightly assumed that many of the women who were interested in him were more interested in his money than his personality. Bill and Allen both had been supervisors for RJ Reynolds Tobacco Company and had not only made nice salaries, but had received excellent benefits, pensions and stock options when they retired. They were set financially for the rest of their lives. Now, they just wanted to have a life.

The two old friends went to the same high school in Winston-Salem together, graduated together, and went to Appalachian State University together. They were in each other's weddings and played golf, softball and fished with each other—all their lives. They worked together nearly forty years before retiring. Allen's retirement party was held at Ryan's, one of the most exclusive restaurants in town. His wife arranged it all and nearly everyone from their church and social groups had come to celebrate the big day.

Bill, unlike Allen, had turned in his retirement notice to his Vice-President and the Human Relations Department and asked them to keep it quiet. He didn't want anyone to know. On his last day at work, he walked around and visited some of his long-time co-workers. He told them how he enjoyed their friendship and dedication. He didn't tell them he was retiring—even when they asked if he was retiring. He just didn't show up for work the next Monday morning. His phone rang off the hook that Monday, but he never answered a single call. Even when Allen drove over to his house and knocked on the door, he didn't answer. He had no party and no celebration, other than he drank a Coors Light and had an Iron Maiden as he sat and remembered all the years.

Now, the two old friends were about to embark on an epic journey. Bill had no idea where they were going or how long they'd be gone. Allen sort of knew where they were going, but he, too, had no idea how long it would take. Neither cared about time, neither cared about an agenda . . . they only cared about what was important in life—that you live.

The morning after the initial phone call, Allen rang Bill again. "Can I please speak with Bill?"

"Yes."

"Is this Bill?" Silence on the other end. After giggling to himself, Allen then asked, "Do you care where we go?"

"No."

"Is there anything or anyplace you'd particularly like to visit?"

"No."

"Okay, then I'll plan everything."

"Fine."

"I don't want to hear any complaining or griping about my choices." Allen waited a few seconds for a response, but he knew there wouldn't be one. "There'll be no grumbling, whining, weeping or malcontent behavior on this trip. Do you understand?"

"Oh, shut up. When do we leave?"

"I can't believe you actually asked a question. I'll have to mark this day down in history. If it's okay with your social calendar we'll leave Saturday morning. There's a certain young lady I have to service Friday night before we go—if you know what I mean."

Bill knew Allen had not even thought of a woman since his wife died eight months ago. "I know exactly what you mean: you need to service your hemorrhoids Friday night, in preparation for the trip. See you Saturday morning. Goodbye."

2

ALLEN THOUGHT HE SHOULD CALL his two children to let them know he'd be on a trip for a while. He wasn't really sure if they would care or not, but just the same, he'd tell them. They both pretended to care about him because they each knew they stood to inherit a good sum of money one day. Actually caring was something else altogether.

He called his oldest first, his daughter, Anna, named for the main character in one of his favorite books, "Anna Karenina." She answered on the first ring, "Dad, great to hear from you. Is everything okay?"

"Yeah, honey. I'm great. Have you got any plans to come visit your old man anytime soon?" He wanted to make sure before he told her of his upcoming trip. But since she hadn't actually visited him in nearly three years, he felt he was pretty safe. Apparently, the trip from New York to North Carolina was just too much for her and her "busy" husband to fit into their schedules. Before his wife, Barbara, died, Allen and she would visit their daughter in New York at least two to three times a year.

"I'm sorry, Dad. David's job keeps him so tied up we're not able to do anything anymore. We seldom leave the house."

"I understand, honey. I wanted to let you know I'll be going on a trip for a few weeks and won't be home." He then wondered how to explain the trip to her, since he didn't actually know how long he'd be gone, or exactly where he was going.

She made it easy for him by answering, "Okay, Dad. I hope you have fun. Call me when you get back, okay?"

"Sure, honey. I love you. Tell David I said hello."

"Will do. Bye, Dad."

Now the call to his son, John, who lived across the country in Reno, Nevada. Allen wanted to name his son after his favorite author, Ernest Hemingway, but his wife protested that she would not have a son named

6

Ernest. So they compromised and chose the name of an author they could both agree on, John Steinbeck.

He waited an hour or so, because of the time difference, then called John who still sounded rather sleepy when he answered the phone.

"Hey son, did I wake you up?"

"Dad?"

"Yeah, how many other people call you son?"

"Why are you calling so early? Is everything alright?"

It was 11:30 on the east coast, making it 8:30 in Reno. Allen didn't think this was early. "Yeah, son, sorry about the time thing, everything is fine. I wanted to let you know that I'll be out of the house for a bit, I'm taking a trip and I wanted to let you know."

His son yawned and said, "Wow, you and Anna both taking trips at the same time. That's great. I hope you have fun."

Anna taking a trip? Allen just spoke with Anna, she told him they were "too busy" to make any trips. He asked his son, "I forget, where did Anna say she was going?"

"She and David are going to New Orleans for a week, then driving over to the casinos in Mississippi for a few days. Should be a great vacation for them."

Allen was silent for a moment or two . . . thinking. He son asked him, "You still there, Dad?"

"Yeah, son. I'm still here."

"Well, I have to get ready for work, Dad. I hope you have a great trip. Send me a postcard."

Neither of his children even asked where he was going. Neither of them said, "I love you, Dad." One of them blatantly lied to him, the other one probably did, too. But they were still his kids and he loved them. He only wished they were nicer people.

Bill called the post office and the newspaper to let them know he'd be gone. They were both friendly and wished him well. Each of the representatives asked him where he was going on his trip and how long he'd be gone. Bill sat back and thought of some of the trips he and his wife used to take together. Sweet dreams. Then he got out the old DVDs of their trip to Hawaii fourteen years ago and watched them for two hours. Even though she left him twelve years ago, he is still unable to turn his heart off. He has found it nearly impossible to stop loving her.

Allen went to the Ford dealership and picked up his leased Ford F-150 pickup truck. He'd never driven a pickup before, but had always wanted one, as all men have dreamed of at one point in their lives. He was surprised by how plush it was inside—much better than his old Buick. He then drove out to Davie County to pick up the small camper he was leasing. They hooked it up for him and gave him some instructions (which he didn't pay attention to), then asked if he needed any help learning to back up the camper. Most people could drive forward okay, but backing up a camper or trailer was a whole different ballgame.

Allen assured them he was fine. He'd had a riding lawnmower once that had a wagon behind it to haul mulch on. He'd had no problems with it and was sure he'd have no problems with the camper either. The camper and RV center was smart enough to ensure that all new and leased campers were situated on the lot so that all the new owners and lessors had to do was drive straight out to the road. No backing up was needed on the premises. They were an experienced dealership.

Allen drove home, quite proud of his new pickup, pulled in the driveway and got out to admire his new man-toys. This was a great day. This was going to be a great trip. He couldn't wait to get going. He missed his wife so much he wanted to cry. He went inside and finished packing and hauled a bunch of stuff he wouldn't need out to the camper. When he finished everything he went back inside and drank a glass of sweet tea and called Bill.

"Hello."

"Can I speak to Bill, please?"

"What do you want?"

"Are you ready to go?

"Now?"

"No, not now. Sometimes, Bill, you can exasperate the poop out of someone. I've got a good mind to disinvite you from my trip."

"Fine. I'll go on my own trip."

"Really? And just how would you get anywhere without me to drive you and guide and show what to do and make sure you didn't get lost? How do you think you'd do out there all by your lonesome self?"

Bill was silent for a few seconds, then said, "I'd probably enjoy the conversation a lot more."

Allen huffed, "Just be ready when I get there. I ain't waiting on no grumpy, ugly, old man."

Allen pulled up in front of Bill's house promptly at 8:00 in the morning. He got out of his new truck and walked around the front of it. He was admiring his new man-toy when he saw Bill come out his front door carrying some luggage. Bill walked down the steps and set his luggage down while staring at the camper. Allen thought Bill was admiring his new truck, so he walked up to him and said, "That, my friend, is what a man drives."

Bill pointed to the back of the camper and said, "That, my friend, is the bush from your front yard."

Allen jerked around and saw the bush Bill was pointing at. Sure enough, that was the bush his wife had planted next to the driveway about ten years ago. It was stuck underneath the camper, wedged half way in. "Holy crap!" Allen yelled, "How'd that get there?"

Bill was still grinning and said, "Probably some Muslin terrorist came during the night and planted it there trying to get you in trouble with the agriculture department."

It took them both about fifteen minutes to un-wedge the bush from underneath the camper. Then they loaded Bill's stuff in the back and got in the Ford F-150. Allen looked over at Bill and said, "Last chance."

Bill looked back and replied, "If I shot you when I wanted to, I'd be out by now. Take off before I go get my gun."

3

THEY DROVE DOWN TO THE STOP SIGN at the end of the street and Allen said, "Well, my friend, which way?"

Bill replied, "Where's your map? And where is it you're taking us first?"

"I ain't got no map and we ain't got no agenda. We got Mr. Google here to help us if we get lost, but since we don't know where we're going, it'd be hard for us to get lost . . . now wouldn't it? So, tell me, old-timer, where do we go—to the left, where nothing's right? Or to the right, where nothing's left?"

So they took off and got on the road that required the least amount of turns—it happened to be headed south. After they'd driven for a bit Allen asked, "Is there anything in South Carolina you want to see?"

Bill said, "I didn't know there WAS anything in South Carolina."

Allen thoughtfully answered, "Good, cause I ain't going to no Myrtle Beach. But there is a place I'd like to visit in Georgia, if it doesn't upset your plans."

Bill said, "I don't have any plans. And just for the record, why have you started using double negatives in your language and the word 'ain't' in every sentence? If your wife heard you talking like that she'd pop you one."

"Well, I AIN'T working no more. I AIN'T in college no more and I AIN'T got no one to correct me. So, tough!"

Bill smiled and said, "Oh, I don't care. It doesn't bother me at all that you want to sound like some uneducated geech from the back woods of South Carolina. In fact, it rather suits you." They made the uneventful trip through South Carolina and almost stopped to look at a large water tank that was painted to look like a peach. Allen started to say something about it, but changed his mind and adjusted his sunshade instead. When they crossed the state line into Georgia they decided to stop at a Cracker Barrel because they were both hungry and had to go to the bathroom. Over lunch Allen said, "There's a place near here I'd like to see that's been on my mind." Bill looked up from his bowl of pinto beans but didn't say anything. So Allen continued, "I want to go to Macon and visit the Allman Brothers Museum and the Big House where they lived."

Bill stopped eating and looked at his friend and replied, "Good, I loved Duane Allman."

"I know you did. I remember some of those nights in our apartment in Boone. You weren't nearly so quiet in those days my friend. I bet you listened to the Eat A Peach album a thousand times."

Bill set his fork down and said, "And the Fillmore East album too. It still makes me sad about Duane and how good a band they could've been."

They both stopped eating momentarily and reminisced about old times and old days and old friends. They both knew that with the right music, you either forget everything or you remember everything. Bill first kissed his wife-to-be listening to the song Little Martha by the Allman Brothers— he'd never forgotten that. Allen knew this about his friend, that's why he suggested Macon as their first stop. That's what friends do.

They arrived in Macon late in the afternoon and after Googling the address of the museum, they found it to be closed for the day. That wasn't even the bad news. It wasn't open on Sunday and they would have to wait until Monday for it to open again. They found a small diner and had something to eat, then located a campground and drove out to set up their temporary home. Neither of them had a clue how anything worked with the camper. Allen should have paid better attention to the instructions.

It would seem as though two college educated men, with over eighty combined years of experience in manufacturing would be able to figure out how a small camper works. You would think so. Apparently it takes a lot of cursing, kicking, and sweating to get the thing operational. But they finally did. As they laid down in their little beds for the first time, Allen looked over at his friend and said, "I really wish you hadn't eaten that plate of pinto beans today."

Bill was giggling to himself as he answered, "Shut up. Just be glad they weren't pork and beans." They didn't sleep well, but they slept enough. Nobody who is sixty-nine years old sleeps well, it's all a matter of relativity at this age. Sleeping was the least of their problems. At home, when nature called, all they had to do was get up and walk a few steps to the bathroom. Not here. Their camp site was at least fifty yards from the showers and restrooms. Another fact of life at sixty-nine: you must go pee at night. You have no choice and there's nothing you can do about it.

The next morning Allen said he was going to get a 2-liter Pepsi bottle to pee in so he wouldn't have to walk to the public bathrooms. Bill told him to "shut up," while silently thinking that was a great idea. After breakfast they roamed around Macon and visited the site of Duane's motorcycle accident, then they visited the site of the band's bass player, Berry Oakley's, motorcycle accident. Two tragedies that stripped the band of a third of its members and more importantly, its very soul.

They found Macon to be a pleasant little town, but they were anxious for Monday morning so they could visit the museum. It didn't open until 11:00 and they were the only people there when a man older than either of them opened the door. The large three-story Tudor house had been restored into the museum it now was. Back in 1970, Berry Oakley and his wife, Duane and his girlfriend, and Gregg and his girlfriend all lived in the big house (with kids) which they rented for $225 a month. They all had rooms on the upper floors and the band practiced on the lower level. From time to time other members of the band and road crew came and went as semi-regular tenants.

It was a big, happy family affair until October 29, 1971 when Duane was killed in his motorcycle accident. Berry Oakley tried to keep the vibe going, but something died in him with Duane's death. He began having nightmares and became depressed, all of which culminated in his own motorcycle death a year later on the streets of Macon.

Allen and Bill saw some of Duane's old guitars and other memorabilia, and each of them bought a tee shirt to remember their visit. At the exit was a picture of Duane doing what he loved most—playing guitar. They each stared at the picture for a few moments. It took all Bill's will power to hold back the tears he felt coming. Allen put his arm around his friend's shoulder and they walked out to their camper parked there on the street, in front of the Big House at 2321 Vineville Avenue, Macon, Georgia.

Neither of the friends spoke as they rode out of town. Finally Allen said, "I wish I had a doobie on me."

Bill looked over at his friend and could do nothing but laugh. Then he said, "Where are we going next, Mr. Doobie?"

"Over the rainbow, my friend. Over the rainbow."

4

"WE'RE CLOSE TO FLORIDA. Do you want to go down there?"

Bill looked over at his friend and asked, "What's in Florida?"

"A bunch of old people, like us."

"If they look anything like you, then I think I'll pass on Florida."

Allen nodded and said, "Good choice. Time we headed west anyway."

"Any place in particular? 'West' is a pretty broad term."

"Yep," Allen answered, "we're going to Tuscaloosa, Alabama. Home of the Crimson Tide, kings of the college football world."

"And just what are we going to do in Tuscaloosa?"

"We're going to eat some world famous BBQ and tour the campus, then take a look at football's Holy Grail—Bryant-Dennehy Stadium. That's what we're gonna do."

Bill didn't reply right away. He simply looked over at his friend until Allen noticed he was looking at him. Allen said, "What?"

"You knucklehead. Tuscaloosa isn't world famous for BBQ—where'd that come from? And it's Bryant Denny Stadium—not Dennehy. Sometimes you amaze me."

Allen smiled back at his friend and said, "I knew all that. I was testing you to see if you knew."

"Oh, shut up and drive." And they did. They drove in silence as they passed forests and plains, very similar to the land in North Carolina. They went through a few small towns and stopped in one to get something to drink and use the toilets. Then they drove some more. After more than thirty minutes of complete silence, Allen looked over at his friend and quite suddenly asked, "Why are we here, Bill?"

"Because you're driving and this is where you took us."

"No, not that. Why are we HERE?"

Bill knew what he meant. But he didn't know the answer Allen wanted to hear. They were both Christians, but Allen wondered why God chose to take his wife from him. That wasn't fair and he was mad at God for some time afterwards. He knew his wife was in a better place, but why did God punish him? Why was he left alone? It was not fair and he was still looking for answers. Bill knew the answer, but was certain his friend either did not want to hear it right now, or did not want to accept it right now. Either way, he decided to keep quiet for the moment and wait for a more opportune time to approach that subject.

They drove around the campus at the University of Alabama, but could not find a BBQ restaurant to stop at anywhere. They went to the football stadium, which dominated the skyline around the area, and took a guided tour through the press box, the VIP level, and down to the field itself. Allen was happy he was able to stand on the same sideline where Bear Bryant once stood as he directed the Tide all those years ago. He even bought a hounds tooth hat in the gift shop in Bear's honor. He doubted he'd ever wear it, because it looked corny, but he'd display it on the dash of his new Ford F-150 for everyone to see.

They left Tuscaloosa and found a semi-deserted campground on the shores of a small lake for the night. Allen forgot to bring himself an empty 2-liter Pepsi bottle, but they did find a camping slot closer to the bathrooms. They took showers, put on their Allman Brothers tee-shirts, sat outside under a shade tree, and drank a couple of Coors Lights—dreaming of those far away mountains they'd see before this trip was over.

The next morning, while eating pancakes at IHOP, Bill asked, "What's next on the agenda, senor?"

Allen put his fork down and said, "You ain't Mexican."

Bill then put his fork down and said, "But I'm American, and since America is about half Mexican now, I have a right to speak our national language, if I so desire."

Allen took a handful of pills out of his pocket, looked back at Bill, and said, "Sometimes you make a little too much sense for me. Eat your pills too and let's adios."

They started driving west, when Allen asked, "Anything else you want to see in Alabama?"

"Nope."

"How about Mississippi?"

Bill said, "I heard they have some nice casinos on the Mississippi coast. I might like to see that."

Allen, remembering that his daughter lied about visiting him while she planned on vacationing at the Mississippi casinos, roughly said, "NO!"

Bill was taken back a bit by the rough answer and said, "Okay, suit yourself."

"I'm sorry, Bill. I didn't mean it like that. I just can't go there. I'll explain later."

Bill understood. Not totally, but he knew enough. "Well, is there anything else in Mississippi?"

"Yes. I've always wanted to see Vicksburg. They have these high cliffs over the river there, and during the Civil War General Patton used that advantage to beat back the Yanks and win our freedom. I'd like to see 'em."

Bill did not attempt to comment or correct his friend. He knew Allen majored in American History at Appalachian, and he was pretty sure Allen knew the correct history of Vicksburg, as well as who General Patton was, and exactly who did win the war.

They consulted Mr. Google and headed for Vicksburg.

During the drive Allen explained his outburst to Bill. He told him about the phone calls to his daughter (who lied to him) and to his son. Before Bill could comment, Allen started talking about his wife . . . and he continued talking about his wife until they decided to stop early at a nice looking campground they saw. After they checked in and set everything up, they decided to unhitch the camper and drive down the road to look for something to eat. The only problem with that plan was that neither of them knew how to unhitch the camper from the Ford F-150.

Well, they probably could have, being two college graduates and all. But they were afraid if they got it unhitched, they might not be able to hitch it back. So they checked out their cooler and were happy to find they had a couple of Coors Lights left as well as three Diet Pepsi's. They also had a bag of pork rinds and some Doritos left over from yesterday. Obviously, this trip was not a "heart-healthy" vacation.

They had a nice camp site, only three spots down from the bathrooms and under some big oaks for shade. They pulled out their camp chairs and had a Diet Pepsi to unwind with. Their plan was to save the Coors Light for a nightcap, to help them sleep better. As bad luck would have it, the people camping next to them soon started cooking several different kinds of meat on their portable grill. The sweet aromas of chicken, hamburger and sausages soon had Allen and Bill in a state of frenzy. The pork rinds they were nibbling on were not an adequate substitute for the tasty meals they were imagining.

Fortunately, Allen had never met a stranger. And very soon he was best friends with Gurney and Margaret, who were on a trip of their own to visit their grandchildren in Texas. They soon invited Allen and Bill to join them for dinner—they assured the boys they had plenty and wouldn't take no for an answer or accept any sort of payment either. Bill saw their Pennsylvania license plates and thought to himself he'd have to change his opinion of those people from the northern tier of states.

Gurney and Margaret told them all about their daughter, who was married to an Army lifer, who was currently stationed in San Antonio at Fort Sam Houston. They bragged about how smart their grandchildren were, what grades they were in, what sports they played, and then they showed the boys about fourteen hundred pictures of the grandkids. But that was okay. Grandparents should be proud of their grandkids. And the grilled chicken was mighty tasty.

Gurney asked Allen where they were headed to next, after Vicksburg, and Allen answered, "I don't have a clue, Gurney. Wherever the mood strikes us I guess. Do you have any suggestions?"

Gurney and Margaret could not understand how two grown men, college educated, and apparently fairly intelligent, could just take off without any plans. However, Gurney secretly thought to himself, "I wish I was going with them."

Margaret spoke up and said, "Why don't you go to San Antonio, you'd love it. They have a River Walk there and the Alamo is there . . . trust me boys, you'll love San Antonio; it's not like the rest of Texas." So it was decided right there at the camp site, eating grilled chicken and corn on the cob, that they would visit San Antonio (not the rest of Texas) after they finished their tour of the bluffs in Vicksburg.

5

VICKSBURG IS SITUATED ON HIGH BLUFFS above the east bank of the Mississippi River. During the Civil War, or as we southern boys call it, The War Between the States, Vicksburg was an impregnable fortress located high on those bluffs. The Union army, hereafter known as Yanks, decided to starve them out since they couldn't beat them. The good old boys held out for forty-seven days before they did indeed run out of food.

They finally surrendered on July 4, 1863. Robert E. Lee surrendered at Gettysburg the following day. These two events marked the turning point of the war. The cliffs are still there, but now there are casino boats on the shores of the Mississippi River instead of Yankee troops. Allen and Bill parked their Ford F-150 in a lot downtown and took a trolley down to the river where Allen walked to the edge, stuck his hand in the water and felt the muddy river slowly sliding by. He'd always wanted to touch the Mississippi and now he had.

They both stood there in awe of the mighty river. Bill finally spoke saying, "I remember my grandmother teaching me how to spell Mississippi: M, I, crooked-letter, crooked-letter, I, crooked-letter, crooked-letter, I, hump-back, hump-back, I. Funny how you remember things like that." Allen smiled and nodded in complete agreement. They each picked up a rock and had a rock-throwing contest into the river—Bill won, but Allen filed an official protest—to be determined later.

They walked into one of the casino boats and had a bite to eat at the buffet while they watched several scantily clad waitresses who kept bringing drinks to the people at the slot machines. Allen suggested they go try their luck. So, Allen sat down in front of a quarter slot machine while Bill ambled over to a $5 dollar Blackjack table.

On the first hand Bill bet the minimum of five dollars and was dealt a 10 and a 6—a terrible hand in blackjack. The dealer had a face card showing, which was even worse news for Bill. When asked if he wanted another card, or if he wanted to hold, Bill held—against all odds. The dealer turned over his other card and it was a 2. Then he took another hit and turned over a face card—busted! Bill won his five dollars, got up from the table and went to the cashier to cash out his five dollar winnings.

Allen was down $4.50 when Bill found him. He said, "One more quarter and we leave." He deposited the final quarter and picked up his "free" drink the scantily clad waitress had brought him and they walked out of the casino on the Mississippi River. Together, they were up twenty-five cents on their gambling expedition, which was a lot better than most people could ever claim.

When they got back to the truck Allen looked over at the bridge and said, "Do you think that there thing can hold this here Ford F-150, hauling a Bear Bryant hat, and two he-men from North Carolina?"

Bill took a deep breath and said, "I sure hope so, cause I do not want to drive all way back across Mississippi again." They crossed the bridge, uneventfully, and asked Mr. Google for the most direct route towards San Antonio, Texas.

The most direct route took them, unfortunately, across Louisiana. The only thing of remembrance in Louisiana was a bug storm they ran through. The flying insects were so thick and splattered the windshield so badly that Allen had to turn on the windshield wipers for about five minutes so that he could see. Bill said, "How in the world does anybody live in this state?"

"They don't. People only live in New Orleans, which is really not a part of Louisiana. They seceded during the Revolution and have their own government, parliament, and king."

Bill nodded and took a sip of the Diet Pepsi he was holding, then asked, "Well what about LSU? People live in Baton Rouge don't they?"

"No, not at all. They commute there from New Orleans. In fact, their football team actually lives in dorms at the Superdome in New Orleans and they fly them to the games in Baton Rouge on a private jet."

Bill said, "How do you know so many interesting facts about Louisiana?"

"I dated a girl from New Orleans once. Met her in a nightclub at Myrtle Beach. She was a true beauty and she told me all that stuff and she also told me I was the handsomest man she'd ever met."

Bill thought about this a moment, then said, "Well, every girl I've ever met in a nightclub at Myrtle Beach has always told me the truth. So, except for the part about you being handsome—I believe her."

Allen smiled and said, "Trust me, son. You'd believe anything this girl told you."

The boys decided to take a break from camping and find a nice Holiday Inn to spend the night. They found a Hampton Inn instead, which was a tad nicer, with a much better free breakfast in the morning. At the hotel bar that evening there was a young lady playing a guitar and singing songs for entertainment. She played a few unknown tunes then asked for any requests from the nine guests in the bar area. No one spoke up so Allen stood up and said, "How about Blue Bayou by Linda Ronstadt?"

The girl said, "I don't know that one. Any others?"

Allen replied, "When Will I Be Loved."

"Sorry, I don't know that one either."

"Well how about anything by Linda Ronstadt?"

The young girl strummed a chord, then looked up and asked, "How about anything from this century?"

Before Allen could erupt, Bill took his arm, pulled it, and said, "Calm down, big boy; it'll be alright."

Allen sat down and told his friend, "I loved Linda . . . heck, I think I still love Linda. That girl needs a spanking and a history lesson and a singing lesson!"

"I know. Young people suck. Let's go to bed."

The Hampton Inn had two very comfortable queen sized beds—at least they felt very comfortable after several nights in a camper. As they lay in their queen sized beds after showering, Allen asked Bill again, "Why are we here, Bill? And I don't mean here in the Holiday Inn."

"We're in a Hampton Inn."

"Quit stalling and give me the answer."

Bill took a few seconds, then said, "We're here to glorify God and serve Him."

Allen then also took a few seconds and replied, "All of us Christians want to serve God, son. That's easy."

"Not really. Many of us want to serve God, but only as advisors."

Allen thought about this statement and realized the truth in it, but didn't want to admit it. Then he rolled over and turned the light off and asked Bill, "Well if you're so smart, what's your goal in this crazy, ridiculous thing we call life?"

Without any hesitation at all, Bill replied, "To glorify Him and hopefully die young as late as possible. Now go to sleep."

They finally hit I-35 around Dallas and started south towards San Antonio. Allen had turned over the driving chores to Bill and was finishing a bacon and egg biscuit when he suddenly yelled out, "Wait. Stop! Turn around, I forgot something."

Bill said, "Too late now brother, we aren't going all the way back to the Hampton Inn just because you forgot your toothbrush."

"Not my toothbrush, I forgot something in Dallas. Something I want to see there. Turn this monster around."

Allen didn't have to explain any further; Bill knew what he wanted to see. He wanted to see it too, but he had also forgotten about Dealey Plaza. They turned around and programmed Mr. Google to take them to the infamous site that no one who was alive in 1963 would ever forget. They found a parking lot about three blocks away and walked over to the roadside. They stood on the spot they'd seen in thousands of photographs, and they walked up to the area known as the "grassy knoll." They were both surprised just how small this area is that had such a large impact on America and the world. They stared up at the School Book Depository just down the road. They stood and stared for quite a while.

After untold and unknown minutes, a woman walked past them and saw them staring at the building and said, "They have a nice museum in there and you can even walk up to the sixth floor if you want to."

They didn't want to. It was hard enough forgetting all the things they'd already seen this morning. They didn't need anymore. They walked in silence back to their Ford F-150 and found the southbound lane of I-35 once again. San Antonio had to be better than this.

6

ALLEN HAD DOZED OFF, and Bill enjoyed the time alone with his thoughts while driving down the interstate. As always, when his mind had time to wander, it kept wandering back to Eliza, his ex-wife. He couldn't help it. He had re-lived their last conversation over and over throughout the years. He thought of so many things he should've said and wished he had said—but didn't. It all seemed to happen in a flash. She simply said she didn't love him anymore and that she was leaving. Unbeknownst to him at the time, she had already moved out a lot of her personal stuff beforehand.

He had loved her from the first time he kissed her during that Allman Brothers song. He never stopped loving her a single day during their marriage—or since their divorce. He couldn't help it. Some ladies from his church used to keep in touch with Eliza before she moved to Hilton Head. But after she left Winston, she cut ties with all her old friends. Bill hadn't heard a word or a rumor from her in the last six years. Nor had his feelings for her changed in the last six years.

He didn't tell anyone his thoughts, especially Allen. None of them would understand. They'd only think he was living in a dream world. But for Bill, his imagination was the only weapon he had in the war against reality.

He glanced over as he saw a little movement from Allen—he must be waking up. Allen did indeed yawn and stretch his arms before he spoke, "Well tell me this, smarty-pants, if John Wilkes Booth didn't shoot him . . . who did?"

Bill shook his head and thought, "There is no way under this Texas blue sky that I'm going to open up that can of worms."

"How much farther?" Allen asked.

"We're close. What do you want to do first?"

"First, I want to pee. Then I want to go to that River Walk old Margaret told us about and sample some genuine Mexican food."

Bill nodded and said, "Okay. You do realize that 'old Margaret' is younger than us don't you?"

"Only in years, buddy. Only in years."

Finding a suitable parking place for the Ford F-150 and camper in downtown San Antonio was not easy or cheap. But it was worth it. The River Walk has been described as "The American Venice," and it's easy to see why. The sights, sounds, and flavors of Old Mexico, the Wild West, and Native America all blend effortlessly into a flowing, festive atmosphere that could charm anyone. The boys first decided to get a Coors Light and take a riverboat tour up and down the "river." Hotels, bars, restaurants, and all sorts of shops and specialty stores lined the banks.

They disembarked at one of the bars next to the river to relax and enjoy the scenery and have a plate of nachos with their Coors Lights. As Allen strained himself watching a group of college-aged girls pass by, Bill looked at him and said, "Remember, son, you're still a Christian."

Allen never took his eyes off the college girls and replied, "Yep, I'm a Christian alright, but I ain't blind or dead yet either."

They walked along the banks of the river and stopped at another bar, then at a restaurant. Their waitress was a young Hispanic girl with a beautiful smile and wearing a very short skirt. Allen told the young waitress to give him the hottest sauce they had on his burrito. No amount of Coors Light, no matter how cold it was, could stop the burning in his mouth when he bit into that burrito. Bill laughed and the young waitress apologized as Allen found it difficult to catch his breath. After much wheezing and coughing, Allen finally recovered enough to take a long, soothing drink of ice water. Bill, looked at him and said, "Well? How was it?"

Allen took another drink of ice water and replied, "Nothing adventured, nothing gained." The young waitress brought him another burrito, one that was suitable for an old man from North Carolina, and it was very good. She told him she was worried about him, after his wheezing and coughing episode, and she kept asking if he was okay. Allen left her a sizeable tip and some wise advice: "Worry less, smile more."

They walked up and down the walkway and stopped at several bars and public areas along the way. They didn't drink any more Coors Lights because they weren't twenty-five years old anymore and they didn't get in any trouble either, because they weren't twenty-five years old anymore. Bill stopped in one tourist shop and bought a Tim Duncan tee shirt. He'd briefly met Tim at a sub sandwich shop in Winston-Salem when Tim was in school there at Wake Forest. Bill had been wearing a white ball cap at the time, and Tim signed the bill of the cap for him. It was still one of Bill's prized possessions.

They decided they'd better get some sleep so they'd feel good in the morning when they visited their last stop in San Antonio, The Alamo. They were both looking forward to that. As they ate bowls of cereal in the morning, Allen began filling Bill in on the Alamo's history as only Allen could tell it. "The Mexicans were mad at us because we wouldn't build a wall to keep out all the Americans from crossing the Rio Grande and going down there to steal all the beautiful women. They were mad we were taking the pretty ones back to the U.S. and leaving the ugly ones for them. So they decided to attack us and teach us a lesson. What they didn't know was that John Wayne, Gary Cooper, Daniel Boone and Davey Crockett had set up the Alamo to withstand all enemy rockets and submachine gun fire.

But those crazy Mexicans listened to their leader, Fernando Valenzuela, and kept attacking us anyway. After seventy-two hours of non-stop fighting, both sides called a truce and we came to an agreement. We promised to not come down there and steal any more women and they promised to only invade California in the future. And since California wasn't actually a state yet, nobody cared. In hindsight, we shouldn't have been so careless, but Daniel Boone was the commander in charge and they all trusted him. And that, my friend, is the story of The Alamo. And we're going to see it this morning."

Bill never commented or corrected his friend. He just nodded and ate his cereal while looking forward to visiting the "real" Alamo. They weren't sure how long it would take to actually drive to The Alamo, but they set the directions in Mr. Google and took off. Turns out they found The Alamo in about four minutes. Incredibly enough, The Alamo is in downtown San Antonio surrounded by skyscrapers, parking lots and doughnut shops. It was a tad bit disappointing.

Apparently, the city had grown up around the famous old fort and totally engulfed it, which certainly took away some of the mystique and romance from Allen's story. But they visited the old fortress and felt the bullet holes in the walls and listened to the tour guides tell their version of what happened here. (Allen liked his version better—so did Bill.)

26

Although the Alamo was a little disappointing, they were still glad to have seen it. Before leaving town, they decided to take the elevator to the top of San Antonio's space needle and have a drink at the bar up there. They were much more impressed with the space needle than the Alamo, but neither would admit it. On the elevator ride back to the bottom, Bill asked, "Okay brother, what's next?"

Allen, who hadn't thought of what's next, was reading a tourist pamphlet he'd taken from the top of the space needle about an artsy little town in Texas called Marfa. He looked up at Bill and said, "Marfa is what's next, my friend. I'm going to introduce you to some Texas culture."

Bill said, "Marfa? What's Marfa and where is it?"

Allen answered, "Marfa is the new age cultural, renaissance center of the west. Says so right here."

"Okay," Bill says, "how far is it?"

"It's not far. Just tighten your saddle bags and we'll be there in no time."

They drove all that day and most of the next day, seeing nothing but brown, scrubby, desert wasteland. Bill said, "And John Wayne fought Fernando Valenzuela for this?"

Allen answered, "I think Fernando pulled one over on the Duke."

They finally arrived in Marfa . . . they knew this because Mr. Google said so, and they saw the town's city limit sign. After stopping for something to eat and drink, they walked around and visited a few artsy places and painter's galleries. Most of the so-called art galleries were not what Bill and Allen would call art. But they were indeed sixty-nine years old and in the hinterlands of Texas.

Finally they came upon one gallery that at least had some paintings they understood—some desert scenes and sunsets. They walked in and saw a woman who was probably in her fifties, but dressed like she was a teenager. She was the only other person in the building. After mulling around looking at the paintings, which didn't impress them at all, they approached the woman. She looked at them, and turned around, walking away without saying a word.

Allen said, "Good morning, miss." But she totally ignored him and went behind a counter at the other end of the store where she plopped down on a stool and started reading a book. The boys, trying to be polite, took their time walking around looking at the paintings, then started for the door, passing by the woman.

As they passed her, without looking up from her book, she said, "Tourists . . . always walking around and looking, never buying anything."

Allen stopped and started to say something to this wannabe teenager, but Bill grabbed his arm and jerked him towards the door. When they were outside, Allen said, "If she had anything in there that was worth a crap, maybe somebody would buy it—Texas cow!"

He looked at Bill for affirmation and his friend replied, "Truth."

They got back in their Ford F-150, and left Marfa. As they drove out of town, Bill looked over at his friend and said, "Nice choice."

Allen shook his head, leaned over to spit out the window, then looked out over the barren landscape and said, "Truth."

After a few minutes of silence, Bill said, "I heard that Santa Fe, New Mexico has some nice art galleries and stuff. It's sort of on our way, do you want to go there?"

Allen said, "Santa Fe, New Mexico you say?"

"Yep."

"More art galleries?"

"Yep."

Allen looked at his friend and said, "Sorry, buddy, I don't know how to spell Santa Fe to put it in Mr. Google. Maybe next time."

Bill thoughtfully replied, "Works for me."

7

THE LONG DRIVE AND DISAPPOINTMENT of Marfa left the boys a little tired so they found a nice campground near El Paso with a view of some mountains, and set up their little home. The campground was nearly deserted, being that this was not a major tourist area, so they were able to park in the slot next to the showers and bathrooms. There were two other campers parked down a bit from them. Both looked like they'd been there for a while. Each camper had a layer of dust coating the outside and neither was actually hooked up to any vehicle. One camper had an old VW van parked next to it, and the other one didn't have any vehicle near it at all.

Allen set up the camp chairs and Bill roamed around and picked up some dead limbs for them to start a small fire in the grill pit. They weren't going to cook anything, they just wanted the fire for the company and the attraction. When the fire finally took, they sat and stared at it, sipping Coors Lights. Allen was thinking of his wife that he'd never see again on this side of heaven; and Bill was thinking of his wife that he wished he would see again on this side of heaven. Each of the friends knew what the other one was thinking . . . they didn't have to ask.

After a suitable time of reflection, Allen said, "You know, there is a big difference between a human being and being human. Only a few folks understand that."

Bill nodded and actually understood what his friend meant, but he didn't comment one way or the other.

Ignoring the silence, Allen asked his friend, "How do you feel about getting old? And don't give me some Freudian crap either. I want to know how YOU feel."

Bill took a sip of his Coors Light; then he took another sip and answered, "The tragedy of old age is not that one is old, but that one is young. But to answer your question, I'd have to admit that I don't really think age matters a lot to me."

Allen leaned forward and spit towards the fire and said, "I definitely agree that age doesn't matter, unless of course you're old like us."

Bill silently stared at the fire, adding a couple of more sticks to keep it going. Then Allen asked him, "Are you afraid of dying?"

"No, sir, I'm not. I don't think any of us particularly want to die, but I'm not afraid of it either. I know this earth isn't my home . . . I'm just passing through here."

"But how can you be so sure about that, Bill? How do you know?"

Bill set his Coors Light down and picked up a stick to stir the fire again. He looked up at his friend and said, "I believe it just as I believe that the sun will rise in the morning: not because I'll see it, but because by it I see everything else."

Allen didn't really know how to respond to that, but he didn't have to because about that time they saw an old pickup truck coming down the road stirring up a dust tail about a hundred feet high. They watched as the pickup pulled up next to the two campers. Three people got out of the truck's cab and two more hopped out of the back of the pickup. It looked like there were three young women and two guys unloading back packs and assorted junk from the bed of the truck.

Allen and Bill gave a neighborly wave to them as the young people were clearly staring at them now. After they carried all the stuff inside their campers, all five of them started walking towards Bill and Allen. Allen said, "Did you bring your gun with you?"

"Shut up old man and be nice."

Allen greeted them, "Howdy folks, it's a beautiful evening isn't it?"

All the young people were smiling and the least dirty looking of the men said, "It sure is sir, I hope you're well. We've been here almost two weeks and you're the first people we've seen."

Allen said, "What in the world would you be doing out here in the middle of nowhere for two weeks?" But as he finished saying that, he noticed just how pretty the three girls were standing in front of him—which pretty much gave him the answer to that question.

"We've been climbing those mountains. We're trying to scale them all before we go back to school."

Bill jumped in and asked, "School? What kind of school?"

One of the girls answered, "UTEP, University of Texas at El Paso. We're taking a mountaineering and orientation course. We go up in the mountains and stay for about a week, then we come back and write what we've done and how we did it." She took a couple of steps closer and said, "My name's Callie. This is Bev, Candy, Danny, and Chris."

"Nice to meet you all. I'm Allen and the old man over there is Bill." Everyone laughed, including Bill. Then Callie, who seemed to be the leader of the group, said, "We're going to get cleaned up and get something to eat. Why don't you come over and join us for a drink later?"

"We'd love to Callie, thanks for asking. We'll come over in a little bit."

When the young people headed back to their campers, Allen turned to Bill and said, "Dang, she was pretty. Heck, they all were."

Bill said, "I don't know if we should go over there or not. We're used to having a couple of Coors Lights. They'll probably be downing shots of tequila or something like that. You know how young people are. We'd better be careful."

"Look, old man, it doesn't matter what they're doing. It only matters what we're doing. Quit worrying so much."

There was nothing to worry about. "Drinks," to these young people meant herbal tea and coffee. They were all very respectful to Bill and Allen; a lot of "yes sirs," and "no sirs." And, like most young people, they were very idealistic and wanted to do their part to "change the world." It was unclear if any of them were boyfriend/girlfriend, girlfriend/girlfriend, or even boyfriend/boyfriend. Or, if they lived in a communal type atmosphere where anything goes. They never hinted at anything, and Allen and Bill didn't ask—none of their business.

The three girls were passionate about having the courage to help save the environment and the planet. The two guys were more interested in helping the poor and homeless and downtrodden. Bill and Allen listened and drank coffee. They weren't here to argue; they just listened. As the evening ended, one of the girls asked them for any advice since Bill and Allen had a lot more experience in life than they did. The two older men stared at each other. Then Allen said, "Fill your life with adventures, not things. Have stories to tell, not stuff to show."

Allen looked at Bill, and without hesitation, Bill said, "Courage, like you've been talking about, is what it takes to stand up and speak; courage is also what it takes to sit down and listen—learn them both."

They shook hands with the guys and each girl gave them a hug as they rose to leave. As they walked back to their camper, Allen said, "I think that girl Candy had a thing for you."

Without any hesitation, Bill replied, "I know she does. She asked me if there's any way I could get rid of you tonight. I said 'Permanently?' And she said, 'Whatever it takes.'"

They left the campground early in the morning, before any of the young people had stirred. Bill was driving and asked, "Okay Carnac, look into your crystal ball and tell me which way to go?"

"West, my friend. Always go west. I want to see the giant saguaro cactuses growing fifty feet tall and skin my legs on the prickly pears, leaving a trail of blood along the slickrock to show that I've been there . . . that I've conquered this unconquerable land and survived to live another day. To make a long story short, follow the sun my compadre, and don't stop until the sun sets in the ocean."

Bill glanced over and said, "You have no idea in the world how to make a long story short."

8

BILL SAW THE ROAD SIGNS FOR I-40, which would take them west. But when they came to the intersection, Allen said, "Don't take it just yet. Keep driving north into New Mexico." Bill looked over at him and asked, "I thought we were going west?"

"We are, my friend, but since you've plainly told me that you don't care where we go, I decided to visit a little place that I've always wondered about—if you don't mind."

Bill replied, "Fine with me, sir, I have nowhere to be and all day to get there. What exactly is this place that you want to see so much?"

"Truth or Consequences, my friend."

"And why do you want to visit Truth or Consequences, New Mexico?"

"To find out which it is: truth, or indeed what the consequences might be."

Bill nodded and said, "I can't wait."

On the ride up north Bill googled Truth or Consequences and learned that it was originally called Hot Springs because of the natural springs there. But they changed the name in 1950 because of the old TV show, Truth or Consequences. They followed the Rio Grande River northward until they arrived in the little town where they found signs for "hot springs" at nearly every corner.

They stopped at a small café as they came into town and went inside for something to eat and to get some information. Fortunately for them, there was only one other table of customers. As they picked out a table near the window, a middle-aged woman with curly hair came over to them and handed them a menu. Before she could speak, Allen said, "It's a beautiful day in Truth or Consequences, isn't it young lady?"

She looked at Bill first, then back at Allen and replied, "That depends . . . are you ordering food or just coffee?"

"Food, my dear, and coffee. I'd like the biggest breakfast you have, and my friend here would like a side salad."

She looked over at Bill to confirm the salad order and he just shook his head and told her he'd have a plate of pancakes. When she came back to refill the coffee cups Allen asked her if she liked living here. "Not really, there's nothing to do, not really any jobs, and it's not close to anything."

Allen said, "Well, why don't you leave?"

"Because its home. It's all I know. My two kids left for Albuquerque a couple of years ago and my husband works in one of the spas here, so I guess this is where I'll always be." She had that resigned look on her face that almost said, "I give up."

They asked her about the spas, and she told them they could rent bathing suits and try out any of the hot springs in town. While they ate breakfast, the idea of visiting a hot spring became more and more inviting. Neither of them had ever been in a hot spring before. So why not? The sad looking waitress refilled their coffee cups again and they each left her a nice tip. As they were leaving, Bill walked past her, and she gave him a wry smile, he half stopped and said to her, "Young lady, don't forget to live before you die."

They rode down the street and saw a sign for "Thermal Hot Springs." So that is the one the boys chose to visit. They rented some loose fitting bathing suits and listened to instructions from a teenager manning the desk, then waded out into the pool area. It was hot! Initially, they didn't think they'd be able to actually wade into the pool of steaming water, but slowly and carefully they kept inching in until they were able to reach an area where they could sit and relax with most of their body being in the water. The longer they remained in the water, the better it felt.

They sat in solitude and silence until Allen asked again, "Bill, why are we here?"

"I've answered that question as adequately as you'll allow me to, son. Do you want me to elaborate?"

"No," Allen said, "why are we here? In Truth or Consequences? I'll tell you why . . . because I'm always looking out for your welfare and making it my goal on this trip to MAKE you have fun—whether you want to or not. That's why."

Bill splashed a little of the hot water on his face and then said, "Well, keep it up."

Lounging in the hot springs for a while did make them feel better somehow. They weren't exactly sure why or how, but they felt energized and refreshed. When they finally exited towards the dressing rooms, the teenager handed them a coupon for 10% off on their next visit. Allen said, "I'm sorry, son, but we have to keep moving. I have a date with a saguaro cactus over in Arizona and I don't want to stand her up."

The teenager looked puzzled and said, "Huh?"

Bill patted him on the shoulder and said, "You're doing a great job, son. Keep up the good work. We might come back someday . . . you just never know."

★★★

After leaving the hot springs they pulled off the side of the road near the Rio Grande River on the edge of town. Bill looked at his friend with a question mark on his face, and Allen said, "Rematch. Get out and find you a good sized rock."

Bill said, "You'll be sorry, brother."

"Yeah? We'll see about that. You go first so I can see how much energy I need to expend."

Bill threw his rock almost all the way over the narrow river channel. Allen looked out at the spot, dropped his rock and said, "You cheated. I ain't playing with no cheaters."

"How did I cheat? I threw the rock just like you told me to."

"You know what you did." Allen said. "Just get in the truck and drive. It's my turn to take it easy for a while instead of driving you all over New Mexico and half of Texas. Let's go!"

Bill started driving westward towards Arizona. He saw a sign for the turnoff to Alamogordo, New Mexico. He woke up Allen from his nap and asked, "Do you want to visit Alamogordo, where the first atomic bomb was tested?"

"Alamogordo? Not really, I saw enough death and destruction during the Vietnam War, I don't care to be reminded of it anymore."

"But you weren't actually in the Vietnam War. In fact, you weren't even in the Army."

"But I watched Walter Cronkite every night and felt like I was there—that was enough for me. Just keep driving, old man . . . I want to see those saguaros before they all wilt away."

So they continued their journey across southern New Mexico and into Arizona where they located a campground for the night. It was a fancy one at that: swimming pool, ping-pong tables, and video games. The bad news was they couldn't find an empty space near the restrooms. The good news was that Allen had purchased a couple of 2-liter Pepsi's and had saved the empty bottles just for a predicament like this.

It had been a clear, warm day in southern Arizona. However, Bill noticed a few clouds starting to gather as they neared the campground. Then the clouds starting getting darker and half way through the camper setup, the clouds burst open and rain starting pelting down in torrents. Allen and Bill had to get in the Ford F-150 to escape the fury of the storm. Fifteen minutes later, the storm had passed. Thirty minutes later, and it was impossible to even tell that it had rained. After finishing the camper setup, Allen walked over to a couple of saguaro cactuses growing on the edge of the campground. He felt them; he sniffed them to find out if they had any odor—they didn't. He wanted to hug one of them but the prickly, thorny hide of the cactus prevented that.

Near the recreation center a cookout for all the campers was being held. Bill and Allen bought a couple of hot dogs and hamburgers, along with chips and a Diet Pepsi. They sat in the community chairs and listened to and watched all the other campers. There was a couple from Everett, Washington who had just retired from Boeing and were crossing the country on their way to Florida. Allen asked the husband why he was going to Florida. But before he could answer, the wife said, "Because I want to be near an ocean where I can actually go swimming and not freeze to death."

They had a little dog with them that wouldn't stop yapping, so Allen and Bill quietly moved away and sat next to two women who seemed to be a few years younger than them—maybe early sixties. The women seemed to be alone and were very friendly, asking Allen and Bill about life in North Carolina. They were from Sausalito, California and had never been east, except to New York City once for a wedding.

Bill sat back and listened to Allen describe North Carolina better than any travel brochure ever could. He told them of the rolling Blue Ridge Mountains and the beaches. They asked him about the Outer Banks, which they'd heard of, but had no true idea what they really were. Allen described places along the road there where you could almost throw a rock into the ocean from one side of the road, and into the sound on the other side. He rarely exaggerated his descriptions—he didn't have to.

The women then told of life in Sausalito and northern California. Trips to Yosemite and the redwood forests, how San Francisco used to be and how charming Carmel by the Sea is now. Then the girls excused themselves to visit the restroom, telling the guys they'd be right back. When they walked away, Allen said, "I think they have the hots for us."

Bill whispered back to him, "You're crazy, old man. They're gay, can't you tell that?"

"Gay? Ain't no way in the world they're gay! Why would you think that?"

"Look . . . they're travelling alone. They never mentioned anything about husbands. They're from Sausalito, for Christ sake, and they're wearing wedding rings. You know they have gay marriage in California—they're married to each other."

Allen thought for a few seconds, then said, "We're travelling alone. We never mentioned to them anything about wives. We have on wedding rings—they probably think we're gay—you ever think about that, Jimmy Swaggart?"

Before Bill could respond, even if he had known how, the two women came back to join them. When they arrived, one of them said, "It's been really nice talking to you boys, but we'd better be getting back to our camper. We're leaving early in the morning. I hope you enjoy the rest of your trip and you've almost convinced us to keep driving over to North Carolina. Good night, boys."

After they left, Bill said, "Well, I guess we'll never know now."

Allen looked down at his hands and took a moment, then said, "Oh, they're not gay. Look at this."

He handed Bill a small piece of paper with some handwriting on it, which Bill couldn't read since he left his glasses in the Ford F-150. He handed it back to Allen saying, "What is it?"

"When they left, the dark headed one dropped this in my lap. It's a note that gives their camper lot number and describes their camper."

Bill was dumbfounded. He said, "Really? You're not messing with me are you?"

"Nope. What do you want to do?"

They both sat there thinking about that question. Bill finally said, "Ahh, they're gay. Let's go to bed."

Allen took a deep breath and replied, "Maybe you're right, son. But, maybe you're not."

The two boys from North Carolina got up and started walking back to their camper, each of them straining through the darkness to see any movement at all in the camper from Sausalito, California.

9

THE NEXT DAY WAS SPENT RIDING through the winding roads of Saguaro National Monument. In addition to the saguaros, they saw teddy bear chollas, jumping chollas, barrel cactus, hedgehog, fishhook, prickly pear, and organ pipe cactus. They knew they saw all these because of the tour guide pamphlet they picked up at the ranger station. The only thing that surprised them was all the varied vegetation out here in the desert. They thought it would be . . . well, a desert.

They walked several of the trails and spoke with a young female ranger who told them not to touch any of the cactuses, and then answered their questions about rattlesnakes. "Yes, they're dangerous; but unless you turn over some rocks or stick your hand down in a hole, you'll probably never see one."

Apparently, Allen didn't believe what the young lady ranger said about not touching any of the cactuses. He wanted to "feel" one; so he did . . . and, now he has the sharp end of fishhook cactus stuck in his finger. Fishhook cactuses are so named because they have a barb like a fishhook that won't let you easily pull it out once it's stuck in you.

After unsuccessfully trying to pull it out and crying like a little girl about it, they drove back to the ranger station for help. A middle-aged, grumpy-looking man in a ranger suit that was much too tight around his stomach, looked at the situation and said, "Hold on."

He went to the back room and came back with an unidentified bottle of something—Allen was hoping he didn't have to drink it. He said, "Come here." Allen walked over to a small sink in the back and the ranger poured the liquid from the bottle on to Allen's finger, which caused it to wrinkle up and turn a little pinkish. As soon as it turned colors, the ranger took a pair of tweezers and yanked the barb out of Allen's finger. Allen expected it to hurt, but he didn't even feel it.

The ranger said, "There you go. You'll be fine. Didn't anyone tell you not to touch the cacti?"

Allen glanced over at Bill and said, "No sir, but I'll know now. Thanks for your help."

When they walked back outside the ranger station Bill said, "Why did you lie to him? You know that young lady ranger told us not to touch any cactuses."

"It ain't a lie if he doesn't know it's a lie. It's only a lie if he knows it ain't true and catches you."

Bill turned to look at him and said, "I think that stuff he poured on your finger has affected your brain."

"Well, the good news is that it's the finger on my non-throwing hand that's injured. Because I'm warning you, old man, the next river we come to is when I'm going to exert my dominance over you in the rock throwing world."

Just before getting back to the parking lot where the Ford F-150 was, Bill "accidentally" bumped his friend off the sidewalk and said, "Oh, excuse me. I didn't see you there. I thought you were still living in your dream world."

"I'll get you for that, old man. Now just get in and let's go; you're driving while my finger heals."

They followed the road signs for Tucson, only because they wanted to see what the city looked like. They had no plans to stop there. But just before they arrived, Allen asked, "Do you want to go by the university and see where the Sun Devils play?"

Bill answered, "The Sun Devils play in Phoenix. The Wildcats play here in Tucson. I thought you used to be a sports fan?"

Without hesitation, Allen said, "I know that, smarty pants . . . I meant where the Sun Devils play when they come down here to whup up on those worthless Wildcats. Do you want to see it or not?"

"No, let's just find a cool place and get something to eat and drink."

"Sounds like a plan to me. WAIT! Pull over."

Bill was startled by this sudden outburst from his friend. He asked, "What's wrong? Are you okay?"

"Yeah, I'm okay. Didn't you see that sign back there for the Gila River? You're trying to avoid your fate, aren't you?"

Bill pulled the Ford F-150 over to the side of the road just before a small bridge. They each got out, and found a rock on the ground, and walked up to the bridge. Standing there, they stared out into the distance, and each wondered what in the world had happened. There was not a drop of water in this so-called river . . . nothing but a bed of sand and dirt and pebbles, with a few small limbs and debris scattered around. Allen spoke first, "That sign back there plainly said Gila River. RIVER!"

Bill was still wondering where in the world all the water went. They stood there another minute or two and didn't notice that a local police car had pulled up behind them. The policeman walked up behind them, startling them both. He said, "Are you gentlemen okay?"

Bill spoke for them, "Yes sir, officer, we just stopped to take a look at your river—but it's gone."

The officer smiled and said, "Well, come back during the winter when the rains come, and you'll see it. Or, if we get a big thunderstorm, it'll come back to life for a while. You sure you're both okay?"

"Yes sir, we're fine. A little surprised, but we're fine."

When the policeman left, the guys continued to stand there staring at the dry river bed . . . wondering. Finally Bill said, "Okay, pick up your rock and give it your best shot."

Allen looked at him and exclaimed, "This ain't no river! I said the next RIVER we came to—then I'll teach you a lesson, old man."

"This is a river, it just doesn't have any water in it right now."

Allen answered, "To be a college graduate, you sure can be stupid sometimes. Look up in your Google machine there and find the definition of a river. I guarantee you it will say something about WATER!"

Bill tried to argue, "What difference does it make, water or sand? We'll still see who wins."

"It's the principle of the thing, professor. I ain't throwing no rock into a sand pit—it ain't American."

They dropped their rocks and stared for a few more minutes before climbing back into the Ford F-150 to continue their journey.

They decided to bypass Tucson and miss most of the traffic. They hit Interstate 17 North towards Phoenix looking for a nice place to eat and have a cold drink. Somewhere north of Tucson they saw exit signs for Black Canyon. Allen asked Bill to Google it up real quick and they learned it was a scenic overview of the surrounding mountains and valleys. Sounded nice to them, and since it was right on the interstate they decided to take a look.

When they pulled off the exit, there was a convenience store and market together, so they went shopping, after they bought gas for the Ford F-150. Allen saw a cold watermelon in the cooler section and bought it. Bill picked out some cherries and grapes, and they got a couple of six-packs of Coors Light and Diet Pepsi. This would hold them until dinner later tonight.

They followed the signs up the winding side roads to the summit of Black Canyon. There was a small parking section with a couple of picnic tables conveniently located in a shady area near the chasm. Allen took a couple of plastic knives they had from a previous restaurant stop, and carried the watermelon over to one of the picnic tables. He dropped the melon lightly on the ground; but it didn't break open. So he lifted it a little higher and dropped it again and in broke into pretty equal halves. They each took a half and dug into the watermelon with the plastic knives. As they were sitting at the picnic table, on the edge of Black Canyon, staring into the abyss, they each thought to themselves how lucky they were to be where they were and who they were with.

After they'd eaten all the watermelon they could comfortably hold, they walked over to the edge of the canyon and sat on a couple of rocks. They watched three or four buzzards float by below them. It was hard to tell if they were looking for lunch, just having fun enjoying the scenery, or perhaps asleep, floating with the currents. Finally, Allen spoke, "Barbara and I thought about coming out here several times. We just never found the time. We kept saying when the kids were grown we'd travel around and see everything we'd always dreamed of." He took a few moments to gather himself, then continued, "But all we ever did was go to the beach—not that it wasn't fun, but . . ."

After a few more moments, he added, "Then she got sick and didn't feel like going anywhere . . . and then it was too late to go anywhere. There's not a day goes by, Bill, that I don't wish I'd have done more for that woman. Doing the same thing forty-four years in a row and calling it a life was not fair to her."

Allen wiped away a few tear drops, hoping Bill didn't notice. He couldn't speak any longer without them being very noticeable. But Bill did notice and understood exactly how his friend felt. After a few minutes of staring and silence, Allen asked his friend, "When you were married, did Eliza like travelling?"

"She loved it. We only came out west once, though. She wanted to go to Hawaii one year, so we did. It rained every day we were there, but we still loved it. As you know, she loved traveling to Europe and that's where we went most years on vacation. She loved France for some reason. She could speak enough French to get us into trouble, but she loved it just the same. We visited all the countries in Europe at least once, but she always wanted to go back to France."

For a while, they were each left to their own thoughts. Then Allen asked his friend, "Bill . . . what happened with Eliza?"

"I wish I knew, Allen. I truly wish I knew. I would have done anything to change things. I'd have done whatever she asked, but I never had the chance. She just walked in that day and said she was leaving. She didn't accuse me of anything. Didn't say she loved someone else. Nothing—just that she was leaving. I still don't know to this day why she did what she did."

"Would you take her back if she came back?"

"In a second. She was the world to me. I can't stop feeling the way I feel . . . I just can't."

They sat for several minutes longer, each thinking of the woman they once loved and the woman they still loved—neither of them able to do anything about it. Then Allen got up from the picnic table and picked up a nice sized rock and threw it as hard as he could over the edge of the canyon. He turned back to his friend and said, "Beat that, old-timer."

Bill looked at him, then looked over the edge where the rock disappeared, and said, "Can't." That's what friends do.

10

THEY COULD TELL THEY WERE NEARING PHOENIX because traffic on Interstate 17 had nearly stopped. Bill said, "Okay, tour guide, what's your thoughts on Phoenix?"

"Charlotte on steroids—that's my thoughts on Phoenix."

Bill nodded and said, "This next exit up here is the by-pass around the city—let's take it."

It did take them around the downtown part of Phoenix, but the traffic in the outlying regions was just as bad. Phoenix had apparently spread all over the desert and outstripped the road's capacity to adequately handle the traffic. Allen asked, "Where do they get water from? What do they drink? The rivers are all dried up; there's no ocean anywhere. I haven't seen any lakes. How do all these people exist here?"

Bill knew that question was unanswerable for him. Maybe Mr. Google could figure it out, but right now they just wanted to get out of the mire, muck, and quicksand that was suburban Phoenix. After clearing the worst of the traffic they started thinking about a campground. But quickly decided to find a nice Holiday Inn with efficient air conditioning instead. They didn't see a Holiday Inn, but did find a nice Best Western that looked modern and comfortable.

They parked the Ford F-150 and went to the lobby to check in. There was a man of Middle Eastern descent behind the desk. When they walked up he said, "Good evening ladies and gentlemen, how can I be of service?"

Bill started to say something, but Allen stopped him and took over, "We're from the U.S. Geological Survey team and we need a room for the night. Do you have anything suitable?"

"Oh, yes sir, we do. Do you want the government rate for your room?"

"No," Allen said, "We're here on unofficial business and don't want to stir up any questions about the nature of our work."

The man said, "Is it a secret? This nature of your work?"

"Well, not really a secret, but it might upset a lot of people if they knew what we were doing."

Allen knew he had the guy going now—and he did. The man lowered his voice and asked, "What ARE you doing?"

Allen looked behind him, then over both shoulders and motioned for the guy to lean in closer to him. When they were close, Allen half-whispered to him, "We're here to survey this part of the country again. This whole area might have to go back to Mexico. The Mexican government is pitching a fit and they want this land back." Then Allen put a finger up to his lips and said, "Shhh."

The man gave them key cards for the room but forgot to ask for their credit card. Allen handed him his Visa card anyway, but again put his finger to his lips and went, "Shhh."

He processed the Visa card and handed it back to Allen, then said, "You can trust me ladies and gentlemen—not a word will I speak."

Allen shook his hand and thanked him for his patriotism, while Bill was trying his best not to laugh out loud. After carrying their stuff into the room, they walked down the street to a burrito place they noticed driving in. It filled them up, and they went back to their room and watched television and munched on the grapes and cherries they had bought earlier.

In the morning, over a breakfast of cereal and sweet rolls, Allen said, "How does the Grand Canyon sound to you, old-timer?"

"It sounds grand. Is that our next stop?"

"Not exactly, I know how fond you are of artsy, new-age crap, so I learned of a place on the way that's supposed to be the epicenter of that junk here in Arizona. I thought we'd stop over and let you check it out."

Bill thought a moment, then asked, "Prescott?"

"No," answered Allen, "that's just an old cowboy town. Sedona is where I'm talking about. Red rock country, new-age spiritualism, hocus-pocus with a western flair. Sounds great doesn't it?"

"Yeah, downright groovy."

Sedona wasn't far off the interstate. The scenic red rock formations in the area immediately drew their attention. They stopped in the little town, and walked around doing some window shopping, and having a cup of coffee. Walking into a bookstore they saw books on spiritualism, self-healing, parapsychology, extrasensory perception and a dozen other new-age philosophies. They didn't buy anything.

On the way out of town they noticed a pull-off for a walking trail . . . a two and a half mile loop overlooking a river and canyon. They stopped and after a little discussion decided to take the two and a half mile walk. About twenty minutes into the walk Allen looked over to Bill and said, "I think I have to poop."

Bill stopped walking and said, "Well, do you or don't you?"

Allen scrunched up his face and answered, "I'll probably be alright."

Five minutes later Allen stopped again and said, "I ain't gonna be alright. It's all those cherries you made me eat last night, they're running right through me."

"I made you eat cherries last night?"

"You knew I had the bag and was eating 'em, you should've taken that bag and eaten some of them yourself; then I wouldn't have the squirts right now."

Bill ignored that nonsense and asked, "Can you make it back to the truck?"

"What good will the truck do? It ain't got no toilet. I need help now!"

They both stood there quietly while Allen was holding himself and squirming a little. Then he said, "You watch out for me; I'm going over there behind those rocks."

Bill firmly replied, "You can't take a dump over there, they'll arrest us both."

"It ain't technically a dump. I told you I had the squirts. Now let me borrow your handkerchief."

"What?" Bill exclaimed. "I am not giving you my handkerchief. Use your own."

"I didn't bring one. All I have is some Kleenex—it won't be enough."

"Alright, here. But you're not borrowing it. It's all yours now—I DON'T want it back."

Allen took the handkerchief and started to go behind the rocks when a young couple came over the hill and walked up to them. They stopped and the young guy said, "It sure is beautiful out here, isn't it? Where are you guys from?"

Allen tried to hold himself while not being noticed and Bill answered, "We're from North Carolina. Where are you two from?" As he said this, Allen indiscreetly elbowed him in the back.

"We're from Michigan. First time in Arizona—it's amazing!"

Allen starting doing a little shuffle and Bill asked them, "What part of Michigan?"

The girl answered, "Kalamazoo . . . we're in school there."

Then Allen interrupted and said, "Well that's great, but we've got to be moving along, don't we buddy?"

Bill ignored him and asked the girl, "What school is that? I'm not familiar with Kalamazoo."

Allen elbowed him again, a little more sharply as the girl answered, "Western Michigan, the Broncos."

Allen interrupted again and said, "I just got a text from the girls, buddy . . . they're waiting on us. Nice to meet you guys. I hope you enjoy the rest of your trip. Let's go buddy."

The young couple smiled and continued their walk, Allen turned to his friend and said, "Butthole! Watch out for me."

He went behind some rocks and returned a few minutes later with a relieved expression on his face. He stuck his hand out towards Bill and said, "Thanks for helping me out and keeping watch."

Bill took a step back from Allen's outstretched hand and said, "No thank you. Where's the handkerchief I donated to you? I hope it's not in your pocket."

"I buried it with the cherry poop under some dirt and rocks. My donation to the new-age mysticism of the occult."

As they neared the end of their scenic walk, Allen once again tried to shake hands with Bill, who once again refused. Allen said, "It's just cherries—they're natural."

"Yeah, right. Go over there to the restroom and wash your hands, Mr. Natural."

Before they left Sedona, Bill picked up a smooth red rock from the desert area near a stream and placed it on the dashboard next to the Bear Bryant hounds tooth hat. Allen looked at it but didn't say anything. On the other side of Flagstaff they saw a nice campground and decided to stop early and relax before driving on toward the Grand Canyon the next day. The campground was nearly full, but didn't seem that way because it was located in a pine forest with trees separating most of the camp spots.

They bought a few snacks at the little store to go with their Diet Pepsis and Coors Lights, plus a small bundle of wood so they could stare at a fire tonight as they sat around and thought about life and their adventure. After getting things set up and starting the little fire in the grill pit, the boys popped open a Diet Pepsi and had a pre-packaged roast beef sandwich with potato chips.

Sitting next to a fire, having something to drink, being with your best friend, having nowhere to be, and nothing to do . . . it was a good life. They stared alternately at the fire and at the stars, which seemed to be a little brighter here north of Flagstaff at nearly six thousand feet in elevation. They each had to put on a light jacket as the sun set for the day. They said hello to several people walking by but not much more than that.

After an extended period of solitude, Allen asked, "Are you glad you're here?"

"You mean here in Arizona, or here on earth?"

"Neither. Here with me."

"Can't think of anywhere on earth I'd rather be right now."

The two friends smiled and sipped the last of their Diet Pepsi before calling it a night.

11

THE ROAD AND THE RIDE UP TO THE GRAND CANYON was actually pretty boring. There's a gradual rise in elevation from just over five thousand feet in Flagstaff to over eight thousand feet at the south rim of the canyon, where everyone goes. And I do mean EVERYONE! It was crowded beyond belief. If it hadn't been the GRAND Canyon, the boys would have turned around and left. But they didn't name it the GRAND Canyon for nothing. Not only is it grand, it's also magnificent, awesome, gorgeous, resplendent, brilliant, excellent and imposing. But Grand Canyon sounds a lot better than "imposing canyon."

They had to park the Ford F-150 about two or three miles away from the actual rim and take a bus to the viewing area. Neither Allen nor Bill had ever visited the canyon before, but Bill did see it once from thirty-seven thousand feet up in an airplane. Neither of them were prepared for what they saw. When they actually walked up to the rim and gazed into the vastness, it nearly took their breath away. They temporarily forgot about the thousands of other tourists and Germans milling all around them.

From where they stood it was over a mile, nearly straight down, to the Colorado River, and almost eighteen miles across the canyon to the north side. With shadows and colors and rock formations and layers of rocks all exposing their senses to something they were not prepared for. Allen thought, "I wish Barbara was here to see this."

Bill thought, "I wish Eliza was here to see this."

They walked along the rim trail and continued to be amazed at what they saw. It was beyond belief. Allen said, "I had no idea it was like this."

Bill concurred, "This is beyond my wildest dreams. I can't believe how big it is."

They walked along the rim all afternoon. Each viewing area being different from the one before. Their senses were on overload, and they ran out of descriptions to impress each other with. They eventually got a little tired and went into a gift shop at the main area and bought a Diet Pepsi and some peanuts to take out to a bench and stare into the void. No sooner had they sat down than a big, fat, red squirrel came up from the edge and stopped about five feet away from them. Bill said, "I've never seen a squirrel that big before. Or that red."

Allen nodded and said, "I wonder what he wants."

"He wants your peanuts, doofus."

"Nah, he's a squirrel, he doesn't know we've got peanuts."

They opened their peanut packages and the squirrel came closer, looking up at them. Bill said, "Throw him a peanut."

"You throw him one, I'm hungry."

So Bill threw him one and he caught it out of the air and stuck it in his jaw while continuing to stare at them. Bill said, "Did you see that? He caught that peanut right out of the air."

Allen whistled to the squirrel, then he threw a peanut which the squirrel caught as well. Then both boys started giggling to each other and alternated throwing peanuts to the squirrel. As far as they could tell, it didn't eat any of them. The squirrel just kept packing them in its jaws until they were about to burst. Just as Allen was set to throw another peanut, a voice from behind them said, "Don't feed the animals, fellows. It's against the rules."

They both turned and saw a young female park ranger staring down at them. They looked back at the squirrel, but it had disappeared. Bill said, "We're sorry miss, we didn't know."

She pointed to a sign about six feet away that read, "Don't feed the wildlife."

All Bill could say was, "Oh."

She walked around in front of them and explained, "If people feed them, then they start expecting free food. And when bad weather sets in and there's no tourists to feed them, they'll starve. Trust me, fellows, they can feed themselves; they don't need you throwing them snacks."

Allen spoke up and said, "Don't worry ma'am, I won't let him do it anymore."

She smiled and started walking over to where some little kids were getting a little too close to the edge of a thousand foot drop off. They finished what was left of their peanuts and drank all the soda before going back in the gift shop. Bill bought a hat that had a scene of the canyon stitched on the front. Allen bought a tee shirt that simply read, "Grand Canyon."

They walked over to the park ranger's information desk and asked the older gentleman several questions (all of which he'd answered ten thousand times before). Then Bill finally asked the question the old ranger knew was coming, "How long does it take to walk all the way to the bottom—to the river?"

He replied, "Most folks can walk down in three or four hours . . . some quicker, depending on how much you stop."

Allen said, "I want to walk down there and stick my little toes into that wild Colorado River."

The old ranger just grinned a little, but didn't say anything. Allen looked at him and said, "You don't think a man my age can walk down there?"

The ranger said, "No, I'm pretty sure you can walk down there. Just as I'm pretty sure you can't walk back up."

They both looked at him with quizzical looks and he explained, "Like I said, three to four hours to walk down there; but, four to eight hours to walk back up."

Allen said, "What?"

"Yep. You have to remember, you're going down in elevation about a mile to the bottom, but the winding trail is about eight miles long. Then coming up its still eight miles long, but every single solitary step is uphill. It's like climbing steps for eight miles. And there's no water fountains, no break rooms, no bathrooms, no first aid stations . . . no nothing but dirt and rocks."

Allen nodded and said, "Maybe I'll take the donkey ride to the bottom."

The old ranger said, "Good luck with that. You'll need a reservation at least six months in advance."

They stood there not knowing what to say next. But there was a group of people behind them waiting to probably ask the ranger the same questions, so they stood aside and the ranger looked at them and said, "You boys have a good day and don't do anything stupid."

★★★

They went back outside and stared some more into the canyon, which seemed to change shape and color as the sun set and cast shadows across the layers of rock. Allen said, "You ain't in no hurry are you?"

Bill replied, "Nope."

"Good. Let's come back here tomorrow and walk down the trail, into the canyon, for as far as we feel comfortable. You okay with that?"

Bill thought about that, then answered, "I'm all for coming back here tomorrow . . . but even though I can walk down that trail, I'm not sure my knee will allow me to walk back up the trail. But I want you to go. One of us has to check it out and come up with a story we can tell people someday. And you're better at story telling than I am."

"Deal." Allen said, "We'll come back and I will venture down into the unknown depths and explore the unforeseeable and experience the uncharted and desolate land below."

Bill looked at him and said, "Lord have mercy, son."

★★★

They had to drive nearly all the way back to Flagstaff to find a campground with an open spot for the night. It was dark when they arrived and by the time they set everything up, they were ready for bed. Their neighbors were not. In the camping lot next to them were several tents with a lot of young people milling around drinking, laughing and talking very loud. Allen and Bill could hear it all, which made trying to sleep nearly impossible. Finally, Allen said, "I'm going over there to speak to them, see if they can tone it down a little."

Bill said, "Leave it alone, you know how young people are, they aren't going to listen to anything you say. You'll only make it worse."

But Allen wouldn't listen. He walked outside and saw a big group of them standing around the fire drinking and laughing. He walked over to them and waited until they noticed him, then said, "Good evening fellas. We're trying to get some sleep next door and wanted to ask if you could tone it down a little for us."

A skin-headed guy with no shirt on, stepped away from the group and said, "We're just having a little party old man. What's it to you?"

"Just trying to ask a small favor is all. Not asking you to stop whatever it is you're doing, just to tone it down a little."

The skin-headed guy said, "I think you should go back to your retirement home old man and leave us alone."

By this time, Bill had come out of the camper to join Allen and see what was happening. Bill walked up to the group and said, "Is everything okay here?"

The skin-headed guy said, "I suggest you two gaybos go back in your gay camper and do whatever it is that gay people do to each other."

Allen started to say something, but Bill grabbed his arm and took a step towards the skin-headed guy and said, "Listen punk, that man behind me was a Green Beret over in Vietnam while you weren't even a dream yet in your mama's mind. He can't even remember how many Vietcong he killed with a knife in hand-to-hand combat. He might be a little old now, but he hasn't forgotten how to use that knife he has strapped to his leg either. And even though I wasn't a Green Beret, I still know how to use the .38 I have strapped to my ankle. Now we're going back to bed, and I hope you'll choose to show some consideration and respect for others around you and stop acting like a bunch of spoiled, college punks."

Bill stared at the skin-headed guy until the punk turned around and went back to his friends. Bill and Allen walked back to their camper shaking a little bit, but very happy with the outcome. When they sat down on their beds, Allen said, "Green Berets? Where in the world did that come from?"

"I was just trying to appeal to his sense of preservation and common sense. He may have acted tough, but I saw a couple of his friends wearing UCLA tee shirts. I seriously doubt any pampered, college kids wanted to tangle with an ex-Green Beret who knew how to use a knife . . . and his crazy, gay partner who had a gun."

After their hearts stopped racing a bit, they noticed a considerable decrease in the noise level next door. Allen was quite proud of his friend for handling that situation. Bill was hoping Allen didn't see him sneak the nitroglycerin pill beneath his tongue as he turned off the lantern for the night.

12

ALLEN AND BILL ROSE EARLY the next morning, excited about returning to the Grand Canyon and still a little psyched from the events of last night. Of course, the college punks were still sleeping it off. Allen started packing up the camper while Bill walked over to the bathrooms about sixty yards away. When he returned, he asked Allen to take the Diet Pepsi bottle they used last night to pee in and dump it in the toilets. Allen said, "I've already taken care of that."

Bill looked at him and asked, "What do you mean by that? You haven't been to the bathroom yet."

"Don't worry about it . . . it's taken care of. Get your ducks ready and let's go."

Bill knew something was up; he just didn't know what. As they pulled out of the camp driveway and slowly passed the college boys' driveway where several vehicles were parked, Allen said, "That's a nice looking Jeep Wrangler over there, isn't it?"

Bill wondered why he asked that, but answered, "Yeah, looks nice."

Allen smiled and said, "I bet it smells nice too."

Bill quickly looked over at him, but Allen had started whistling an old Beatles' tune as they drove away.

They parked the Ford F-150 in the lot and took the shuttle back to the rim where Germans, Italians, Englishmen, and a few natives were all staring at the canyon in awe at something they'd never imagined. Allen had a small backpack with him which included a bottle of water, an orange, some Advil, a pre-packaged sandwich, and some raisins. Bill walked to the edge of the Bright Angel Trail with him and said, "Good luck, buddy. Stay away from the edge, don't make me take the rest of this trip by myself."

Allen smiled and said, "It's not uncommon for most people to spend their whole life waiting to start living . . . but, old timer, not being dead isn't being alive." And with that, he turned and started down the trail. Bill watched him until he turned the first of the many switchback corners on the way to the bottom. He knew Allen wasn't going all the way down, but he still wished he was going with him.

Bill walked the little path along the canyon's rim, and whenever he came across a telescope, he paid the twenty-five cents and scanned the trail for his friend. But he never saw him. He went beyond the little path and made his way through some scrub pines to a secluded area with an indescribable view of the canyon. He looked all around him to make sure he was alone, then he picked up a good sized rock and threw it over the edge as hard as he could. He said to himself, "Beat that one, old man!"

He then found a nice sized boulder and sat on the ground, leaning back against the rock which had probably been in that spot for six thousand years or more. He watched some large birds floating with the currents above him and below him—having fun and doing exactly what God had created them to do. He thought about Eliza. He thought about her a lot. He imagined sitting here with her right now, holding her hand and feeling the magic that her touch and the Grand Canyon could have had on his senses. He also spoke to her: "I miss you so much, Eliza. Sometimes I don't know how I'll make it through the day without you. Whatever I did to drive you away, I apologize a million times over. I wish I could go back in time and change it all. I'd jump over the edge of this big hole if I only knew that I could hold you in my arms one more time, honey. I love you so much."

He took a deep breath to keep from crying, when he suddenly heard a noise behind him. He half rose and looked over his shoulder and saw a deer nibbling on the leaves of a scrub oak. The deer stopped, looked at Bill, but perceived no danger and continued its morning snack. Bill watched it until it moved on further into the forest, apparently unconcerned with the beauty out beyond the back of beyond. After a suitable time of reflection and a short, unplanned nap, Bill rose and started back towards the masses. He hadn't gone too far when he walked up on a couple of teenagers kissing each other behind a clump of trees. They stopped, looked at him, and Bill said, "Carry on," as he walked on down the path.

The first building he came to had a small store where he bought a large Diet Pepsi, some peanuts, nabs, and a book about two men who took a trip together down the Colorado River years ago. He intended to find a secluded bench where he could read the book while he waited on Allen to finish his trip. He sat down, and before he opened his snacks another squirrel hopped right in front of him. He was at the last bench before the trees, away from most of the people, and didn't see any rangers patrolling the area. He took out three or four peanuts and threw them on the ground. Unlike the other squirrel, this one was apparently hungry because it ate them right away.

Bill looked at the squirrel and said, "No more. I'm not getting in trouble because of you." Obviously the squirrel didn't understand him because it never moved. Instead, it did something Bill had never seen a squirrel do before: it laid flat on the ground, spread its legs out in all four directions, and stared up at him. Bill opened his nabs and ate a couple of them while reading the first few pages of the book. He looked down at the squirrel, who was just lying there, staring back at him. Bill said, "No more!" The squirrel ignored him.

Bill read a chapter and a half before his eyes got tired. He finished the nabs and most of the peanuts; he couldn't bring himself to eat them all. The squirrel never complained, never begged; in fact, it didn't do anything but lie there with its feet all splayed out and stare at Bill. To keep from falling asleep, Bill figured he'd better get up and walk around some. When he rose, the squirrel jumped to attention, but didn't run away. Bill looked around for any rangers, then left several peanuts lying on the park bench as he walked back towards the Bright Angel Trail. After about ten steps, he turned and looked back at the bench . . . the peanuts and the squirrel were both gone.

Allen walked about an hour and a half down that lonesome trail. He had to stop twice and let a pack train of donkeys carrying German tourists pass him. He stopped intentionally three other times simply to enjoy the moment. There weren't many places to actually stop and sit. Probably ninety-five percent of the trail is just wide enough for two people to comfortably walk side-by-side . . . sometimes not even that much. Added to that is the fact that on one side of the trail there is usually a drop-off of anywhere from a couple of hundred feet to over a thousand feet. It demands you pay attention to what you're doing and watch for rocks that may trip you.

He remembered what the old ranger had told him about the trip back up the trail. Sure enough, without exception, all the people he met coming back up the trail had the most painful looks on their faces. Going downhill everyone is laughing, whistling, telling jokes, and loving it . . . not coming back up. Allen was smart and remembered that. When he finally decided to stop and turn back, he was sure he'd have no problems—he was wrong. Fifteen minutes of walking up hill, every step left him exhausted. When he came across a rock to sit on, he'd stop and rest. He took ten steps, stopped and rested . . . twelve steps, stopped and rested. That was his routine.

Unfortunately though, he didn't ration his water efficiently and ran out half way back up the trail. He was sitting on a rock when he took the last little swig of water in his bottle. He held the empty bottle in one hand and the cap to the bottle in the other hand, thinking to himself, "What am I gonna do now?"

Almost as if by divine intervention, three young men came up the trail behind him speaking some sort of foreign language he couldn't understand. They stopped and spoke to him, but he had no idea what they were saying. All he could do was hold up his empty water bottle. Two of the guys took their backpacks off and got their own large water bottles. Each of them poured some of their precious water into Allen's empty bottle. He shook their hands, thanked them profusely, and watched them head on up the trail, still not understanding a single word they ever said.

Allen finally made it to the top, and Bill was sitting on a bench near the trail head reading a book, waiting on him. Allen yelled over to him, and Bill came over to meet him, saying, "Hey, old-timer. How was it?"

Allen half smiled at him and answered, "Piece of cake."

As soon as he finished that sentence he half bent over and threw up. It happened so fast Bill couldn't get out of the way, and some of the residual spew went on his tennis shoes. Bill helped his friend over to a bench, and they sat down. Bill said, "Are you okay? Do I need to go get some help?"

Allen answered, "Nah, I'm fine. I could use some cold water though."

Bill went and bought his friend a cold bottle of water and sat with him for a bit while he recovered. A ranger came over to ask how he was feeling. But by then, Allen had perked up a little and replied, "I could do this all day long!"

They caught the shuttle bus back to the parking lot and rode back to the Ford F-150 in silence. As soon as Bill started driving them back towards Flagstaff, Allen fell asleep and didn't wake up until Bill shook him in the parking lot of a Best Western on the outskirts of town. Bill checked them in and made sure his buddy was okay. He waited for him to shower and flop into bed, then he went downstairs to the restaurant for dinner while his friend slept off the adventure of a lifetime.

13

AT THE BREAKFAST BAR IN THE BEST WESTERN the next morning, the two friends were each eating a bowl of cereal when Allen looked up and told Bill, "Well, buddy, I stared death in the face and lived to tell about it."

Bill set his spoon down, looked at his friend, and said, "What?"

"No need to worry about me now, though," Allen continued, "I think I'm okay."

Bill still didn't pick up his spoon and said, "You stared death in the face?"

"Yep . . . I'll never forget it, buddy."

Bill then ate a spoonful of Raisin Bran and said, "Was that before or after you puked on my shoes?"

"You don't realize how close I came to giving up down in that canyon . . . just laying down and letting the buzzards pick my bones. I was totally out of water and was saved only by divine intervention."

"I thought you said some Germans gave you water. Now, it's the Lord who saved you?"

Allen nodded and answered, "I'm not sure they were Germans. I don't know what they were . . . maybe angels, but I am sure the Lord sent them to me at that point in time to keep me from dying."

Bill shook his head and continued eating his Raisin Bran, wondering if his friend was still full of cherry poop or had, in fact, been given divine intervention from the man upstairs. He looked back up at his friend, who was still looking at him in between bites of Frosted Flakes. They stared at each other, then nodded, and continued eating.

After they checked out and loaded up the camper and truck, Allen asked Bill if he would continue driving so he could regain his strength. Bill answered, "Of course, grandpa. Which direction should I point us in? Or, has your near death experience fogged your decision making?"

"Not at all, my Green Beret friend . . . get us out to I-40 and point us west. When in doubt, always follow Horatio Hornblower's advice and 'Go West' young man . . . always go west."

Bill shook his head and was hoping Allen's suggestions were only the culmination of a long, confused life and not from the lingering effects of lunacy. At any rate, he pulled the Ford F-150 onto the westbound lane of I-40 and watched his friend quickly doze off.

Allen slept soundly until he felt the Ford F-150 slowing down and coming to a stop. He opened his eyes and said, "Where are we?"

Bill said, "This is the exit towards Hoover Dam. I thought it might be cool to see that sucker."

"Since when did you become the decision-maker on this epic voyage?"

"Since the time you decided to sleep across half of Arizona."

Allen yawned and said, "Okay, I give you permission to go to the Hoover Dam. But then, I'm back in charge."

"Oh, shut up, and go back to sleep."

Allen closed his eyes and said, "Just wake me up when we get to the Colorado River. I've got a rock throwing lesson to teach you, buddy roe."

The dam itself woke them both up—big time. They knew of the Hoover Dam, but they didn't KNOW the Hoover Dam. It startled them with it's vastness and it's location, set in the rocky river channel of the Colorado. Lake Mead, on their right, about thirty feet below the top level of the dam, and the Colorado River on their left, about six hundred feet down the contours of the dam. Awesome!

They decided to park and take the guided tour of the dam, which included an elevator ride to the bottom. They exited the elevator, which was inside the dam, and found themselves at river level. They looked back up to the top of the dam and could hardly imagine that Lake Mead was indeed on the other side of this pile of concrete. But it was. Held back by tons and tons of concrete and good old American ingenuity and fortitude. It made them proud to be American; but it made them even happier to ride the elevator back to the top and emerge safely from the bottom of Black Canyon.

They walked back across the dam to the parking lot and saw a very heavy woman walking a very small dog on a leash. The dog stopped, lifted a leg, and peed on the wheel of the Ford F-150. Allen, who was about twenty yards away, yelled and said, "Hey! That's my truck. Can't you control your dog?"

Allen's words didn't seem to faze the heavy woman in the least. As the boys came close to her, she said, "It's just pee; it didn't hurt anything."

Allen didn't understand it at the time, but that remark made him angry. Without thinking, he said, "Well, let him pee on your leg next time, since it doesn't hurt anything."

Her beer-gutted husband then walked over and picked up the little dog without saying a word. The heavy woman stared at Allen, and he stared back at her. Bill hit the automatic unlock on the Ford F-150, breaking the standoff, and they each went their separate ways. Bill started the truck and looked at his friend and asked, "Did you mean to say that to that woman?"

Allen kept looking out the window towards the woman's car and answered, "I always mean what I say . . . I may not always mean to say it out loud, but I always mean it."

Bill starting pulling out of the lot and said, "I might just take you back to the Grand Canyon and dump you back in that hole."

Allen smiled and said, "Why? You know I'll just climb out again."

Allen wasn't exactly sure where they were or how to get back to the interstate, but Bill steered them toward the sign for Boulder City. Allen then asked, "So I guess we're going to Boulder City?"

"I am. You can always get out and hitchhike. I'm sure that heavy woman and her husband will pick you up."

Allen rolled up his shirt sleeve a little and said, "With these guns, there ain't a woman in Arizona that would pass me by."

"Maybe, but since we're in Nevada now, you might want to just lay back and take another nap."

Allen then bolted upright in his seat and said, "Turn around!"

Bill took his foot off the accelerator and said, "What?"

"You purposely made us miss throwing a rock across the Colorado because you knew I'd beat you. Turn this monster around. I want my revenge."

The truth was that the sight of Hoover Dam made them both forget about any rock throwing. Allen's revenge would have to wait as Bill said, "Shut up and go back to sleep, old man."

Boulder City wasn't far, and they stopped at a new-looking restaurant on Main Street that had easy parking (meaning you didn't have to back up). When they started to get out, Allen reached in the glove compartment and took out a plastic bag full of quarters he'd been saving just for this occurrence. Bill looked at him, and Allen said, "Slots. I'm going to play a few quarters while we order our food."

They walked in the restaurant, which was cool, clean, and very spacious, but totally void of any slot machines. The boys didn't really understand why there were no slot machines here, because they thought there were slot machines everywhere in Nevada. They had a very nice waitress and a delicious meal. When they finished, she thanked them for stopping in and Allen asked her where the nearest slot machines were. She said, "Vegas."

Both boys stopped in their tracks when she said that. Allen said, "Las Vegas?"

"Yeah," she said, "it's only about thirty minutes away."

Then Bill asked, "But we're in Nevada now, aren't we?"

"Yeah, you're in Nevada alright, but Boulder City does not allow gambling. You'll have to go to Vegas for that."

Neither Bill nor Allen knew what to say. Finally Bill said, "I thought you could gamble anywhere in Nevada."

She smiled at them and replied, "Not here."

They walked out of the restaurant and Allen said, "I don't believe that. Let's walk down the street."

They walked down one street and up another street. No slot machines anywhere. They finally decided to walk back to the truck, which was parked at the restaurant. When they arrived, their waitress stuck her head out the door and said, "Told you."

Even Allen had no response to that. They got in the truck and slowly drove through slot-less Boulder City on their way to a place where they were pretty sure there were more slot machines than people.

14

DRIVING THROUGH HENDERSON, NEVADA, which is a suburb of Las Vegas, Allen suddenly said, "Hey, this is Michael Chang's hometown."

"You mean the tennis player, Michael Chang?"

"Well just how many other Michael Chang's do you know, grandpa?"

Bill said, "How do you know he lives in Henderson?"

Allen answered, "You'd be surprised at all the stuff I know."

Bill glanced at him and said, "Yes, I truly would."

They took the exit for Las Vegas Boulevard, the infamous "Strip." Bill drove the Ford F-150 slowly down the crowded street while gawking at all the people and the famous hotels they'd always heard of: Caesar's Palace, Bellagio, The Venetian, Harrah's, Paris-Las Vegas, Bally's--on and on and on. As they neared the end of the "Strip" Allen said, "I have something I need to tell you."

It was such a serious tone from his friend that it had Bill a little concerned as he replied, "Okay. What?"

"I won't stand for any whores, prostitutes, or women-of-the evening degrading my camper—I might as well get that out front right now."

Without any pause, Bill answered, "It's not your camper—you're only renting it."

Allen said, "Oh, that's right. In that case, pull over here and let's see what ten dollars will get us."

Instead, they pulled into a glitzy hotel off the strip for the night. It had a nice bar, Sonny and Cher impersonators, and plenty of slot machines. The boys decided not to venture out into the Las Vegas night; they'd do their exploring the following day. They each ordered a Coors Light from a middle-aged, yet very attractive waitress, and listened to Sonny and Cher sing a few off key songs.

Business was slow in the bar so Allen worked up a conversation with the waitress, who could have been anywhere from thirty-five to fifty-five years old—depending on the light and the amount of makeup she had on. But she was very friendly. She told them her name was Loretta Martin, and she was originally from Boise, Idaho. She'd been in Vegas for almost fifteen years now. Her husband was a blackjack dealer at Circus Circus downtown, and they had a teenaged son who was a star soccer player on the local high school team.

She asked about their trip and where else they were going. Allen replied, "We really don't know, Loretta; but we'll find out when we get there." That logic was too difficult for Loretta to understand.

A young couple came in later and sat at the table next them. Bill had on his Allman Brothers tee shirt, and the man from the couple said, "You like the Allman Brothers?"

Bill nodded and said, "I sure do, son. They were quite a band."

The girl then spoke and said, "They're all dead aren't they?"

"Well, not all of them . . . yet."

She giggled a little and said, "Right, I mean the brothers, John and Paul."

Allen was thinking to himself how ignorant young people were . . . not even knowing the difference between The Allman Brothers and the Beatles. Then being unable to control himself, he said, "Well John is dead, but Paul still tours with Lynyrd Skynyrd."

"Oh wow," she said, "I'd like to see them."

At that moment, Loretta came back by their table, and facing away from the couple, said to Allen and Bill, "You guys have a little red devil in you, don't you?"

Allen grinned and looked up at her saying, "He does, Loretta. I'm just a good old mama's boy."

Loretta smiled at them both and replied, "I'm sure that's true, boys."

After a nice leisurely breakfast in the morning, Allen and Bill took a walk down the "Strip" and visited most of the big casinos. They would walk in, play a few quarter slots, see if they could get a free drink, then go to the next hotel. At the Bellagio, they walked out back to the pool area, found a table in some shade, and watched the local scenery. It was very interesting . . . not at all like they portray it on television. In fact, it looked pretty much the same as the pools looked anywhere: overweight people, ugly people, others overdressed, and some unfortunately, underdressed.

On nearly every street corner there were young guys handing out pamphlets for either nude dancing, escort services, or legal brothels—truly living up to the reputation of "Sin City." They stopped for a late lunch in the Luxor, which is a pyramid-shaped hotel, modeled after ancient Egypt. They went to the buffet where every type of food imaginable was available. They sampled a lot of it, but were most impressed by the desserts—especially the key lime pie.

They played a few slots at the Luxor, but the big meal had made them drowsy. So they took a cab back to their hotel and took a nap. Waking up refreshed, or as refreshed as two sixty-nine year olds could be, they decided they'd seen all they wanted to see of Las Vegas. The decision was made to stay in their hotel that evening and see the Wayne Newton impersonator later in the lounge. Turns out the Wayne Newton impersonator was the same guy who was Sonny, from Sonny and Cher last night—with a different wig.

They didn't stay long and went back to the bar area to do some people watching. They were sitting at a small table when a man who seemed to be a little older than each of them stopped to talk. He looked a little run down and tired, like he needed a shower and a good night's rest. Allen introduced himself and Bill, then asked the man what his name was. His answer was unintelligible, or else so foreign they couldn't understand it. He told them he was a professional gambler and had been in Las Vegas for over twenty years.

This news got their attention. Neither Allen nor Bill had ever met a professional gambler before. He told them his long, sad story of boom and bust at the tables . . . of his wife leaving him and his children abandoning him. And, finally, of his struggle to make ends meet when the tables were unkind to him. He lived in a small apartment on the edge of town and ate all his meals in the various hotels at the buffets, where he would sneak out enough food to last him for the next meal.

Allen and Bill felt certain the old guy would eventually ask them for some money, but he didn't. When he finished his sad story, he got up and shook their hands, saying he needed to get over to the casino and test his luck again. When he left, Allen looked at Bill and said, "I thought Vegas was supposed to be fun—not depressing."

They went up to their room and watched a soccer match on television, even though neither of them liked soccer. They finally laid down in their beds, with the lights turned off, and after a few moments of silence, Allen said, "Did I ever tell you the last thing Barbara said to me before she died?"

"No. What was it?"

"She had been mostly unconscious for several days. Sometimes she'd drift in and out, but never made any sense when she did wake up. We all knew she wouldn't last much longer; the doctors had prepared us. At that point I just didn't want her to suffer anymore. She would breathe in these deep gasps like she was in pain—that just tore me up. Then, that last morning, things seemed different. She was breathing normally and all of a sudden she woke up and looked at me. There were no nurses or anyone else in the room, just me. I wasn't really sure if she was actually conscious or what, but she looked at me and made eye contact. I took her hand and she smiled at me. Then she said, 'I love you.' Before I could say anything back to her, she closed her eyes and stopped breathing."

Allen didn't say anything else—he couldn't say anything else. Neither could Bill. They eventually drifted off to sleep, and fortunately for each of them, they didn't dream about a thing . . . nothing.

15

AFTER LEAVING THE HOTEL THE NEXT MORNING, they stopped at a gas station on the outskirts of Las Vegas for fuel and supplies. As Bill was putting the gas cap back on the truck he asked Allen where they were going next . . . after their less than exhilarating time spent in Vegas. Allen said, "City of Angels, grandpa. I've always wanted to see where OJ lived when he . . . well, you know."

Bill cocked his head a little and said, "You don't think he did it?"

"Ain't my position to say yes or no. The jury said he didn't, so that's that."

"Well, the second jury said he did do it. So what do you think: yes or no?"

Allen walked back to the passenger door, opened it, and answered, "I also want to see Dodger Stadium and the Coliseum, if it's not too much trouble, and you can work it into your plans."

Bill ignored the last comment and said, "You do know that the house OJ lived in at that time has been torn down don't you?"

Allen frowned and asked, "What about the fence around the house where Jack Ruby hid the gloves?"

Bill smiled and said, "Yeah, I think the fence is still there. We'll check it out."

The drive from Las Vegas to Los Angeles was long and boring—very boring. Nothing to see but sand, dirt, rocks, and scrubby little bushes. Allen commented, "How does anybody live out here?"

Bill said, "Look around brother, there isn't anybody living out here. We haven't seen any houses or signs of life for hours. The only things living here are rattlesnakes and scorpions."

Allen then asked, "Why in the world would a bunch of lawyers and politicians want to live out here?"

They drove in silence for a while until they saw a sign on the road that read "Deadman's Wash." Allen got excited and said, "Pull over . . . that's the sign I was looking for."

Bill eased the truck off the road, looked at his friend and asked, "What are you talking about? What sign?"

"That one! I was waiting on a sign from above to tell me when I should put you in your rock-throwing place. This is it—Deadman's Wash. Get out and choose your weapon."

It was hot, dry, and dusty as they walked around choosing a suitable rock to throw. When they each made their choice, Allen said, "Go ahead, rookie. Give it your best shot."

Bill picked out a fairly round, dark colored rock, limbered up his arm and shoulder a bit, then slung his rock way out into the wash where they saw it land, creating a little dust cloud. He said, "Anh, wasn't my best, but I really don't need my best, now do I?"

Allen stared at him but didn't say anything. Then he stared out at the little dust cloud still hovering where Bill's rock hit. Instead of throwing overhand, like he always had before, he threw his light-colored flat rock a little side armed so it would ride the wind like a Frisbee. It was a magnificent throw, better than Allen had imagined he could throw. His rock landed a few yards to the right of where Bill's did and also created a dust cloud when it landed. Upon impact, Allen yelled, "Gotcha! We have a new champion, ladies and gentlemen, boys and girls. One worthy of the title, 'Champion.'"

Bill was silent, but immediately started walking out to the rock landing area. Allen followed and asked, "What are you doing? You saw me beat you fair and square."

Bill never spoke, but stopped when they reached the spots in question. It was easy to see where the rocks had landed—all the ground around them had been smoothed over by the wind. They looked at the two spots and Allen said, "See? Clearly shows I won."

Then Bill went to the spot that clearly had not won and picked up the smooth, flat rock that Allen had thrown. He turned and handed the rock to his friend, still without saying a word, and started walking back to the truck.

Allen held the rock, then looked at both spots, and knew he'd lost again. He ran a few steps to catch up with Bill and said, "You just wait till we get to the Pacific Ocean! I'm gonna really embarrass your old, wrinkled up self."

When they reached the truck, Bill walked to the passenger side and finally spoke, saying, "Loser drives."

They arrived on the outskirts of Los Angeles and decided to stop at a Holiday Inn for the night. It was actually a Hawthorne Inn, but by this point in the trip they'd given up on Holiday Inns. And apparently, they were in a little town called El Monte, not Los Angeles. The Hawthorne Inn had an adjoining restaurant, so they stayed in and rested after the long drive from Vegas. At some point during the night, either fire crackers or gunfire woke them. Bill said, "Did you hear that?"

"Yeah, what was it?" Allen answered. He sat up and turned on the lamp between the two beds.

Bill immediately yelled, "Turn the light off! If it was gunfire, don't give 'em a target to shoot at!"

Allen quickly turned the light off, hoping the noise was just firecrackers. Neither of the boys slept much the rest of the night. And didn't even take time to enjoy the free continental breakfast in the lobby in the morning. They were happy to get on the road towards safer ground as quickly as possible. It was Saturday morning, so the traffic wasn't as bad as it could have been. It was still bad . . . terrible by North Carolina standards.

They Googled directions for 360 N. Richardson Ave. in Brentwood. It was a ritzy, quiet neighborhood that hinted of money and prestige. As they drove slowly down the street, it became evident to them that many other tourists were also riding by. They stopped and parked behind several other cars, then got out and walked up the street where a few tourists were taking pictures of a big house behind a high wall. There was no address anywhere on the wall or street, but Mr. Google assured them this was 360 N. Richardson—OJ's address all those years ago.

They stood there with the others and Allen whispered to Bill, "Are you sure that's not the house OJ lived in?"

Bill answered, "Why are you whispering? I told you they tore down OJ's house. This one is a new house built by some millionaire."

They kept staring, with the other tourists, then Allen asked, "But that's the original fence, right?"

Bill knew it couldn't be the original fence. It looked too new and tall, but still, he told Allen, "Yep, that's the original fence alright; said so on Google." That's what friends sometimes do for each other.

Allen said, "Wow. I can't believe I'm standing here." He looked over at Bill and continued, "Just think . . . right over there is where Keno hid the gloves and where Mark Fruton planted evidence."

Bill didn't reply to the obvious historical blunders, but a fellow tourist who overheard Allen said, "Really? Right over there?"

Allen answered, "Yep, right over there behind that wall is where they found the knife, the scarf, and the letter."

The male tourist said, "I didn't know they found the knife?"

"Oh yeah," Allen said, "Fruton found it and hid it; that's why OJ got off . . . because they tampered with the evidence."

The tourist was trying to somehow make sense of this gibberish and finally asked Allen, "What was the letter you said they found? I don't remember that."

"Oh yeah," Allen said, "There was a letter wrapped in a scarf . . . in OJ's handwriting where he tried to pin the blame on Charles Manson. But, before it got to trial, Johnny Cochran had the letter disbarred—he was a slick dude. That's really what saved OJ."

The male tourist was gawking at Allen, trying to comprehend this nonsense, and finally said, "Wow. I didn't know any of that."

Two other cars pulled up slowly and Bill said, "Let's get out of here before they arrest you for perjury." They started walking back to the Ford F-150 and Bill asked Allen, "Why did you tell that guy all that nonsense?"

"Because he got out of that car from Missouri over there. They're the 'Show Me' state . . . so I showed him."

Bill laughed and said, "You ain't no good at all, boy."

They drove about two miles and stopped in front of a condo complex on Bundy Drive. Allen said, "Why are you stopping?"

Bill looked up the driveway at the condos and replied, "Cause right there is where it happened. Nothing happened back at OJ's house. It all happened right there, brother."

Allen then realized this was the spot where Nicole and Ron Goldman were actually killed. They both stared up the drive for a few minutes, thinking about that tragic day back in 1994, and wondering why all the tourists were at OJ's old address and not here.

16

THE NEXT DAY THEY DROVE DOWN TO VENICE and the beach area. Allen had on shorts showing his very white legs, whereas Bill kept his khakis on. They walked through the beachfront area, had a drink in one of the bars, and sat outside while watching anything and everything you could imagine walk by. Allen said, "If I was twenty years old again, I'd come out here and live."

"I'd like to see that." Bill replied, "You with blue hair, tattoos all over your body, nose and ear and tongue pierced. Riding a skateboard down the sidewalk, being pulled by a pig on a leash." Bill hadn't made that up—a guy matching that exact description just came by them—on a skateboard, being pulled by a pig on a leash.

Allen said, "They're not all like that . . . this guy walking up right here is fairly normal." They waited till the guy passed, then Allen said, "See . . . he was okay."

Bill elbowed him and said, "You dumb redneck. That was a girl."

Allen turned back to look at the guy (girl) walking away and said, "No way."

Bill said, "She had boobs! Or didn't you notice that?"

Allen hopped up from his seat and started walking briskly after the person in question. After a minute or two he caught up and slowed his pace considerably as he tried to determine the actual sex of this person. Bill nearly lost sight of them in the crowd and had to stand up to follow the scene. He saw Allen pass by the person, then sort of stop and pat his pockets, like he'd lost something, then turn around right in front of the guy/girl.

After this charade, he walked back and joined Bill at the table, shaking his head. Bill said, "Well?"

Allen took a sip of his cold drink and said, "Walks like a guy, talks like a guy, acts like a guy . . . boobs like a girl."

They continued to sit and stare at the scenery. After a few minutes, Allen commented again, "I ain't never seen so many pretty girls in one place before."

Bill nodded and added, "I guess old Brian Wilson was right when he wrote, California girls—best in the world."

They argued for a few minutes about who actually did write that song and exactly what the lyrics were . . . but whoever wrote them, they were right. They finished their sightseeing on the streets of Venice and made their way over to the Los Angeles Coliseum before it got too late. There was nothing happening at the coliseum that day and it didn't have any tours, like the Alabama stadium did. So they just walked around it a little, remembering all the times they'd seen it on television over the years . . . OJ, and his Southern Cal teammates, running wild; the Los Angeles Rams, with the Fearsome Foursome; and the Olympics in 1980. Allen said, "I remember those Olympics like they were yesterday. Muhammad Ali lighting the opening torch and all . . ."

"Wait, wait, wait, wait, wait . . ." Bill said, "Ali didn't light the torch in those Olympics."

"He most certainly did! I can see him in my mind doing it."

Bill stopped walking and said, "Look, I'm not from Missouri and I'm not believing these crazy stories you're telling. He lit the torch once, but not here—not in 1980."

Allen thought to himself, "Could Bill be right?" No, he remembered it as plain as day. He told Bill, "Nope, you're wrong and I'll bet you. If I'm wrong, I'll buy dinner tonight. But if I'm right, then you'll buy me dinner at one of those fancy restaurants in Bel Air."

They rushed back to the truck and fired up Mr. Google. Muhammad Ali did light the Olympic torch at the games in 1994—in Atlanta. Bill didn't gloat because he knew his friend really thought he had that one right. So he said, "You know what . . . I bet only about one person in a million even remembers Ali lighting the torch at any Olympics."

Allen smiled at that and said, "Yep, I bet you're right. Dang, my memory's good." Friends being friends . . .

It had been several nights since they actually slept in their camper, but they still hauled it around Los Angeles with them. And once again they opted for a hotel room for the night near the beaches. They found a nice place near the Santa Monica Pier and, soon after checking in, they found the entire area to be quite busy and active. The pier itself had a small amusement park on it and several bars and restaurants.

After a dinner of pizza and Diet Pepsi, they walked out to the end of the pier and spoke to a couple of middle-aged guys who were sipping Coronas while tending four or five fishing poles they had in use. They were local guys who just liked getting away from the wives and spending time alone on the pier. Allen asked them what they were fishing for. He was unfamiliar with the marine life in the Pacific. The guy with the bushy mustache answered, "Anything that's out there. We don't care. We throw it all back in anyway. You'd be crazy to eat anything that came out of these waters."

The two fishermen offered them a beer, but they politely declined and headed back to the hotel for the evening. They debated whether to stay another night here, but finally decided to check out Dodger Stadium in the morning, then keep on going north. The next day before they left, Allen wanted to walk over to the beach again, which was only two blocks over. When they arrived, each of them took their shoes off and rolled up their pants, then waded in the water up past their ankles. They stood there silently watching the waves roll in while their feet slowly sank in the soft California sand.

After several thoughtful and reflective minutes, Allen said, "Find you a nice one and give it a whirl."

Bill was confused and said, "What?"

"Find you a rock and throw it as far as you can . . . Japan, if you can hit it."

Bill walked back up the shore a little ways and found a good sized rock. Allen had already picked his out and was waiting. Bill asked, "You ready?"

"Go!"

Bill threw it good and hard, out past where the waves were breaking. Allen looked out at the spot, then looked at Bill and said, "Nice try, gramps, but not good enough. Stand back and watch this."

He had picked out another flat, skinny rock, similar to the one he threw at Deadman's Wash. He was hoping to ride the air currents there on shore.

However, he miscalculated the strength and direction of the wind. He threw it side armed again and started it a little too high. The ocean breeze caught it and almost started bringing it back to them. It finally fell only about fifteen feet out in the surf. Bill started laughing as Allen kicked the sand and turned around, walking in disgust back to the Ford F-150.

Before leaving town they drove out to Dodger Stadium and took a guided tour through the old ball park. Even though it was built in the early 1960's, it looked new. They were allowed to walk out on the field and sit in the dugout . . . and dream. The tour ended with a visit to the Dodger Hall of Fame underneath the stadium. Neither of them had actually been Dodger fans, but they both loved Sandy Koufax. So each of them bought a Dodger's tee shirt with Sandy's number 32 on the back.

As they walked back to the truck, Bill spoke, "Well, we've gone as far west as the truck will take us. What are your thoughts now?"

Allen stopped in front of the truck, thought for a moment, then said, "I'm having the time of my life, but I don't know what your thoughts are. I never really know what you're thinking. Are you tired? Do you wanna go home? Are you bored? Do you miss your life? Do you wanna keep going? What is it, old-timer?"

Bill went around to the driver's side door and said, "Yes."

Allen opened his door and replied, "Yes, what?"

"Keep going."

17

THEY DECIDED TO FIND ROUTE 1 and take it up the coast of California. They knew that eventually they'd run into San Francisco, but they really didn't know what was in between Los Angeles and San Francisco. What they found was a lot of beauty in between those two points. The winding road alternated between the ocean and the coastal mountain range. Once they were away from the city, the country became more rural and scenic and fun. They stopped at nearly every pull-off available to gaze into the Pacific. Sometimes the road would be at nearly sea level, whereas other times, it would climb the mountains and be skirting three or four hundred foot cliffs.

Between all the viewing stops and other stops for food and rest, they weren't even halfway to San Francisco at the end of the day. They found a scenic campground near Morro Bay with a view out into the ocean and an inlet that was dominated by a large haystack shaped island. There were no campfires allowed here, but the boys didn't really mind—a chair with a cold Coors Light and that view was just fine with them.

As the sun was getting low and almost kissing the ocean, Allen looked over at Bill and asked, "So you're not regretting this trip, huh?"

Bill took a small sip of Coors Light and said, "You know . . . it's better to look back on life and say, 'I can't believe I did that!' Than to look back and say, 'I wish I had done that.'"

Allen nodded and added, "I know what you mean, brother. I think about my kids and a lot of the friends we used to have and wonder about what they're thinking or doing."

Bill pointed out to a sailboat in the ocean, then said, "Brother, learn to let go. Not everyone in your life is meant to stay. Happiness depends on ourselves."

As the sun was nearly halfway down into the ocean, Allen said, "You know, just sitting here looking at that incredible scene out there makes me realize that most people lose the small joys in the hope for the big happiness. Just like with me and Barbara . . . now I only regret the vacations we didn't take."

They watched the sun settle below the horizon and leave that entire end of the world in a reddish, yellow glow. Allen asked his friend one other question, "Have you liked all the places we've visited?"

Bill smiled and said, "I get a strange feeling when we're about to leave a place we've visited. Like I'll not only miss the people we met, but that I'll also miss the person I am at that time and place . . . because I'll probably never be at this place, or this way, ever again."

In the morning, after packing things up, they found a diner on the highway that was literally built on stilts over the cliff side. When they got out of the truck, they walked over to one side, then the other side to look at it and see what was actually keeping the diner from falling down the cliff. They weren't completely and scientifically satisfied, but the coffee and the grease from inside smelled too good for much resistance.

They sat in a window booth that overlooked the ocean and were a little surprised when the waitress appeared so soon to take their order. She said, "And how are you two gentlemen doing this morning?"

"Well, young lady, I'm doing very well. And I'll be doing great if this restaurant doesn't fall down the cliff while I'm eating flapjacks."

She smiled back at Allen and replied, "We'll be alright . . . as long as there's not an earthquake, or a truck runs off the road and hits us, or those wooden beams holding us up don't rot away. Other than that, we're good." Until she laughed, the boys didn't know what to think—and even then, they weren't a hundred percent sure.

She took their orders . . . ham and eggs for Bill, and flapjacks for Allen—with two coffees. When she brought the coffees to them, she asked, "Where are you gentlemen headed today?"

Allen pointed toward the window and said, "That way."

She smiled again and said, "I guess you've been everywhere else, huh?"

"We haven't been everywhere, but it's on our list."

Getting nowhere with Allen, she turned to Bill and asked, "Okay, but what's your destination today?"

Bill set his coffee cup down and quite seriously said, "Our destination is not a place, young lady, it's just a new way of seeing things."

She refilled their cups, put one hand on her rather broad hip, and said, "Got room for one more?"

The boys weren't entirely sure if she was serious or not, but she left for the kitchen before they had to answer that loaded question. After they were completely filled of eggs and flapjacks, they went outside and looked at the diner again, and Bill said, "I'm glad we're outta there."

As they came upon the town of Big Sur, Allen said, "Let's stop and check this out . . . see if there's any 'free love' still floating around from the sixties."

Bill eased the Ford F-150 into the exit lane, looked at his friend, and said, "And just what would an old man like you do with some 'free love?'"

"It would depend on just what the flower child was offering. I can be pretty particular with the love I take, because you know the love you take equals the love you make."

Bill remembered that song, and added, "And in your case, if you took any free love, it would definitely be The End."

They both giggled at that memory from long ago as Bill pulled the truck into a parking space along a side street. They walked down a street with a few businesses, but not much else. Allen asked, "Is this it?"

"Surely this can't be all there is to Big Sur." Bill said, then continued, "The town must be at the next exit."

They walked about three blocks, then turned the corner and went towards the ocean. The view was mostly blocked by tall pines and other growth, but they found a few spots where they could actually see the water. On their way back to the truck they met a teenager on a bicycle and asked him if this was indeed Big Sur.

The teenager asked, "What do you mean?"

Allen again asked, "Is this Big Sur? All of it?"

The teenager looked as though Allen asked him to explain the theory of quantum physics. He finally said, "I guess so." Then he pedaled away, looking back over his shoulder at what must've seemed to him to be quite an oddity.

Bill looked at Allen, then pointed to the teenager pedaling away and said, "That, my friend, is the product of some 'free love.'"

Allen answered, "If God couldn't use him, he wouldn't be here. Let's head up the road, old timer."

They had driven in silence for a few miles when Allen suddenly remembered something, "Hey, remember those two old girls from Sausalito we met back at one of those campgrounds?"

"Yeah, I remember them—the two gay girls."

"Why do you want to be like that? They weren't gay. I wonder if they'd be home now? We should be passing through Sausalito before too long."

"Home?" Bill asked. "They were going the other way from us. Texas or Florida or somewhere like that. Plus, we don't even know their last names or a phone number or anything."

"I was just wondering. They were alright, weren't they?"

Bill answered, "For two gay girls, they were pretty good."

The traffic started to pick up as they got closer to Monterey and the bay area. They stopped at a small restaurant and saw a young guy with a beard sitting across from them wearing a tee shirt that read University of Santa Cruz . . . and right under that, it read, Banana Slugs. He had a pretty girl sitting with him, but they weren't paying attention to each other. They were each too busy texting someone else.

Finally, when Allen noticed a break in the texting storm, he said, "Excuse me, sir, but I was noticing your tee shirt. What is a banana slug?"

The young guy smiled and said, "It's the name of our school, University of Santa Cruz Banana Slugs."

Allen said, "Yeah, I get that. My question is: What is a banana slug? Seems like an odd thing to be calling yourselves."

Then the girl stopped texting and answered, "Years ago we were 'The Seals,' and nobody noticed us. Too plain and ordinary. Now everybody notices us— like you just did."

Allen nodded and started to ask his question again, but the guy interrupted him and explained, "It's sort of like a bug, or a slug, that's yellowish and looks like a tiny banana. Sort of common in this area."

Allen smiled and said, "I'm gonna get me one."

The boy and girl went back to texting, ignoring them and each other. Allen and Bill had burgers and fries, with apple pie for dessert. The boy and girl must have finished their meal already because all they had on their table were tea cups. Soon, a waitress came to their table and asked, "Are you ready to order yet? Or is the tea going to be all?"

They looked up from their cell phones, then looked at each other, and the boy said, "I guess that'll be all."

As Allen and Bill were finishing their dessert, they noticed the boy and girl whispering to each other. Then the boy rose and went up to the front of the restaurant and came back with a handful of these little one or two ounce containers that hold milk for coffee and tea. He laid them down on the counter, and the girl quickly opened them all up and dumped them in her empty tea cup. They took turns sipping the tepid milk until the cup was empty again.

Allen and Bill remained quiet until Bill said, "Well, you ready to hit the road, partner?"

They took their tickets to the front register and when they got there Bill said, "I also want to place an order of two cheeseburgers, fries and Pepsis for those two young people back there—I'm paying for it."

The waitress smiled at him and said, "You don't have to do that, they'll be alright."

Bill said, "I know I don't have to—I want to."

As they walked outside to the Ford F-150, Allen said, "I can't wait to get back home and tell everybody what an old softy you are."

Bill opened his door, looked at Allen and said, "Bite me."

18

WHEN THEY ARRIVED IN THE CENTER OF MONTEREY, they stopped and Googled "Bed and Breakfast," and found hundreds of possibilities. Bill said, "How about The Seven Gables Inn? That sounds interesting."

It was also close . . . only four blocks away. It was an old Victorian house right on Monterey Bay with seven gables facing the ocean. They counted to make sure. Walking in they found the place temporarily deserted, but there was a table in the next room with cookies, pastries, and drinks sitting on it. Allen said, "Go get us a cookie while I wait here."

"I'm not going to steal their cookies, old man. If you want one, you go get it."

Without hesitation, Allen walked into the next room and picked up two cookies, biting into one of them as he walked back in the room with Bill. As he was handing the other cookie to his friend, a woman came in from the back room and saw them. They looked at her; she looked at them, and said, "I was going to ask if I could help you, but it seems as though you're helping yourself."

Allen tried to mumble something, but his mouth was full of cookie. Bill said, "It was him young lady. I told him not to."

She laughed at both of them and said, "It's okay, that's why they're there—for you to enjoy. Now . . . how can I really help you?"

They told her they were looking for a place to stay and her house looked interesting—and they loved the name. She said, "You two must be the luckiest guys in California. This place is booked up at least six to eight months in advance all year."

Allen frowned and asked, "How does that make us lucky?"

"Because I just got a cancellation call about an hour ago. I never, or seldom, get cancellations. I have the one room available, but it only has one queen-sized bed, and there's a three night minimum stay. But if you want it, I'll give you a good deal."

Allen looked at Bill . . . Bill looked at the woman and asked, "One queen-sized bed you say?"

She nodded and said, "Well, are you two . . . "

Before she could finish, Bill blurted out, "No! We are not gay. I can assure you of that, miss."

She smiled and continued, "I meant to ask, are you two committing to the three nights? If so, then I could get you a roll-away bed as well."

They looked at each other and she said, "There's a lot to see here: the Aquarium, the bay, Carmel . . . you'll need more than three days to see it all. And, I make the best breakfast in the entire state."

Without any further discussion, Allen said, "Sold. Sign us up." He looked over at Bill and asked, "Okay with you, darling?"

Bill just shook his head and answered, "We'll flip for the queen-sized bed."

They visited the world famous Monterey Bay Aquarium first. A truly unique venue, not only in the various exhibits, but it also incorporated the actual sea into the aquarium. A large glass wall extended from the aquarium itself out into the ocean, creating an exceptional viewing experience for visitors. Allen's favorite exhibit was the large tank with a great white shark. The aquarium would take in injured great whites, then nurse them back to health and release them back into the ocean.

Bill's favorite part was the entire section devoted to jellyfish. The lighting in the tanks highlighted these creatures to give off an almost surreal glow to them, mesmerizing the audiences. Both guys loved the kelp forest, which allowed the underwater plants to grow twenty to thirty feet tall. They spent several hours visiting all the exhibits, and when the left, they bought souvenirs from the gift shop to remember this day. Bill bought a small clock for his bedroom, and Allen bought a porcelain great white shark. He didn't know what he'd do with it, but he wanted it.

From the aquarium, they walked the streets of Monterey and fell in love with the quaint little town. They stopped in a book shop and learned that the aquarium itself used to be an old fish cannery in the middle of what was known as "Cannery Row," the location and inspiration of John Steinbeck's epic novel of the same name. Allen bought a copy of Cannery Row, and Bill bought two Steinbeck novels: Cannery Row and East of Eden.

After that, they took a break at an outdoor pub where they had a Coors Light and some chips. As they sat and watched all the other tourists walk by, Allen suddenly said, "Wait here. I'll be right back." He walked across the street to a tee shirt store and came back with University of Santa Cruz, Banana Slugs tee shirts for each of them. He handed one to Bill and said, "I didn't want to forget these. When we get home, we're wearing 'em out together first chance we get."

Bill smiled and held his tee shirt up in front of him, saying, "I can't wait."

They took all the stuff they'd bought back to their room and saw more cookies and pastries set out in the lobby of the Seven Gables Inn. They helped themselves to the snacks and took a plate full up to their room. After getting a Coors Light from the refrigerator in the room, they went out on the balcony, sat in some old, very comfortable rocking chairs, and ate cookies and pastries while watching the ocean waves crash against the rocky shore. It would be hard to find a more beautiful, peaceful, and happy place to be with your best friend.

All the day's events, plus the Coors Lights, cookies, and the fact that they were indeed sixty-nine years old, made the decision to stay in and rest an easy one for them. The windows were open and the cool, ocean breeze ruffled the curtains and quickly put the boys to sleep . . . each one hoping for dreams they could never forget, or would never want to forget.

★★★

Breakfast was indeed one of the best the boys had ever eaten. The owner, Susan, checked on them and asked, "Well, is it as good as I promised?"

Allen said, "If you weren't so young and so married, I'd take you home to North Carolina to cook for me."

Susan smiled at that comment and replied, "Just cook?" Before Allen could respond, even if he'd known how, she continued, "North Carolina? Isn't that part of South Carolina?"

But before either boy could get too riled up with that comment, she smiled and went back into the kitchen. They ate all they comfortably could and were sipping their last cup of coffee when two other guests came into the dining room. One lady was near their age and the other lady was thirty or so. Both of them were very attractive. They introduced themselves as Sara, the mother, and her daughter, Christine.

Of course, Allen started talking to them like he'd known them his entire life. He told them about his wife who had died, about North Carolina, and about the epic adventure he and Bill were currently on. Christine was happy to let her mother answer back and talk as much as she wanted. Which was quite a bit. Her husband had died earlier that year and her daughter, Christine, had not yet married, although she had been dating the same guy for several years now. Sara explained this last bit of information throwing a few icy stares at her daughter.

Sara and her husband were from Sacramento and had honeymooned here in Monterey many years ago. In fact, she volunteered that she thought Christine had been conceived here in Monterey—a fact that made Christine blush, yet remain quiet. Sara and her husband would come back here nearly every year of their marriage and had fallen in love with the Seven Gables Inn several years ago. When she said this, she sipped a cup of tea and stared off into eternity for a few moments. Christine then finally spoke and said, "Are you okay, Mom?"

Her mother smiled, but Allen answered the question for her, "Yeah, we're fine. Sometimes we just need to remember some things."

19

SUSAN'S HUSBAND VOLUNTEERED to unhook the camper from the Ford F-150 so the boys could do some easy exploring. And he also offered to hook it back up for them before they left. They took their time and drove around Monterey Bay until they came to the scenic, pricy town of Carmel-by-the-Sea. This area was the home of some of the most famous and gorgeous golf courses in the world, the most famous being Pebble Beach. Susan had told them to find a coastal road known as "The 17-mile Drive," which is supposed to be the most beautiful drive in California.

Susan had not exaggerated. Describing the views on this road would be impossible. You just have to see it. They stopped every quarter mile or so, got out and stared at what Steinbeck called, "The most beautiful meeting of water and land in the world." They parked and walked into the clubhouse at Pebble Beach where they each bought an overpriced golf shirt that had Pebble Beach on the front and on one of the sleeves.

When they walked out of the clubhouse, they were close to the first tee on the golf course. A group had just started walking down the fairway so the boys scurried up to the tee area and stood there looking towards the green, imagining what it must be like to actually play on this course. As they walked off the tee area, Allen told Bill to follow him. They walked back into the pro shop, and Allen walked up to a guy behind the counter and said, "How much would it cost a couple of old men to play this course?"

The young pro smiled and answered, "I could probably get you on late this afternoon for the senior rate of three hundred and ninety-five dollars."

Allen nodded and thought to himself, "That's not really that bad for us to play Pebble Beach." But as he was still thinking, the golf pro continued his sentence: "Each."

Bill grabbed Allen by the arm and said, "Let's get outta here before they charge us for standing up on the tee box."

They finished their tour around the peninsula and were extremely impressed by the 17-Mile Drive. When they came back out to the main road, Allen asked Bill, "Have you ever seen anything like that?"

Bill, who was driving, said, "It was only thirteen miles—not seventeen."

Allen looked at his friend and said, "What?"

"The road signs said it was the '17-Mile Drive.' It wasn't. It was only thirteen . . . I measured it."

Allen frowned and looked at Bill, saying "You crazy redneck. That's just the NAME of the road, not the measurement of the road. Seventeen just sounds better than thirteen. Nobody wants to live on a road called 'thirteen' . . . it's unlucky. If you saw a sign for a road called, 'Blue Jay Way,' you wouldn't expect to see blue jays on it, would you?"

Bill thought about arguing, but he couldn't . . . so he just said, "Well . . ."

They drove a couple of miles and parked in the little town of Carmel and walked the streets—it was like being in a dream. Allen had picked up a travel brochure and saw a place he wanted to visit, a bar/pub named The Hog's Breath Inn that was once owned by Clint Eastwood when he was the mayor of this little town. It was only two blocks down the street, but easy to find because all the other tourists wanted to see it as well, and there was a gathering of people outside.

They walked in but couldn't find any open seats. So they walked around and looked at the pictures on the walls of Clint with various other famous people and beautiful women. They finally found a small table outside and grabbed it before a fat man and his wife could waddle over to it. A young girl came over and handed them a drink menu and left without saying a word. There was nothing, including a Coors Light, on the menu for less than twelve dollars a drink. They sat there at least fifteen minutes and the young waitress never came back. Finally, Bill stood up and waved to the fat couple to come over and take their seats. He looked at Allen and said, "Screw this! Clint or no Clint, let's get outta here."

Allen really wanted to stay and somehow steal a glass from the pub that had Hog's Breath Inn written on it. But he knew Bill well enough to know when to argue with him and when to say, "Yes, sir." So, he said, "Yes, sir," and they left Clint's old bar, on the streets of Carmel-by-the-Sea.

They made the traffic-congested drive back to Monterey, and just before they came to their exit Allen saw a sign that read, "Snowhill Drive, 1 mile." He pointed at the sign and started to say something, but Bill noticed him and said, "Shut up."

They decided to get some take out tacos and Coors Lights and sit out on the balcony again tonight. As the sun started to sink into the Pacific, they had to put on a light jacket to keep the chill off. They were talking about nothing in particular when they heard a woman's voice say, "Excuse me."

Allen looked at Bill and asked, "What was that? Did you hear it?"

Bill got out of his rocking chair and walked over to the rail and looked down. He saw the woman, Sara, from breakfast this morning, waving back to him. She said, "I heard you guys up there . . . would you mind a little company?"

Bill said, "No, that'd be great. Come on up."

Allen looked at him and asked, "Is she coming up here?"

"Yeah. Is that alright with you?"

Allen had his pants unbuttoned and his zipper half way down as he relaxed in his rocking chair. He jumped up and started zipping his pants and said, "You wouldn't care if she saw me half naked would you?"

"No. I wouldn't care at all, but I'm sure it would greatly disturb her."

Bill met her at the door. Her daughter had carried the rocking chair up the stairs for her so she could sit outside with the boys. As soon as Bill took the chair from her, she said, "Have fun, Mom." Then before she left, she looked at Bill and continued, "Don't let her bore you too much with her stories."

As Bill closed the door, Sara looked at him and said, "She's such a prude."

Sara had brought a glass of wine with her, plus a half full wine bottle. She offered the boys a glass, but they were happy with their Coors Lights. Sara wanted to know about North Carolina and Winston-Salem. She had been to Charlotte once with her husband on a business trip. They never left the city though, except to take a tour out to the Charlotte Motor Speedway which she hated. And they had taken one other trip to the Grove Park Inn in Asheville for a friend's wedding. That trip she liked. Sara raved about Asheville and the Grove Park Inn and always wished she and her husband could've revisited that place on their own.

Allen and she took turns telling stories, while Bill mostly listened and smiled. As Sara neared the bottom of her wine bottle, her stories became a little more colorful. She told of hiking up the wilderness areas around El Capitan in Yosemite with her husband and skinny dipping in the Merced River, then making love in a field of wild flowers and clover.

Allen followed with his own story of being on vacation at Ocean Isle Beach one year, and he and Barbara jumped in the pool naked one night about 3:00 A.M. She got scared though and quickly got out and went back to the room. He put his trunks back on and was sitting in the shallow end finishing his beer when two well-dressed black guys came out and sat in some lounge chairs near him. They were surprised to see him, and Allen quickly started a conversation with them. They were part of Wilson Pickett's back-up band and had just finished a concert at UNC-Wilmington.

Bill had heard this story several times before. Each time Allen told it, the sequences, times, and names were different. The first time Allen told it to him, the guys were members of The Four Tops, and he met them in the hotel bar. But, all that was unimportant. All that mattered was that his audience enjoyed the fable—which they always did.

After a short respite from story-telling, Bill looked over at Sara, and she was fast asleep. He took the wine glass from her hand so it wouldn't fall and break. Allen saw him do this and whispered, "You're not feeling her up are you?"

Before too long there was a knock on the door. Sara's daughter had come to check on her mom. They gently woke Sara, and she thanked them for a wonderful evening. Bill picked up the rocking chair to carry it back down the stairs for her, and they all went over to the door. Sara's daughter went out first, then Sara stopped in the doorway and turned back towards Allen and half-whispered, "I wish he would have."

It took the boys about three seconds to figure out what she was referring to, then all three of them started giggling. Christine stopped, turned around and said, "What?"

Sara looked at both of the guys and replied, "Nothing dear, just old people talk. Let's go to bed."

20

WHEN IT WAS TIME TO LEAVE the Seven Gables Inn, Susan's husband hooked up the camper for them as they loaded the truck with their luggage and souvenirs. Susan made them a plate of oatmeal-raisin cookies to take with them and gave each of them a big hug before they left. As they were in the front yard, Sara and Christine came out to say goodbye as well. They all said their farewells and the boys promised to come back and stay again at the Seven Gables Inn. As they were getting into the Ford F-150, Sara walked a few steps closer to Bill and said, "Last chance."

The boys drove away from the Inn with grins on their faces and cookies on the dash, sitting next to a Bear Bryant hounds tooth hat and a rock from Sedona. They stopped at a gas station to fill up the tank, and the cooler with Coors Lights and Diet Pepsis. Bill asked his friend, "Well . . . that was fun. What's next?"

Allen was screwing the gas cap back on and answered him with a question, "Have you ever been to Berkeley?"

"Now, old man, you know good and well I've never been to Berkeley."

Allen grinned and said, "Me neither. I wanted to go out there during the sixties and protest something, but I was too lazy and too broke."

"What exactly did you want to protest?"

"It didn't matter. Whatever they were protesting at the time. I just wanted to be a part of it and check out some of those female flower children."

Bill looked at him and replied, "So the social unrest of the day really meant nothing to you . . . you just wanted to score with a hippie girl? Is that right?"

Allen rolled his head back slightly and said, "Yep, that's about it."

They programmed Mr. Google for Berkeley and were both wondering if this cauldron of the center of social unrest in the sixties still had any fire burning today. The University of California at Berkeley was huge. They didn't know where to go or where to stop, so they chose a parking lot with plenty of room for the Ford F-150 and camper. They got out and started walking. The campus looked like any other college campus to them: geeky and nerdy-looking guys, girls in short skirts and even shorter shorts. And there were many, many Asian students; none, apparently, who spoke English.

After walking around campus for about fifteen minutes, they noticed a crowd of people gathered in a grassy square between some buildings. There was a small stage with a few people gathered around it, and one guy was speaking into a microphone. The boys stood off to one side and tried to understand what was going on and what the speech was about. The guy on stage was dressed in long pants with shirt and tie—no coat. From what they could understand, he was railing about social injustice, the federal budget, taxes, the deficit, and all the other problems people usually complain about.

At the end of each comment, half the crowd would applaud and the other half would boo. Then another guy took the stage. He was dressed in a suit and started talking about the same stuff. But nearly everyone booed at everything he said. There was a young guy standing next to Bill who didn't applaud or boo, so Bill asked him what this was all about.

"It's supposed to be a debate with these two Congressmen about all the problems our country is facing."

Bill asked, "Are those guys on stage United States Congressmen?"

"Yes, sir. They're both from our district and running for re-election."

Allen said, "Let's get outta here, this stuff is useless and pointless."

Bill said, "In a minute . . . I want to hear what the guy in the suit says."

Soon, the crowd starting chanting something, and one side was yelling at the other side. Then Allen noticed a camera crew coming up behind them to get a better picture of all the ruckus. There was a young Asian lady speaking into a microphone, and the cameraman was filming her against the backdrop of the speeches. She kept moving while talking and coming closer to where Bill and Allen stood. Allen saw her, because she had on a short skirt; Bill never noticed her.

When she came next to them she said into the camera, "We have two interested onlookers at the rally today. Two men who don't fit the norm of this college setting. Let's see if we can get their take on the candidates and their platforms."

She looked at Allen and asked if she could talk with him. He pulled Bill's arm and said, "Hey, she wants to ask you some questions." Bill turned around, and for the first time saw the cameras and the girl with the microphone.

The young lady said, "Excuse me, sir, have you been listening to the debate?"

"Yep."

"And what is your opinion of the problems our country is facing, and which of the candidates has the best solutions to fix what's wrong?"

Allen started smiling. He knew what was coming. He knew there were very few things that could really get Bill going—this was at the top of the list. Bill totally ignored the cameraman and looked directly at the young Asian girl and said, "Miss, politicians, like these two guys, are the only people in the world who create problems and then campaign against them."

She replied, "I understand," but she really didn't, "what party are you associated with, sir? And which party can fix our deficits most efficiently?"

Bill started getting worked up and replied, "Miss, have you ever wondered if both the Democrats and the Republicans are against deficits, WHY do we have deficits?"

Before she could answer, he continued, "Have you ever wondered about the fact if all the politicians are against inflation and high taxes, WHY do we have inflation and high taxes?"

At this point, she motioned for the cameraman to keep rolling. She knew this was a good story. Bill said, "You and I don't propose a federal budget. You and I don't have Constitutional authority to vote on anything. The House of Representatives does!"

He was talking louder and louder now, "You and I don't write the tax code, Congress does. You and I don't set fiscal policy, Congress does."

The young lady was nodding furiously and waiting for Bill to catch his breath. When he did, he continued, "One hundred senators, four hundred and thirty-five congressmen, one President and nine Supreme Court justices equates to five hundred and forty-five human beings out of about three hundred million Americans, who are directly, legally, morally, and individually responsible for the domestic problems that plague this country."

Allen was thoroughly enjoying the lesson Bill was teaching the young lady. Bill continued, "Those five hundred and forty-five human beings spend much of their energy convincing you that what they did is not their fault. However, this group of people are the only ones that can approve any budget they want! We should replace these five hundred and forty-five individuals as quickly as possible. There is not a single domestic problem that is not directly traceable to those five hundred and forty-five people."

He was rolling now, "If the tax code is unfair, it's because they want it unfair. If the budget is in the red, it's because they want it in the red. If we have troops all over the world, it's because they want them there. Don't let them con you into the belief that there exists disembodied mystical forces like 'the economy,' 'inflation,' or 'politics' that prevent them from doing what they take an oath to do. Young lady, those five hundred and forty-five people, and they alone, are responsible. We should vote all of them out of office and clean up their mess!"

When it was evident Bill had finished, all those around him burst out in applause. The young lady reporter sidled next to Allen and said, "That was great! What's your friend's name?"

Allen smiled and said, "Young lady, that is Jonathan B. Goode and I'm proud to be his friend."

She was gushing now and asked, "And what is your name, sir?"

"I'm Mr. Kite, for your benefit, ma'am. Thanks for your time and interest, but we've got to be moving along."

The young lady tried her best to talk with Bill further, but Allen was dragging him away as all the young people were shaking his hand and giving him fist bumps. When they finally cleared the crowd, Allen said, "Well, you sure stirred up the pot back there didn't you, grandpa?"

Bill smiled broadly and replied, "I sure hope so."

They found the Ford F-150 and were starting to pull out when they noticed the young news woman and her cameraman coming down the sidewalk in their direction. As they passed them, Bill waved and Allen gave the peace sign. The news woman was waving her arms frantically at them—to no avail. They were on their way over the rainbow . . . or the Golden Gate Bridge, whichever came first.

21

I<small>T TOOK THEM NEARLY ALL DAY</small> to get up to San Francisco. It wasn't that far, but the traffic was Californian in nature. And, pulling the camper prevented them from displaying their NASCAR roots and showing off the power in the Ford F-150. They found a parking lot that charged them ten dollars to park. Then they hopped on a cable car—just because they wanted to.

They eventually made it to Fisherman's Wharf, the most touristy of San Francisco's many tourist places, and found a nice café to sit, relax, and have a drink with dinner. It was expensive, but it was worth it. The view from their table was out across the San Francisco Bay, looking towards the ocean through the Golden Gate Bridge. They took their time ordering, drinking, and eating. Eventually, they saw the sun slipping down behind the bridge towards the ocean.

As they were sipping their drinks, they noticed several people in the café pointing in their direction. They assumed these people were pointing past them, out towards the setting sun. They were not. Soon, one young lady and her friend came over to the table where Allen and Bill were sitting, and the one lady said, "Excuse me, I hope I'm not disturbing you, Mr. Goode, but I wanted to tell you how much I enjoyed and appreciated your comments today."

Allen stood up and said, "Thank you young lady. Mr. Goode and I are thankful there are some people out there who have the same sentiments as we do."

She thanked them again and reached down to shake Bill's hand. He stood up and took the young lady's hand and started to ask her what in the world she was talking about, but Allen spoke first and said, "Thanks again for coming over, I hope you have a great evening."

When the two ladies went back to their table, Bill looked at Allen and said, "That was bizarre. What was she talking about?"

But before Allen could respond, a man dressed in shorts and a tank top came up to their table and said, "I saw you on TV today, Mr. Goode. You told them exactly what we all wish we could have told them. Thanks for speaking up, I appreciate it." He shook hands with Bill and Allen and, as he turned to leave, several other people all stood up and started clapping their hands. Soon, the entire café erupted in applause. Allen was halfway bowing and waving his hand in appreciation. Bill was dumbfounded and wondering what these crazy Californians were doing—and also wondering who in the world Mr. Goode was.

When the scene finally calmed down a bit, Allen explained everything to Bill. Neither of them knew the camera woman and film crew were with the local television station. They had no idea the interview Bill did with the young lady was going to be aired and create as much publicity as it did. They were minor celebrities now. Bill even appreciated Allen's quick thinking about giving out false names. He understood Jonathan (Johnny) B. Goode, but he couldn't understand the name Allen gave for himself—Mr. Kite.

Allen said, "Think."

After a few seconds, Bill then remembered the old Beatles' song, "For the Benefit of Mr. Kite." He smiled and said, "Oh, okay, gotcha."

They shook hands with several more people and Bill even signed an autograph for a young kid—he signed it, J.B. Goode. The kid was thrilled. After this eventful dinner and the sun fully set into the Pacific, the boys made their way back to the Ford F-150 and set upon trying to find a Holiday Inn for the night to enjoy their newfound celebrity status.

They drove across the Golden Gate Bridge as slowly as they could without getting a ticket so they could view the city and the bay behind them. They saw several hotels in the Sausalito area, none of them a Holiday Inn. They picked out one named The Bay Bridge Hotel that was located on San Pablo Bay. However, they couldn't see the Golden Gate Bridge from anywhere in the hotel. After they checked into their room they went to the little pub at the hotel for a nightcap and asked the bartender about not being able to see the bridge.

He said, "Sure you can, look right over there."

They looked where he was pointing, but they didn't see it. Bill said, "This isn't even the right direction, the Golden Gate is back that way."

The bartender said, "Oh, you thought the name of the hotel meant you could see the Golden Gate Bridge. No . . . it's the Bay Bridge that goes over to Oakland. That's it right over there."

The boys looked again and did indeed see what he was pointing at. Their disappointment was very evident, but the bartender then said, "Hey, aren't you the two guys from TV today?"

Allen perked right up and said, "Yes, sir, we are."

The bartender insisted on buying them a drink on the house. It was a very nice way to end the evening as the guys sat and sipped an Iron Maiden while staring at the less than spectacular, twinkling lights of the Oakland Bay Bridge.

In the morning they debated about taking a bay cruise on one of the many tourist boats. But the thought of it made Allen feel a little queasy so they decided not to risk it. After they checked out of the Bay Bridge Hotel, they found a parking space near the little downtown area of Sausalito. They were enamored by the quaint little town and all the shops and cafes available. As they were walking, Allen asked Bill, "I wonder where those two girls live?"

He was referring to the two ladies from the campground they met that one night. He doubted Bill would remember them at all. But as soon as he finished asking the question, Bill replied, "I don't know. You should've gotten their names or phone number."

That answer surprised Allen, and he thought to himself, "Maybe there is some hope for my old, lovesick friend after all."

They decided to stop at an outdoor café and have some coffee while watching life pass by on the streets of Sausalito. As they came to a nice place and started to walk in, Allen grabbed Bill's arm and said, "Wait."

Bill stopped and looked at his friend, saying, "You don't like this place?"

Allen didn't answer that question. Instead he half whispered to Bill, "Look over there."

Bill looked in the direction Allen was nodding, and saw two middle-aged women sipping coffee and gossiping. Another table had a young guy and his girlfriend drinking something icy while holding hands, and the only other table in that area had a guy reading a newspaper. Bill said, "What?"

Allen excitedly answered, "That's Johnny Depp."

"What's Johnny Depp?"

"That's Johnny Depp reading the newspaper over there."

Bill couldn't see who the guy was; the newspaper was completely covering his face. He whispered back to Allen, "You're crazy, old man."

"I'm not crazy. I saw him. That's Johnny Depp."

They stood there waiting for the man to move the newspaper so they could see his face, but a woman walked up to them and said, "Can I help you? Do you guys want a table?"

Allen was still speechless, thinking he'd seen Johnny Depp, so Bill answered, "Yes, ma'am, we would. Thank you."

They were seated on the other side of the man reading the newspaper, next to the table of the two middle-aged women. The man reading the newspaper set his paper down, but he had a hat on and sunglasses and was half-turned away from them—they couldn't be sure if it was or was not Johnny Depp. As the waitress brought their coffee and sweet rolls back to them, the young boy and his girlfriend walked up to them and said, "Aren't you the guys from TV?"

Before Allen or Bill could answer, the two middle-aged women looked over and one of them said, "Yes, you are them. I can't believe it. Ava, it's those guys from TV."

Both women then came to their table, along with the boy and girl, and they were all babbling about something when Allen and Bill noticed the guy with the newspaper getting up from his table. He rose, picked up his newspaper and keys from the table, took his sunglasses off, and looked directly at the guys, tipping his hat to them, then walked away. It was Johnny Depp.

They eventually spoke with their new fans and made them all happy as they realized that for a few minutes they were indeed more famous than the movie star, Johnny Depp.

Before leaving San Francisco, there was one other place Allen wanted to visit: Haight-Ashbury. They drove back across the bridge and Mr. Google took them to this famous bastion of the hippie, counter-culture movement of the 1960's. Of course, there were no more hippies and there was no counter-culture movement any longer . . . but there used to be. And this is where it all had happened. It was hard finding a parking place, but they finally found a side street a few blocks away and started walking. San Francisco was not the ideal city to walk around in if you're sixty-nine years old and a little out of shape—too many hills.

They made it to the corner of Haight Street and Ashbury Street, with several other tourists, and stood there . . . thinking. This entire area of the city had gone into decline and disrepair after the sixties and had only recently been revitalized. However, now it was full of shops and cafes and pubs and a very nice place to meet and congregate. No free love, no open drug use, no hippie bands playing on the corners, no flower children—but a nice place.

Allen and Bill found an outdoor café and sat watching all the traffic pass by as they had a sandwich and a Diet Pepsi. An older couple, probably close to their age, sat next to them and Allen started a conversation—of course. He asked if they were from San Francisco and the gentleman answered, "We used to be. But it got so expensive to live here that we had to move out to Daly City. We only come down here now to walk around and see the city—it's still beautiful—don't you think?"

Allen answered, "Yes, it's great. It's my first time visiting, but I always dreamed of coming here—back in the day."

The lady said, "You should've come. You would've had fun. We did."

Allen asked them both, "Were you here in the sixties?"

"Oh yes, this is where we met, one summer day in 1967. It doesn't seem real now." The woman had a wistful look on her face as she said this.

Bill finally joined in and asked, "Was it as surreal and open as the magazines and television made it seem to all us other people around the country?"

The man smiled and said, "It was different back then. Life was different. Values were diverse and a far cry from what they are today."

Allen asked, "You say you met here, how did that happen?"

They both smiled and looked at each other to decide who would tell the story. Finally the man started, "There was some sort of festival going on and a band was playing across the street, right over there. It was summer and an unusually warm day for San Francisco. For some reason, and I don't know why, a firetruck appeared and started shooting water up in the sky and letting it fall down on everyone like rain. It was surrealistic, if you know what I mean."

Then he looked at his wife and she continued the story, "Well, we all got soaking wet, which was good and a lot of fun. And of course back then none of us girls wore bras—it just wasn't done. As our shirts and dresses got wet, well . . . you can imagine what we looked like. A wet tee shirt doesn't hide much. I was completely soaked through and laughing at something. And as I turned around this guy with a beard and beautiful blue eyes, was standing next to me, smoking something, and staring at me. I looked at him and asked, 'Do you like what you see?' He said, 'From the outside . . . yes.' So I pulled up my shirt to show him my boobs and said, 'How about now?' He smiled at me and handed me his, umm, what he was smoking, and we spent the rest of the day and night together."

She looked at her husband and he smiled at her and took her hand and said, "And almost every night since then."

They asked Allen and Bill about North Carolina, but neither of the boys could match that story of a hippie party, with firetrucks, wet tee shirts, smoking, flashing, and falling in love on the corner of Haight-Ashbury back in 1967.

22

THE BOYS DROVE UP THE COAST OF CALIFORNIA, taking their time to enjoy the views and revel in their temporary stardom. They stopped early when they saw a nice looking campground with a view of the ocean near Eureka, California. This campground didn't allow campfires either, which was a downer, but the view of the ocean from the high elevation pretty much made up for it. And, they got there early enough to secure a spot only two places down from the bathrooms!

After setting up everything, and since it was still daylight, they decided to take a walk down the trail towards the ocean. It was a gentle slope, so it wouldn't bother Bill's knees too much. And it was deserted as well—at least in human terms. There were several little tidal pools near the shore that were teeming with marine life—all waiting for the tide to come back in and set them free. The boys sensed some movement in the ocean, other than the waves, and soon saw a pod of dolphins pass by, rising and dipping below the surface. It was impossible to count them, but there must have been at least fifteen or twenty in the grouping.

Several birds, whose species was unknown to them, would land and peck at something in the sand, then fly away. Others would follow the waves as they receded along the shore, then scurry back as the new waves came rolling in. God had provided for them all in His own unique way. They walked down the beach until the sun started lowering near the horizon. Then they decided to return so they could watch the sun set in the ocean from their camp chairs.

As they started back, Allen said, "Find you a nice one and throw it as far as you can . . . if you're up to it."

Bill replied, "Oh, I'm up to it, grandpa."

Allen threw his rock out into the ocean first . . . and it was a good throw. He looked at Bill and said, "Beat that, Mr. Goode."

Bill wound up and really heaved his rock extra hard. As soon as he let it go and grunted with the throw, Allen knew he was probably beat. When the rock was about half way to splashdown, Allen yelled out, "Hey, what's that over there?"

Bill looked where Allen was pointing and, of course, he didn't see anything. He asked, "Where?"

By that time, Bill's rock fell anonymously into the ocean, out of sight. Allen then said, "Oh, sorry, it was nothing. But, ladies and gentlemen, we have a new world rock throwing champion."

Bill looked out into the ocean, then back at Allen and said, "Well, there's no disgrace in losing this way; but there's no honor in winning this way either."

Bill started walking back toward camp, but Allen just stood there . . . thinking. Then Allen yelled out, "Okay, we'll call it a draw and wait for better conditions." He caught up with Bill, and they started back towards camp together. The only problem was they couldn't recall which path they'd taken down to the beach from the camp.

The first trail they ventured up ended in a grove of trees. The second path fizzled away after a few yards. Allen looked at Bill and said, "Well this is a fine mess you've gotten us in."

Bill replied, "I didn't realize you were such a whiner."

"Whiner? Just because I don't want to die out here in the middle of nowhere makes me a whiner?"

Bill said, "As soon as they figure out that two celebrities like us are missing, they'll have the Coast Guard, the National Guard, and CHIPs all out here looking for us."

Allen said, "Okay, Mr. Jonathan B. Goode, whatever you say. But I'm getting thirsty."

They soon found the right path and made it back to their camp in time to open up a cold Coors Light and watch the last half of the sun slowly sink into the Pacific. It was a grand sight indeed. As soon as the sun disappeared, it got chilly. They put on a jacket and wished they could light a fire. As they started on their second and last Coors Light of the evening, Bill broke the silence and asked his friend, "Tell me about your kids, Allen. What's going on with them?"

Initially, Bill didn't think Allen was going to answer him. But after a time of reflection, Allen began, "It's hard to explain, Bill. I love my kids and I would die for them; but we're just not close anymore. I don't want to say they're not good people, because I think they are. They're both successful and smart, but we just don't have a lot in common—it seems that all died with their mother."

Bill only nodded and gave his friend more time . . . then Allen continued, "They were always close to her, especially Anna. Well, John was too. I always wanted John to play sports, but that just wasn't in him. He was happy playing video games and working on the computer, so he and I really never did much together. And Anna was always with her mom. I don't know if I was a bad father or what, but I was just never close to either of them. And now . . . I think they'd be fine to never see me again. It's hard."

Allen picked up a small pebble and threw it down the road and said, "They both know they'll get a good inheritance when I'm gone, so they're nice to me . . . most of the time. But I know they don't want to visit me, or really even speak to me on the phone. I guess every family has problems, Bill. It would've been a lot easier on everybody if I'd been the one who died, and Barbara had lived. But, it is what it is. At least with the inheritance looming, I know they'll sort of keep in touch with me."

Bill could sense his friend choking up a bit, so to lighten the mood, he asked, "Well, speaking about the inheritance and all . . . what are you leaving me?"

Allen took a sip of Coors Light and answered, "I'm leaving you that rock on the dash of the Ford F-150, and I want you to take good care of it."

Bill looked over at him and said, "You can't leave me that rock. It's mine to begin with. I picked it up in Sedona, Arizona with my own hand."

Allen answered, "Well, you ain't getting my Bear Bryant hat—you can forget that!"

They both giggled a little until it was time for Allen to ask his serious question: "Why didn't you and Eliza have any kids, Bill?"

"We tried, Allen. We went to doctors. We did all sorts of procedures. I don't know how much money we spent on fertility clinics and junk like that . . . none of it worked. We just couldn't do it. Lord knows we tried. After Eliza left me I always wondered if that was the root cause of it all—that I couldn't give her any children. But she never said anything, so I guess I'll never know. We thought about adopting one time, but the whole process would take so long, we just never followed through on it. By the time it dawned on us that we'd never have kids of our own, it was too late."

They both sat there staring at nothing. Thinking about everything. Finally Allen spoke and said, "Sometimes life is hard to understand, isn't it?"

"I don't understand things any more than you do, buddy. But one thing I've learned is that you don't have to understand things for them to be."

Allen thought about this comment, then said, "Truth."

They got cold during the night and were not unhappy to see the sun rise in the morning. After packing up quickly, they drove down into the town of Eureka to find a café with hot coffee and greasy biscuits. The Humboldt Diner sat in the middle of town and it had easy parking for the camper and Ford F-150. They sat in a corner booth, and a thin man came from behind the counter carrying a coffee pot. He walked up and asked, "Will you two gents be needing some coffee?"

Allen answered, "Yes, sir. You are a life saver."

He poured their coffee and handed them menus, then said, "My name's Lance, I'll come and check on you in a couple of minutes."

Bill wanted the Fisherman's Feast: eggs, bacon, ham, hash browns, and biscuits. Allen looked at him and said, "Really?"

"Yeah. What's wrong with it?"

Allen said, "Just make sure you find us a camping spot next to the bathrooms tonight."

Lance came back to take their order, and Allen ordered the biscuits with sausage gravy to go along with Bill's Fisherman's Feast. He took their orders back to the kitchen, then came back to refill their coffee cups, and Allen asked him if he'd always lived here in Eureka.

"Sure have, all my life. I love it here."

Bill asked, "Is this your place?

"No . . . my brother-in-law owns it. I run it for him. I used to be a painter, but that was hard work—this is a lot easier."

Allen then asked Lance, "Eureka is certainly unique. How did the town get it's name?"

Lance set the coffee pot down on the table and said, "The first settlers were coming down the Shasta River minding their own business when the local Indian tribe started chasing them. The Indians ran down the river banks shooting arrows at 'em, trying to kill 'em. This went on for a few miles, and the settlers were getting really scared and tired of rowing so hard in their canoes. Then, all of a sudden, the river opened up into the Humboldt Bay here and the settlers rowed out into the bay out of arrow range. When they were safe, one of them stood up and yelled out 'EUREKA!' And the name stuck."

Bill and Allen were spellbound by the story and waited until they were sure Lance had finished. Then Allen said, "Wow! That really happened, huh?"

Lance picked up his coffee pot, grinned at them both and said, "Nah, I'm just messing with you."

Breakfast was great and the boys were getting ready to go when Lance came back over to see if they wanted anything else. They didn't . . . they were too full. Allen said, "Those biscuits were amazing; ya'll make 'em by hand?"

Lance smiled and said, "Yeah, we're famous for those--special ingredients."

Allen took the bait and asked, "Really, what do you put in them?"

Lance looked around to make sure no one could hear him, then whispered, "We add a little cocaine to get you hooked . . . just a pinch."

They were both dumbfounded until Lance started laughing at them. He asked if they wanted anything else, but they declined, saying they needed to be moving on down the road. Rising from the table, Allen asked Lance where the closest gas station was because they needed to fuel up. Lance looked out the window and said, "Is that your Chevy Silverado out there?"

Allen answered, "No, we're driving the Ford F-150 down the street."

Lance had a very serious look on his face and said, "We don't allow Fords to gas up here in Eureka."

There was complete silence until Bill punched Allen on the arm and said, "He's messing with you again."

Lance laughed, Bill laughed. But Allen was a little shell-shocked, and quietly walked out the door. Once they were safely outside, Allen said, "Dang, he was weird."

Bill said, "I liked him."

"Well then, you're weird too, old man. Let's get outta here."

23

THEY CONTINUED UP THE COAST, knowing they would eventually run into Oregon . . . but they didn't know they would run into the biggest trees in the world first. They were stunned to drive through Redwood National Forest and experience these massive trees up close. Most of the trees were ten to fifteen feet in diameter and usually 225-325 feet tall. Some were nearly 370 feet tall—on a football field, that's reaching from one goal post across the field to the other goal post.

Around 1850, there were over two million acres of redwoods in California. Now, there were less than forty thousand acres—most of them protected from loggers—but not all of them. It was hard for the boys to fathom how big these trees really were. Their minds just didn't seem to be able to grasp what their eyes were seeing. Not only the trees, but the growth in the forest was amazing as well. Rhododendrons were everywhere and ferns were growing four and five feet tall. It seemed possible to walk among the ferns and get lost.

They even drove the Ford F-150 THROUGH one tree. The road had been built through the forest, and one tree had the road cut through it, like a tunnel. Stopping in a small parking lot along the way, there was a gift store cut into one of the massive trees. The entire store was inside the tree. Each of the boys bought a tee shirt with a picture of a redwood tree on the front.

One of the park rangers told them of a campground on the coast, which wasn't far from the National Forest where they were. They drove over and were surprised to find no one else there—not even an attendant. It was on the honor system. They set up camp, and since there were no signs preventing camp fires, they gathered up some wood for a small fire later that night.

From where they set up their camper they could see and smell the ocean. Since it was still daylight, they decided to walk down the deserted beach for a while. As soon as they crossed over the small dunes, they saw a man sitting in a reclining beach chair with a cooler at his side and a fishing pole. They looked up and down the beach and didn't see anyone else in either direction, nor did they see any other cars in the campground. Their first thought was, "How did this guy get here?"

They crossed the dunes and started walking towards him just as he reached in his cooler for something to drink. He noticed them coming and threw an arm up in the air waving to them. The boys walked up behind him only to be shocked to find him completely naked, sitting in his chair, drinking a cold Bud. He didn't try to cover up or put anything on, he simply adjusted the fishing pole, which had a line out into the surf. He said, "Howdy boys. Beautiful day isn't it?"

Allen spoke while Bill tried to avert his eyes and look into the ocean, "Yes, sir, it is. Catching anything?"

"I've caught a few small ones, but I threw 'em back. Trying to catch a couple of good ones for dinner tonight."

As far as the boys could see, he had no clothes whatsoever with him or near him. There was his chair, his cooler, and the fishing pole. Unless he had some clothes inside his cooler, he was au natural. He asked Allen, "You guys like a beer?"

"No, we're good. Just out taking a walk, we've been driving all day."

He asked, "Where are you fellows from?"

"North Carolina."

"You guys ever fished the Outer Banks there? I heard it's awesome."

"No, I've never been fishing there." Then Allen looked at Bill and asked him, "Bill, you ever been fishing at the Outer Banks?"

Bill had been fishing at the Outer Banks several times, but he answered, "No." while still looking out into the ocean.

Allen, trying not to look directly at this naked man, but not wanting to be rude either, said, "You live around here?" "About twenty minutes away."

Allen nodded and asked, "Walking or driving?"

"Driving."

This line of questioning was going nowhere fast. Why was a naked man, with no apparent transportation, sitting in a reclining beach chair, fishing on a deserted beach, in the middle of nowhere?

As Allen was desperately trying to figure how to ask his next question, the man's pole snapped forward and he jumped up and ran toward the water. Bill immediately averted his focus away from the water and back to Allen, who just shrugged. The man started reeling in his catch, and the boys tried not to watch. But their curiosity got the better of them. He had some sort of fish that looked to be about eighteen inches long. He looked back at them and yelled out, "There's one! Now I just need one more."

As he started walking back to his chair, they both waved and started walking away as Allen yelled back to him, "Good luck, Sir. Have a great day."

The boys walked down the beach and picked up a few sea shells they found interesting. Then they crossed over the dunes to walk back toward their camp so they wouldn't cross paths with the nude man again. When they made it back to their camper, two other campers were parked down from them, each of them setting up their equipment for the night. As they opened the doors to the Ford F-150 to put their sea shells on the floor, Bill looked over at Allen and said, "Do you think anyone would ever believe us if we told them what we just saw?"

Allen smiled and said, "Nope. Absolutely not."

The next morning, after they warmed up, they continued exploring the roads through and around Redwood National Park. Just outside the park boundary was a small restaurant that was packed with other tourists from the park. They had to wait a few minutes for a table, but it was worth it. The meal was great, all except for a table near them with little kids running wild and screaming while the parents ignored them—apparently too busy texting someone else more important than their own family.

They passed through a couple of other state parks and stopped to admire the majestic redwoods there as well. Late afternoon they came into a small town near the Oregon border and saw a friendly looking bar, so they stopped. They ordered a pizza to share, plus Coors Lights. When the young waitress left, Bill said, "Well?"

Allen knew what he meant, but he had no answer. So he remained silent. Bill kept looking at him, and when Allen finally looked back, Bill arched his eyebrows. Then Allen said, "I don't want to go home yet."

Bill replied, "I don't either. That wasn't what I was asking."

"Well, what were you asking?"

"Continue north to Canada? Start back toward the Rockies and see what's there, or backtrack through the center of California?"

Allen said, "Did you bring your passport?"

"Didn't think about it."

"Me neither. But it would be a shame to be this close to Seattle and not visit Jimi Hendrix's home."

That hadn't crossed Bill's mind. He was thinking about Mt. Rainier, the Olympic Peninsula, and the Space Needle . . . but Hendrix was better than all that. He looked at Allen and said, "Exactly what I was thinking."

24

THE BOYS CROSSED INTO OREGON, not knowing much about the state except what they could see: mountains off to the east and north, with a beautiful, rocky coastline. They found a nice campground and stopped a little early to wash some clothes and clean out the camper. There was also a KFC nearby and they picked up a bucket of chicken for dinner. Tonight they would picnic around their little camp fire—which was admissible here.

It was a crisp night, and they had to wear sweaters and jackets as they sat outside and stared into the fire, eating chicken and sipping their Diet Pepsis. The Coors Light would be their dessert tonight. As Bill was finishing his second chicken leg, he said, "I don't know a lot about Oregon. I like their football team, but that's about all I know."

Allen shook his head and threw a chicken bone into the trash bag, then said, "I thought you went to college, boy. Ain't you learned nothing?"

Bill leaned back and replied, "I learned as much as you did—probably more, since I didn't cut nearly as many classes as you did."

"Well I learned it all so quick, I didn't need to go to class all the time. Only you remedial learners needed to go all the time."

"Shut up. You don't even know what 'remedial' means."

Allen threw his Diet Pepsi can in the trash bag and opened a Coors Light, then said, "I know more about Oregon than you do, old-timer."

"Okay, illuminate me."

Allen started to say something, then stopped, and asked, "You want a flashlight?"

"No, grandpa . . . tell me what you know about Oregon."

"I know all sorts of stuff. It's where Evil Knievel tried to jump over the Snake River in that hoax of a television show back in 1980. It's where Saint Helen's Mountain exploded and killed all those people back in the nineties.

Oregon is where Lewis & Clark got ambushed by Indians and taken into captivity before they bought Alaska. And, it's the birthplace of John Glenn, the first man in space."

He took a big drink of Coors Light, then wiped his mouth with the sleeve of his coat and burped. Bill looked at him like he was from a foreign planet. Bill said, "How can one man get so many facts so messed up, so easily?"

Allen asked his friend, "How do you know they're messed up? You said you didn't know anything about Oregon."

Bill got a little indignant and said, "Not knowing anything and being crazy are two completely different things."

Allen took another swallow and said, "Well, I think I'm right. And since you admittedly don't know anything about Oregon, then I tend to like the facts I do know better than the facts you don't know."

As Bill was trying to understand this ill-conceived logic, Allen threw him a Coors Light and said, "Here, Einstein, see if you can understand this."

★★★

None of the other campers stayed outside, but Allen and Bill enjoyed their fire and the solitude the two friends had with each other. After an extended period of silence, Allen said, "Today is Barbara's birthday." If he'd said anymore, he would've started crying. Then, several minutes later, he asked Bill if he remembered the old Van Morrison song, Crazy Love.

"I remember Van Morrison," Bill answered, "but I don't remember that song."

Allen sighed, "I memorized it and sung it to her every year on her birthday—it was sort of our song, I guess."

Bill said, "Sing it now. For her . . . she's listening."

Allen started singing and made it all the way through without breaking down:

> "I can hear her heart beat for a thousand miles
>
> And the heavens open every time she smiles
>
> And when I come to her that's where I belong

FRIENDS

Yet I'm running to her like a river's song

  She gives me love, love, love, love, crazy love

She's got a fine sense of humor when I'm feeling low down

And when I come to her when the sun goes down

Take away my trouble, take away my grief

Take away my heartache, in the night like a thief

Yes I need her in the daytime

Yes I need her in the night

Yes I want to throw my arms around her

Kiss her hug her kiss her hug her tight

And when I'm returning from so far away

She gives me some sweet lovin' brighten up my day

Yes it makes me righteous, yes it makes me feel whole

Yes it makes me mellow down in to my soul

She give me love, love, love, love . . . crazy love."

When he finished his song, Allen got up and walked down the road by himself . . . all by himself.

25

THEY TRAVELED UP THE COAST OF OREGON and breathed in all the magnificent scenes. It was cloudy and rained some; but it was still gorgeous. They stopped at a curve in the road with a pull-off big enough for the Ford F-150 and the camper. Stepping out into a light drizzle, they looked down a cliff and out into the ocean where there were six or seven little islands not far from shore. Some type of bird was riding the currents off the ocean, floating overhead. It wasn't a buzzard, but it was big like a buzzard. It never flapped it's wings and never soared close enough to reveal exactly what kind of bird it was . . . except, beautiful.

The boys stopped at nearly every pull-off they saw and gazed into the misty distance. By the time they reached Cape Lookout State Park, it was too late in the day to hike the 2.4 mile trail they'd read about on Mr. Google. So they drove into the nearest town and decided to find a Holiday Inn for the night since it was still raining and a little chilly. They settled for the Lookout Hotel instead, and it was a good choice.

The hotel had a nice restaurant that served fresh salmon, caught in one of the local rivers. Bill and Allen had never enjoyed salmon that tasty. It was a new experience for them . . . eating salmon caught fresh from the river that same day. When the waiter came to refill their coffee, Allen said to the young man, "That was indeed the best salmon (which he pronounced s-a-l-m-o-n) I've ever had in my life."

The young man said, "I'm glad you liked it, sir. It was caught fresh today."

When he walked away, Bill half whispered to Allen, "It's pronounced s-a-m-o-n, without the 'L.'"

Allen said, "What? I ain't never heard that before."

"Just because you've never heard it before doesn't mean that it's not right."

"That's not how you say it in North Carolina."

"Yes it is. We just don't pronounce it right."

Allen looked at Bill like he wasn't sure if Bill was just messing with him, or not. Then he said, "Really?"

"Yes, really."

Allen nodded slowly, still unsure if Bill was pulling his leg. When they finished the meal and dessert of blueberry cobbler, Allen handed the waiter his credit card and said, "Excuse me young man. How do YOU pronounce this word?" Allen spelled out s-a-l-m-o-n.

The young man immediately said, "Samon."

When he left with the credit card, Allen shook his head and told Bill, "I can't believe I've been saying that wrong my entire life."

Bill quite sympathetically replied, "Buddy, much of what is said just doesn't matter; and much of what matters is not said."

Allen didn't quite understand the full meaning of that, but he knew Bill did, and he appreciated the thought behind it. The waiter brought their credit cards back and asked if there would be anything else. Allen stood up and said, "Nope. That'll be all. But dang, that was some of the best . . . blueberry cobbler I've ever had."

Their plan for the next day was to hike the 2.4 mile trail at Cape Lookout State Park if it wasn't raining too hard. The peninsula on which the park was located jutted out into the ocean and had very little protection from the wind and rain, which are prevalent to this area.

At breakfast, Allen looked up at Bill and said, "I think I'll have the eggs and bacon—that's pronounced b-a-c-o-n."

Bill picked up a packet of sugar from the table and threw it at Allen, who said, "What?"

After breakfast, it looked like it would start raining any moment. They drove out to the trailhead for the hike around the peninsula anyway. After parking and putting on their raincoats, they looked at each other. Allen said, "Well?"

Bill looked up at the low ceiling of clouds and answered, "Up to you."

Allen said, "No, you decide. Right or wrong, make a decision. The road of life is paved with flat squirrels who couldn't make a decision."

Bill opened his door and said, "Let's go."

They started out in a fine mist, with the wind at their backs . . . not unpleasant at all. However, when they reached the end of the peninsula, about a mile and a half from the parking lot, it started raining with a fury. And, the walk back was into the wind, which was now not playing games. The boys had to walk bent over into the wind, trying to keep the rain out of their eyes. They couldn't see the coast, the ocean, or the shore—they could barely see the path in front of them.

Finally, they made it back to the safety of the park welcome center. When they walked in, a ranger looked at the two soaked men and said, "You guys really like an adventure don't you?"

Allen grinned and replied, "You only live once, but if you do it right, once is enough."

The ranger offered them some coffee while they dried out. The rain had no intention of letting up. The ranger asked where they were from, and he told them he'd once been a ranger at Guilford Battlefield Park in Greensboro, North Carolina. He said during the careers of all young rangers, they must do time in the "cannon-ball parks," as he called them. He spent time at Gettysburg, Fort Sumter, and several other similar parks on the east coast. "After building some seniority, you're allowed to move to the more scenic places out west." he explained.

He told them he'd been at Arches National Park, Zion, Yellowstone, Yosemite and now here, due to a promotion. Allen asked how he liked the weather, since it was currently pouring down rain. The guy smiled and said, "Well, you really never get used to it . . . you more or less just accept it and move on."

Bill asked him for any suggestions for sight-seeing in Washington, and he told them the Olympic Peninsula was outstanding, as well as Mt. Rainier. After thanking him, they ran back out to the Ford F-150 to continue up the coast. They crossed over the Columbia River into Washington and were surprised by how wide the river was. Once they crossed, Allen pulled over into a viewing area on the Washington side and parked the truck. He sat there staring at the river and said, "I bet you can't throw a rock over that sucker."

"Probably can't. But I don't need to either. All I have to do is throw my rock a little bit further than you throw your rock."

When he said that, Allen opened his door and said, "Let's go."

They had to walk out of the parking lot, away from the cars and people, in order to find a decent rock and hide from any authorities who might frown on them throwing rocks into their river. The rain had slacked off a little, but it was very muddy once they left the pavement. They found a spot in an open area that led down the slope to the river. They took a few steps to get closer to the water, but didn't want to risk getting too close because it was so muddy.

They had each picked out their rock and Allen said, "You go first old timer, but be careful you don't slip in that mud."

As soon as the word "mud" came out of his mouth, Allen himself slipped on the muddy slope and fell right on his butt. As soon as he landed, he started sliding towards the river and screaming, "Whoa!"

Before Bill could take even one step to help, Allen had slid down to the rocky shore of the Columbia River. The rocks stopped him from going any further, but he was in water up to his knees. When he stood up Bill saw that his entire back side was covered in mud as well. Allen stepped up from the river and looked at Bill saying, "Great help you were. I could've drowned!"

Bill was trying not to laugh too hard, and replied, "You didn't yell 'Help,' you yelled 'Whoa.'"

Allen finally made it back up the muddy slope and said, "I win by default."

"Whatever you say old timer . . . whatever you say."

Allen got some dry clothes from his suitcase and went into the public bathrooms to change. While he was doing that, Bill went to a vending machine and got them each a cup of coffee and had them waiting in the truck when Allen came out. He handed Allen the coffee and didn't say a word about the mud slide. Sometimes, friends do that for each other . . . sometimes.

26

THE GUYS STOPPED IN A SMALL TOWN in southern Washington for a late lunch. After placing their order, the middle-aged waitress came back to their table to bring their glasses of Diet Pepsi. When she set the drinks down, Allen said, "Can I ask you a question?"

She looked down at him and replied, "Yes, I'm married. And, no, I don't want to party?"

Allen said, "No, no, no . . . that wasn't my question. How do you pronounce this word?" He was pointing to the menu, which had fresh salmon as the special of the day.

She looked at it and said, "Samon. Why?"

Bill smiled, and Allen answered her, "Just curious, I've heard it pronounced different ways."

She said, rather sternly, "That's the only correct way to pronounce it. If you're interested in catching any of them, they're running right now and my husband operates a guide company. He can take you out and almost guarantee two city slickers like you will catch something. Think about it."

She went back to the kitchen, and Bill asked Allen, "What do you think about that?"

"I ain't no city slicker. Why would she think that?"

"Maybe because you're wearing a corny hounds tooth hat inside her restaurant."

Allen had put on his Bear Bryant hat because it was still raining a little, and he hadn't taken it off when they entered the restaurant.

"Crap!" He said, as he quickly took the hat off. "I ain't no city slicker; I've lived in the country all my life."

"Living in a housing development just out of the city limits doesn't count as being in the country, old man."

Allen huffed, "Well I'm more country than you are, John Travolta."

Bill asked, "John Travolta? Where'd that come from?"

"He was an urban cowboy one time wasn't he? Or was that Dustin Hoffman?"

Bill shook his head and said, "You seriously need to go to night school and try to learn something soon."

They took a drink of their Diet Pepsis, which didn't taste exactly right; they thought the waitress might've brought them regular Pepsis instead. When she passed by, Bill said, "Excuse me, miss . . . are these drinks Diet Pepsi or regular Pepsi?"

"Neither. They're Cokes. We don't have Pepsi."

She was not the sort of woman you messed with . . . even though Allen wanted to say something, it was better all around to just swallow those words and let it be. They drank their Cokes and kept quiet. After she left, Bill asked his friend, "Well, mud-man, do you want to go fishing or not? It might be fun."

Allen said, "Son, I'd hate to embarrass you out there on the ocean in front of some complete strangers."

Bill corrected him, "The salmon are running on the river; that's where you catch them—not in the ocean."

Allen thought a moment or two and answered, "In the river you say? That might be okay. You could hide behind a tree when I start pulling 'em in. Yeah, let's do it."

When the waitress, whose name was Carleen, came back with their food, Bill said, "I think we'd like to do a little fishing. We don't have any equipment with us though. Does your husband's company have rentals?"

Carleen said, "Be back here at 8:00 in the morning. He'll take care of everything. And don't be late."

Carleen didn't ask them if tomorrow was okay. She didn't ask them if 8:00 was okay. She was not the kind of woman who negotiated. The boys would be here at 8:00 in the morning . . . or else. When they finished eating and were leaving to pay the bill, Carleen said, "You boys stay at the Fisherman's

Lodge at the end of this street. I'll tell 'em you're coming. And remember—8:00—don't be late."

They were unsure if they should answer, "Yes, ma'am," or "Yes, sir," or "Javolt, Mein Fuhrer."

The Fisherman's Lodge was a nice choice: clean rooms, nice bar, breakfast buffet, and a reasonable price. They called the front desk for a wakeup call at 6:30 and they set the alarm on Mr. Google as well. Knowing Carleen as they did, they did not want to take any chances.

They hurried through a bagel and coffee for breakfast—they didn't want to be late. As they pulled up in front of Carleen's restaurant at 7:45, there was an old Chevy Suburban parked out front with a bunch of fishing poles stuck out the back. A very skinny man got out of the Suburban and said, "You must be Carleen's friends—nice to meet you. I'm her husband . . . my name's Josh."

They all shook hands, and Josh said, "Wait right here, and I'll run in and get Carleen to make us some sandwiches to take with us. I'll be right back."

He went in the restaurant as Bill and Allen looked at each other thinking the same thing: "Nobody tells Carleen to do nothing."

In a few minutes Josh came back out empty handed and said, "She was tied up with something boys . . . we'll get something later. You all ready to go?"

Bill and Allen looked at poor, little Josh and knew he was lying. Poor Josh knew that they knew he was lying, but they all kept quiet and got in the Chevy Suburban to go catch some salmon.

Josh drove about twenty minutes, the last five minutes on a rutted, dirt road that shook the poor Suburban mercilessly—and it's occupants as well. Josh said this was a tributary of the Skyhomish River, and this time of year was always teeming with salmon swimming upstream. When they got out of the Suburban, Allen handed Bill one of the fishing poles and said, "In case you didn't know it, they're swimming upstream because that's where they go to spend the winter months."

Josh looked surprised and corrected Allen, "That's not exactly right. It's where they go to spawn and lay eggs, then die."

Allen said, "Well, six of one, half dozen of the other."

Josh didn't want to be rude to his guests, so he let that absurdity pass. They all took their fishing poles over to the little stream, and Allen asked, "Salmon are going to swim up this little stream? Really?"

The stream couldn't have been but about eight to ten feet wide and looked to be about two or three feet deep. Josh answered, "They'll be here. They have no choice—nature calls."

Bill didn't understand that reference at all; Allen thought to himself, "They come up this stream to pee?"

Josh could see the confusion on their faces, so he explained, "The salmon that are swimming up this creek now were once eggs laid up at the head of this stream. Those eggs hatched, then the little fish swim down the stream, where some are eaten by other fish. Some are eaten by all sorts of wildlife, and some actually make it to the Skyhomish River and out to the ocean. Then they start growing and spreading out. Some of these salmon have been caught across the ocean near Japan."

He stopped to see if the boys had any questions, then he continued, "At some point in time, something inside them, a homing instinct, will start driving them back across the ocean, up the Skyhomish River until they find this little creek again—the same one they were spawned in—then they'll swim right back up here and lay their own eggs. Then die and the whole process will start again. It's truly amazing."

Allen looked at Bill and said, "He's messing with us, right?"

Bill looked at Josh; Josh shook his head no, and said, "Truth."

Josh asked if they needed any help with anything, and Allen assured him they were fine. Josh said he was going back into town to get some drinks and lunch to bring back. The boys baited their hooks and threw the lines in . . . and sat there . . . and sat there . . . and sat there. Not a nibble or a trace of a nibble. Allen finally said, "I'm not so sure I trust old Josh. Do you believe that crap he was telling us? We've had nothing all morning. I can't believe a salmon is going to swim up this little, old creek."

Bill added, "Well, he sounded like he knows what he's doing. He seems pretty smart."

"He married Carleen, for goodness sakes! How smart can he be?"

They continued to sit and think . . . and watch nothing happen with their fishing poles. Then Allen said, "I hope this ain't like that movie Burt Reynolds was in where old Jed Clampett got . . . well, you know what happened to old Jed."

"What movie?"

"The one where they're out camping or fishing or something, and a bunch of hillbilly's catch Burt and Jed and violate their butts."

Before Bill could respond, they heard the Suburban coming down the dirt road. When Josh parked, he unloaded two coolers from the back and sacks of McDonald's biscuits for each of them. Bill asked what was in the coolers and Josh said, "One's full of cold drinks, and the other just has ice to put the fish in."

The boys were a little embarrassed to tell Josh they hadn't even had a nibble, much less caught an actual fish. Allen, a little sheepishly said, "Maybe the salmon got lost and haven't been able to find this little creek."

Josh looked over where they left their poles and asked, "Is that where you were fishing?"

They nodded, and Josh said, "No. Grab your poles and follow me."

Josh walked upstream a few yards to some small rapids and led them to a place where the water had pooled, just below the rapids. He said, "This is where you need to be. I thought you knew what you were doing."

Allen said, "Josh, I just don't think there's any salmon in this little stream."

Josh looked at Allen as though he was speaking a foreign language to him, then said, "Come here."

Bill and Allen followed him to the side of the creek where the water had pooled just before the rapids, and Josh said, "Look."

They looked down into the water where Josh was pointing, and there must have been nine or ten big salmon laying in that pool, all facing upstream. Josh said, "They congregate in these pools to gain their strength back so they can swim up the rapids. This is where you catch 'em."

Allen looked at Bill, then back at Josh, and said, "I tried to tell him, Josh, but he thinks he knows it all just because he stood on a pier at Nags Head and caught some groupers."

Both men looked at Allen and didn't know how to respond. So Allen said, "Get your pole, grandpa, and let's catch us some dinner."

27

JOSH SET THEM UP and showed them where to drop their lines. Within three minutes Bill caught a two-and-a-half footer. They all cheered and laughed and whooped at Bill's success. Josh took the salmon and put it in the cooler. About ten minutes later, Bill caught another one. Then Bill caught another one—Bill and Josh whooped and cheered. Allen sulked. He looked at Bill and said, "You got the good bait."

Josh corrected him, "You've both got the same bait."

Allen grabbed Bill's pole and said, "Switch with me."

About five minutes later Allen's pole snapped forward and he screamed, "See? I told you."

All three guys stopped and watched Allen reel in his catch: an eel. Allen looked at it and screamed, "I caught a snake!"

"No," Josh said, "It's an eel . . . them's good eatin.'"

While they were still looking at the eel, Bill caught another big salmon. Josh was busy taking the eel and the salmon off their hooks, so the boys took a break to get something to drink and eat a biscuit. Bill said, "Man, this is great!"

Allen took a bite of sausage biscuit and said, "Shut up."

They switched poles two or three times, but Allen never caught anything besides the eel. They soon decided that the six salmon Bill had caught was more than enough. Allen walked back over to the little pool of water, just below the rapids, and looked down to see at least five more salmon in there waiting to swim upstream. He reached down and picked up a small pebble and dropped it into the pool of fish, startling them. Two of the salmon immediately jumped upstream and swam off. One other fish swam back down the stream, and one poor salmon got so disoriented that it jumped up on the bank, instead of up the stream. It started flopping wildly at Allen's feet, trying to get back into the water. But Allen grabbed it quickly and started yelling, "I got one! I got one!"

Allen was beaming as Josh came over and said, "That's the biggest one of the day. You oughtta mount that one."

Allen was extremely proud of his "catch." They threw his big one in the cooler with the rest of the others and started loading up the Suburban for the trip back into town. Josh told them to go get cleaned up, and he'd ask Carleen to cook one of the fish for their dinner tonight. He said they could sell the others to some local restaurants, but Bill and Allen told him to keep the fish for himself . . . or he could sell them if he wanted to. They were just happy to enjoy the adventure.

After returning to the hotel to take a short nap, they showered, changed clothes, and had a drink. They went back to the restaurant in the early evening, and a young waitress seated them and told them their salmon dinners would be out shortly. Carleen brought out their meals and everything looked great, smelled fantastic, and tasted heavenly.

They thoroughly enjoyed it all, even their Cokes. Carleen came by and asked how everything was, and they both complimented her on the meal. Then Allen said, "I guess you heard that I caught the biggest one of the day, huh?"

She walked right up next to Allen and looked down at him and said, "Really?"

There are certain times in your life when you know—you absolutely know—to say nothing. Allen recognized this moment as one of those times. He picked up his glass of Coke, took a big sip, and went, "Ahhhh."

The boys spent an uneventful night in the Fisherman's Lodge. They had some laundry done by the hotel staff and they caught up on emails and other matters from back home. After all that business was complete, they popped open a can of Rainier Beer in honor of being in Washington, near Mt. Rainier. It was pretty good. As they sat there sipping and relaxing, Allen said, "You're not mad at me are you?"

"Mad at you? For what?"

"For catching the biggest fish today and embarrassing you in front of old Josh."

126

Bill set his can of Rainier down and said, "You did NOT catch the biggest fish today. That fish flopped up on shore and you picked it up."

"That's right. I caught it. Caught it before it could escape back into the stream. No need for you to get all mad just because I was quicker than you, and my reflexes were better. Anybody can catch a fish with pole. It takes someone special to catch a monster like that bare-handed."

Bill picked up his Rainier and said, "Yeah, you're special alright."

In the morning when they went to check out, there was a message for them to stop by the restaurant before they left. They drove down there and saw Josh's Suburban parked out front. When they walked in, Carleen came out with a bag of biscuits and a mug of coffee for each of them. She said, "Nice knowing you boys. If you ever get by here again, stop in and see me."

They both said, "Yes, ma'am."

She handed them the biscuits and coffee and Bill said, "Thanks Carleen, how much do we owe you?"

"Nothing. Josh sold those extra fish last night and made a good profit. We thank you for that."

Then she yelled back towards the kitchen for Josh. He came out carrying the large salmon Allen had "caught," mounted on a redwood plaque with yesterday's date on it. The boys were overwhelmed and asked how he did that. He told them he did some fish mounting on the side and thought they would like this one. Again, they wouldn't take any money for the work he'd done.

They shook hands again and even thought about hugging Carleen, but . . .

Allen carefully stowed the mounted salmon in the back of the Ford F-150, and as they were driving away, he knew he'd always remember the day he "caught" his salmon on the banks of a little creek, flowing into the Skyhomish River.

28

THEY STARTED DRIVING NORTHWARD towards Mt. Rainier, which was easily spotted from a hundred miles away. The mountain dominated the landscape and filled the windshield as they drove. The guys were unprepared for its massive presence. It seemed as though they drove the entire morning staring straight ahead at the mountain. It just kept getting bigger and bigger. They finally arrived at an exit and drove the winding road up to a welcome center, which was located at the snow line.

The first thing they did was get out and throw snowballs at each other, laughing like two little kids. A van load of young people were all preparing to do some hiking and were quite entertained at the sight of two old men throwing snowballs at each other. The boys walked around a little, but couldn't see much because of the thick cloud cover that had recently descended. After hitting each other again with snowballs, they decided to take the road back down the mountain and keep going toward Seattle.

It was drizzly and cloudy, so they decided to stop early at a Holiday Inn near Tacoma. They actually saw a Holiday Inn, but the Best Western was easier to get to. So that's where they checked in. After unloading everything, they went to the restaurant in the hotel for an early dinner. The restaurant was a large room built out on a platform, with glass windows dominating the walls on three sides. If it had been clearer at that time of day, Mt. Rainier would have filled up the entire viewing area of one side. But the clouds prevented any viewing that day.

After they ate, they moved to the lounge area and sat in two comfortable chairs to enjoy a Rainier beer before going back to the room. They sat quietly for several minutes, then Allen asked, "What is home?"

"Exactly what do you mean by that?"

"I mean that exactly, what is home?"

Sometimes it was hard for Bill to determine when Allen was being serious or silly. Now was one of those times, but he answered, "Home is where the heart is, they say."

"Well what about us, Bill? Our hearts aren't in our homes. My heart is at the cemetery at God's Acre, and your heart is somewhere down in Hilton Head. So I ask you again old sage one, 'What is home?'"

Bill did not have an answer he thought Allen would understand. But he honestly told him, "My home is where I am. Today my home is the Best Western Hotel outside of Tacoma, Washington. It's not an empty house back in Winston-Salem. All that is, is an empty house. Tomorrow my home will be somewhere around Seattle, if the Lord allows us to get that far."

Allen didn't say anything. He didn't agree or disagree or argue—which was very unusual for him. They finished their Rainiers in silence and decided to have an Iron Maiden before they went to bed. As they were sipping their drinks, a group of college kids came into the hotel to check in. Several had on shirts with Olympic College on the front or back. The boys had never heard of that school, but assumed it must be one of the local colleges in this area. The young college kids were about evenly split between guys and girls, and also evenly split between pretty girls and not so pretty girls—but isn't life like that?

They were giggling and having fun with each other, as young kids are supposed to do. Allen and Bill watched and enjoyed them, and remembered what those days used to be like—in another life. Allen looked at his friend and said, "Remember that time we . . . "

"Stop," Bill said, "don't even go there."

"You don't even know what I'm going to say."

Bill set his Iron Maiden down and said, "I do know what you're going to say. You're going to rehash something we did forty-nine or fifty years ago . . . and enhance all the crazy stuff and forget all the bad stuff—that's what you do."

"Well how would you know? You can't even remember that far back, you old goat."

Bill said, "Oh, I remember it . . . that doesn't mean I want to hear your version of things that never happened. I like to remember things as they actually were."

Allen said, "I was just going to ask you if you remembered that night we picked up those two girls over at Blowing Rock and took them back to the frat house?"

Bill corrected him, "We didn't pick up any girls in Blowing Rock. A bunch of people, including those girls, decided to go back to a frat house on campus and we tagged along. We weren't even members of that fraternity."

"But still, we went back to that frat house with those girls, and everybody was getting messed up . . . and we ended up in the same bedroom with both those girls."

Bill sighed and explained, "Those two girls both got drunk and went to that bedroom and passed out on the beds. We went in there and tried to wake them up. But they just kept on snoring, so we left."

Allen thought about that, and replied, "But we could've taken advantage of them if we had wanted to."

"Yeah," Bill added, "and we could've gone to jail too."

Allen said, "You know what your problem is? You don't like a good story. Here I am trying to make you have a good time, and all you want to do is ruin it with the facts."

Bill got up and stretched, then looked down at his best friend and said, "Bite me. I'm going to bed."

They rose and had a leisurely breakfast before starting for Seattle. They figured they should arrive in Seattle around 10:00-11:00, thus missing the morning rush hour traffic. They were wrong. The interstate, I-5, was between five and six lanes each direction, north and south, and traffic was at a snail's pace. At first, the boys thought there must be a wreck somewhere holding everything up. But no, this was how it was both northbound and southbound—all twelve lanes. Allen commented, "If it's like this at 11:00 in the morning, what must it be like at 8:00 in the morning, or 5:00 in the afternoon?"

Bill added, "It couldn't be any worse. We're averaging about ten miles per hour. How do people live like this?"

They decided to take a break from the congestion and stop for a drink and a snack at one of the exits. They went in the convenience store and got a

Diet Pepsi and some chips and asked the clerk about the traffic. He said, "It's always like this . . . night and day, doesn't make any difference what time it is; it's always heavy."

Bill couldn't grasp that, and asked "Why?"

The clerk explained, "Think about it. We have the ocean on one side of us and Puget Sound on the other side. The only way to drive is north and south. There is no east and west traffic. Everyone has to go either north or south—that's why it's always so busy."

The boys took their Diet Pepsis out to the Ford F-150 and dreaded getting back on the constipated interstate. The traffic was so bad they abandoned their proposed trip out to the Olympic Peninsula. But they did continue onward towards the heart of Seattle . . . only because they both loved Jimi Hendrix so much. Hendrix was worth it.

29

MR. GOOGLE HELPED THEM LOCATE THE MUSEUM. Once they got off the interstate, traffic was fairly normal again. As they were getting close, Allen said, "You know, all those guys we liked back then died in 1971. It was pretty strange."

Bill asked, "What guys are you talking about?"

"Hendrix, Duane Allman, Jim Morrison of the Doors, Janis Joplin, John Lennon, and a few more . . . it was really weird."

Bill, who was driving at the moment, glanced over and said, "You're crazy, old man. I know for a fact that John Lennon died in 1980."

"Oh," Allen corrected himself, "I didn't mean John Lennon, I meant Brian Jones of the Rolling Stones, he died in 1971—it's all documented."

Bill drove onward, but thought to himself, "Am I really going to believe this?" Then he answered himself, "No!"

They arrived at the museum parking lot, which was about half filled with cars from all over the United States and Canada. The museum itself looked like an abstract representation of a smashed guitar, one of Hendrix's calling cards. They were walking up to the front when Bill said, "You know, I saw Hendrix in concert once. He'd just had his hair cut; it wasn't all wild like it normally was. He played the guitar behind his neck and behind his back, and then with his teeth. Then he laid it on the stage and set it on fire, and played it while it burned—it was incredible."

That news stopped Allen in his tracks. He looked at Bill and said, "You what?"

"I saw him in concert in Raleigh in, I think, 1970. It might have been '69 . . . I'm not sure."

Allen said, "How come I've never heard about this before? And where was I at the time? You went without me?"

Bill answered, "Eliza got us tickets for my birthday. She surprised me. I don't know where you were . . . probably at a Bobby Goldsboro concert."

"I liked Bobby Goldsboro." Then as they started walking again, Allen began singing, "God didn't make little green apples, and it don't rain in Indianapolis, in the summertime."

Bill stopped abruptly and said, "You nincompoop, that's Roger Miller's song, not Bobby Goldsboro."

Allen never stopped walking and said, "Well I liked him, too."

The museum was fantastic. The Microsoft billionaire, Paul Allen, funded it, and it was top notch. They saw the famous Fender Stratocaster that Hendrix used to play The Star Spangled Banner on at Woodstock in 1969. Then they pressed the play button at the display and listened to Hendrix's version of the national anthem once again. Incomparable!

There was a display case that held memorabilia from the many events of Hendrix's life, including the newspaper headlines of the day he died in London in 1970. When they read that, Bill said, "I thought you told me all these guys died in 1971?"

"Well, all but Hendrix . . . you know he was always first in everything—he was an innovator."

They spent quite a while touring all the exhibits and listening to music in the auditorium. They ended in the gift shop, and each bought a Hendrix tee shirt; while Bill also bought a framed picture with a replica signature. All in all, Hendrix was worth the drive and the traffic. The Experience and the Crosstown Traffic through the Purple Haze were well worth the effort.

They decided to find a hotel in downtown Seattle that had parking for the Ford F-150 and camper. Fortunately, they located a place which was also within walking distance of the Space Needle. After checking in the hotel, they started walking to the famous Seattle landmark, which was built for the World's Fair held in Seattle in 1962. The Space Needle was just as amazing today as it was then.

They rode the elevator up to the top and walked around enjoying the 360 degree views of downtown Seattle, the Puget Sound, Mt. Rainer to the south, and Mt. Baker to the north. They couldn't get reservations in the restaurant up there, but the bar area had some seats available. The entire top of the Space Needle revolved 360 degrees once every hour . . . slowly enough that you never noticed it moving, but enough that the views changed constantly.

They each got a twelve dollar Rainier Beer and sipped it slowly while watching the panoramic view unfold in front of them. Seattle was gorgeous. The ocean, the surrounding islands, and the Puget Sound were all spectacular. The view deserved a second twelve dollar beer. They were sitting next to a husband and wife from Modesto, California who were here celebrating their wedding anniversary. Bill asked them, "Isn't that where Ernest and Julio Gallo have a winery?"

Before they answer, Allen jumped in and said, "Yeah, they used to have commercials all the time back east. Did they go out of business?"

The husband, Matt, said, "No, they're doing well. They don't make the snooty wines, like up in the Napa Valley. They just make good table wines that are reasonably priced and sell good for the common people—like us. Why buy a twenty dollar bottle of wine, when you can get a bottle of Gallo wine for nine dollars?"

Then his wife, Sam, said, "They really stopped advertising back east when all the wineries exploded on the scene about ten or fifteen years ago. Before that, California and New York had the market for wines. Then something changed, and now every state has wineries. So, the Gallos just changed their market to the west coast."

"Yeah," Bill added, "that's right. I bet North Carolina has a hundred or more wineries at least."

Matt and Sam told them about their family and showed pictures of their kids. They talked about their trips to Yosemite every fall. They seemed very happy, almost to the point of making Bill and Allen a bit depressed . . . not because they were jealous of Matt and Sam's happiness, but because of what they each once had, and what they each no longer had.

Even though neither guy had their passports with them, they still decided to drive up to the Canadian border, "just to take a look," as Allen put it. They got off the interstate north of Bellingham and drove the back roads over to the coast, stopping at the border. It was drizzly, foggy and a little chilly, but they could see Canada. They parked and walked down to the rocky coast, and Allen said, "Let's go!"

"I am not going to walk across the border. Don't you think they have people checking on that?"

Allen said, "No, grandpa, grab you a rock and let's go. Give me a chance to double down on you."

Bill smiled and said, "I didn't know you were such a glutton for punishment."

They each picked a good sized rock, and Allen said, "Throw it across the border . . . if your old man arm can throw that far."

Bill surprised himself with his throw. It was by far his best one of the trip. When Bill's rock landed, Allen looked towards the border and said, "Quick, let's go."

He dropped his rock and took off at a brisk walk back toward the parking lot. When Bill caught up with him, Allen said, "That was close . . . I saw one of those border patrol guys looking at you throwing that rock—he did not look happy."

Bill said, "I didn't see any border patrol guys."

"See?" Allen answered, "Saved you from trouble again. What in the world would you do if I wasn't around to save you from getting in trouble?"

Bill laughed a little and replied, "I'd probably win a lot more rock throwing contests."

30

THE BOYS FINALLY DIRECTED THE FORD F-150 BACK EAST . . . only because they couldn't go north or west any further. They traveled on some back roads, with no intended destination and with nothing in particular on their minds. Allen was driving on a deserted, rural, country road in the middle of Washington, and they hadn't passed a town or village in over an hour. Suddenly, he pulled over to the side of the road, surprising Bill, who asked, "What's wrong?"

"I got to pee, that's what's wrong. I haven't seen a town in over an hour and I got to go!"

They both got out, and Allen walked a few yards into a field to relieve himself while Bill walked down the road a bit to stretch his legs. As Bill turned around, he noticed a dust trail rising from across the field and then saw an old pickup truck barreling down a dirt road coming in their direction. He noticed Allen walking back to the Ford F-150 as the old pickup truck came off the dirt road and pulled up behind them.

A man, probably a few years older than them, got out of his truck carrying a shotgun and walked up to Bill and Allen and said, "What do you think you're doing out here on my land?"

Allen answered, "We aren't doing anything. We just stopped to stretch our legs."

The old man snarled, "Looked to me like you was walking across my field and maybe desecrating it."

Allen knew he was caught, so he didn't say anything. Bill said, "We just stopped for a minute, sir. We'll be leaving right now. Didn't know you owned all this land and the road as well. We didn't mean any harm."

"I don't take kindly to strangers, including foreigners, trespassing on my land and relieving themselves on my crops."

Allen spoke up, "I'm sorry about that, sir. I apologize for my behavior. We'll just get in our truck and be leaving now."

The old man said, "You won't be leaving till you pay me for using my land as a toilet."

Bill replied, "Pay you? What are you talking about?"

"You'll pay me a hundred dollars right now for what you did." At that point the old man repositioned his shotgun, pointing it in their direction.

Allen got a little excited and exclaimed, "Hold on now, sir. I admit I did pee in your field, but we ain't gonna pay you a hundred dollars for that."

At that point, they noticed an old Chevy van coming down the same dirt road. They all waited to see who it was. A middle-aged guy got out, started walking towards them and said, "What's going on here, dad?"

"These here guys stopped and peed in my field, and I'm gonna make 'em pay for it—that's what's going on."

The son gently took hold of the shotgun and pulled it away from his dad. He looked at Allen and Bill as he said, "Why don't you guys get in your truck and take off. No harm, no foul . . . okay?"

They both nodded and got in the Ford F-150. As they drove away, they each kept an eye in the rear view mirror. Just before a curve in the road, they saw the son gently put his arm on his dad's shoulder, talking to him, as they rounded the corner and lost sight of them.

Allen finally said, "Dang that was weird. That old man was crazy."

Bill looked over and asked, "Are you okay to be driving?"

"What do you mean, am I okay? Of course I'm okay. That old man didn't scare me."

Bill smiled and said, "Okay, fine. But go ahead and zip your pants up the first chance you get."

They were driving through an area of low rolling hills with many fields planted with what could be wheat, or some other grains. It was a nice fertile region, with very few trees and no mountains. They saw a road sign for Spokane and also one for Gonzaga University. Allen asked, "Is Gonzaga here in Spokane?

Bill answered, "I have no idea. I never hear of Gonzaga except during March madness."

Allen thought, "I was thinking it was in California for some reason."

At that point they saw a sign for Campgrounds of America and decided to pull in for the evening. The campground was located near a small river, with some rolling hills in the distance. There was a small grill at the campground office, and the guys bought some burgers and fries after they'd set up everything. They picked up their camp chairs, and walked down to the little stream to eat and relax. Allen spoke first, "I bet there ain't no salmon in that stream."

A few seconds after he said that, some sort of fish jumped out of the water, probably chasing a bug, and made the boys laugh. They finished eating and were sipping on the last of the Rainier beers they had left, watching the sun fall slowly towards the rolling hills off to the west. Again Allen asked his age-old question: "Bill, why are we here?"

"We're here because you peed in an old man's field and made him mad. And we didn't have enough time to drive into Spokane to a nice hotel."

"Did you want to stay in a hotel tonight?"

Bill smiled and replied, "Nah, I was just messing with you. No hotel can beat this type of scenery."

"Okay then, now that you've used up your one attempt at humor for the month, why are we here?"

Bill took a long drink from his can of Rainier, then answered that question as best he could. "We're here to glorify God and worship Him through our lives and our actions. We're here to witness and testify to His majesty and goodness, so that those who don't believe will hear the truth and repent and be saved—like us, who are the worst of the worst."

Allen sat up and looked at his friend and asked, "You think we're the worst of the worst?"

"If the Apostle Paul said he was the chief of all sinners, then buddy, I guarantee you we're the worst of the worst."

Allen argued, "But we're basically good. What about all those people out there murdering, cheating, stealing and pulling for the Tar Heels? What about them?"

"Those people THINK they're good, which they aren't. The difference with us is we know we're not good, and the only way we can be saved is by the Grace of God . . . not by doing good stuff, not by helping the poor, not by going to church every week, and not by pulling for Wake Forest—no sir! We are saved only by His grace, and His grace alone."

Allen thought about that a moment or two, then said, "Well why did you wait sixty-nine years to tell me all that? I've been being good and going to church every week, and I didn't have to."

Bill opened a can of Coors Light, since the Rainier was gone, and said, "First of all, you haven't been good. In fact, you're an ornery old man. Second, you haven't been going to church every week, and we both know that. Third, and last, I know for a fact that in 1982 you pulled for Carolina to win the national championship against Georgetown—and don't deny it because you know it's true!"

"They had Michael Jordon, Bill!"

Bill just stared at him, not saying a word.

Allen, getting nervous, then said, "But it was Georgetown! Nobody pulls for Georgetown. God'll forgive me for that won't He?"

"I don't know, buddy. I just don't know. Somewhere in the Bible it talks about the 'Unforgiveable Sin.' That might be it."

Allen then opened up a can of Coors Light for himself, and they sat there and watched the sun fade over the burnt hills of eastern Washington . . . next to a small stream, each sitting next to their best friend in the world.

31

THEY STOPPED FOR BREAKFAST at a waffle place on the outskirts of Spokane. Their waitress was stunningly gorgeous and very friendly. Each time she passed by the table Allen would nearly fall out of his seat turning around to look at her. She came to take their order, and Bill wasn't sure if Allen was going to be able to communicate or not; he was so captivated. She said, "Hi . . . my name's Farrah, would you like some coffee to start with?"

When Farrah walked away, Allen said, "That young lady is gorgeous. If I lived out here I'd chase her to the end of the earth and back."

"No you wouldn't," Bill replied, "after a few steps of you chasing her, she'd call the police and have you arrested for being a dirty old man."

"Shut up. You know what I mean. Now hush, here she comes back."

Farrah poured the coffee and asked if they'd decided on anything yet. Of course, they hadn't because they were too busy staring at her. Allen said, "That's a beautiful name you have, Farrah. It fits you."

Farrah smiled, and both guys nearly fainted. Then she said, "Thank you, sir. My father named me . . . he was a big fan of Joni Mitchell."

Allen and Bill understood what she said, but they didn't understand what she meant . . . Joni Mitchell? Joni had a decent voice, but she was nothing to look at. Neither guy spoke in response to Farrah's comment. Then she smiled again and said, "I'm just messing with you, he loved Farrah Fawcett."

Beautiful, great legs, great smile, and a sense of humor! When she walked away, Allen said, "She's just about perfect, isn't she?"

Bill nodded, and added, "Yep, but it really doesn't matter how beautiful a girl is . . . somewhere, there's somebody out there who is sick of her."

Allen looked at him like he'd lost his mind, and said, "Drink some coffee, old man, and pretend you know what you're doing."

Farrah brought their waffles, refilled their coffee several times, and smiled every time she was near them—she knew how to generate good tips. When they finished eating and drinking more coffee than they wanted, Farrah brought them the check and asked where they were traveling to next. Allen swooned, and answered, "If we weren't so old, young lady, we might just stay here."

Farrah smiled once more and winked as she replied, "You're not too old, and it's never too late."

Needless to say, Farrah received the largest tip she would receive that entire week. Bill made sure Allen went to the restroom before they got in the Ford F-150 to continue their journey over the rainbow . . . while they each dreamed sweet dreams of Farrah.

By early afternoon the boys still weren't hungry. The waffles and dreams of Farrah had kept them filled and satisfied. But they were tired. So they stopped in a small town to walk up and down the streets a little and have something to drink. They found a café with outdoor seating and sat there drinking a Diet Pepsi while admiring life in a small town. Finally Allen said, "Well, Mr. Goode, I guess we should sort of figure out where we're going next."

Bill said, "I told you from the start, Mr. Kite, I don't care . . . well, there is one place I'd like to see, if it's possible. But it's way on down the road from here. For now, I don't care where we go or how long we stay."

"I can't believe there's actually a place you want to see. I thought you were going to ride my coattails this entire trip and just copy me in everything. Tell me, Buzz . . . where is this place that you want to go?"

Bill looked quizzically at Allen and said, "Buzz?"

"Yeah, Buzz Aldrin. He followed Neil Sedaka to the moon and back, like you're following me around the world and back. Now tell me where it is you want to go—the suspense is killing me."

Bill smiled and said, "You just beat all, don't you old man? I'd like to visit Lambeau Field and take the tour of that place . . . if they have one. I'd certainly like to see the Packer's Hall of Fame and have my picture taken next to the Vince Lombardi statue there at the stadium. I always loved Coach Lombardi."

"Well, my rock-throwing chump . . . I'll see if I can work that into our schedule for later. But for now, we've got great things to see and exciting things to do."

Bill nodded and replied, "Sounds good to me. What are we going to see next?"

"I have no idea, cheese head. None whatsoever."

Before they got back on the road, they stopped to buy gas and a few snacks to take with them. They asked the cashier about any great places to visit up this way. He thought for a moment and then said, "Well, there's really nothing around here, or in Idaho. But if you keep going east into Montana, Glacier National Park is outstanding. That's where I'd go."

Allen said, "Glacier National Park? I've never heard of it. Are there glaciers there—in Montana?"

The clerk said, "There used to be; they're melting fast with all the global warming now. But I'd still check it out—it's beautiful."

The boys got back in the truck and thought for a minute or two and then decided—Glacier National Park it is! Almost immediately after leaving Spokane, they crossed the Snake River into Idaho. As soon as they crossed the bridge, Allen pulled the Ford F-150 over to the side of the road. "Get out." He said, "We're going to settle this thing once and for all."

Bill never spoke; he knew what was happening. As soon as he stepped outside the truck, he saw a nice round rock lying there waiting on him. He picked it up and gently tossed it up and down in his hand, waiting for Allen to decide on his weapon. They were probably a hundred feet or so above the river itself, which was not as wide as they thought it would be. Allen finally picked a light colored rock with a dark stripe on it and said, "Do you want to go first, grandpa?"

"No, you go first, pilgrim."

Allen looked back at him and snorted, "You ain't John Wayne, old-timer."

"I don't have to be John Wayne to beat a washed-up minor leaguer like you. Heck, Rooster Cogburn could probably beat you, and he was about a hundred and twenty years old."

This fired Allen up. He walked to the edge, spit into his hand for some unknown reason, and then fired his rock out over the Snake River. It was a grand throw, and made it completely over the water, landing in the mud flats on the far side. He smiled at his accomplishment and mumbled, "Rooster Cogburn my butt."

Bill walked over to the edge and threw his rock with the effortless grace that comes only from natural talent. Allen was watching for a splash in the river water, or a plunk in the mud flats where his rock had landed. But he didn't see anything. He turned and looked at Bill with a quizzical look. Bill pointed and said, "Over the edge."

Allen looked over the river, over the mud flats, up the bank and saw the last remnants of a tiny dust spiral floating away—the unmistakable evidence that he'd once again been beaten. He turned towards Bill and said, "Well you should've beaten me; I spit too much in my hand and my rock slipped as I threw it. Any rookie could've won that contest. Now get in the car and let's go—we've got some glaciers to see."

Bill only smiled and replied, "You mean to get in the truck, right?"

32

THEY CROSSED THE BITTERROOT MOUNTAINS into Montana and steered towards the small town of Kalispell, which was near Glacier National Park. They stopped at a roadside restaurant and asked their waiter several questions regarding the park and where they could camp. Fortunately, they learned there were several campgrounds inside the park with plenty of spaces available.

Even though it was getting fairly late in the day, they decided to drive into the park for the evening. The scenery was overwhelming. Allen asked his friend, "How come nobody knows about this place? It's incredible."

Bill answered, "People do know about it . . . just not us. And I hope it stays hidden. Too many tourists would ruin it."

They picked up some information at the ranger's station and started for the first campground in the park, which was located about half way up one of the glaciated peaks. That campground, being so close to the entrance, was full. So they continued up the slope and soon found another campground that had vacancies, along with a lot of snow and ice in the shaded areas. As they set everything up, Allen observed, "I don't think we brought enough clothes."

Bill, who already had on his Allman Brothers tee shirt on top of his Redwood's tee shirt, added, "I know we didn't bring enough clothes. At least it's okay for us to have a fire in the pit over there."

They walked around and picked up loose twigs and small sticks from the surrounding forest, hoping this would save them during the night. The little fire did indeed keep their hands warm, but that was about all. It was too chilly to even think about a cold Coors Light, so they hopped in their beds and covered up with everything they had, taking nothing off except their shoes. And they still froze.

Sometime after midnight, Allen said in a low voice, "Bill, are you awake? Bill? Are you awake?"

"Well, I am now. What do you want? And, no, you can't get in bed with me."

Allen ignored that and asked, "Did you hear that?"

"What?

"That grunting sound. There's something out there."

Bill perked up then and said, "I didn't hear anything. Are you sure?"

"Yes, I'm sure. There's something out there. Open the door and take a look around."

Incredulously, Bill answered, "I'm not opening that door. If there is something out there, I don't want to let it in here! Plus, I think you're imagining things."

Before Allen could answer, they both heard a loud grunting, huffing noise just outside their camper.

Allen excitedly asked, "Where's your gun?"

"I didn't bring a gun, fool."

"What are we gonna do?"

"Nothing. Just sit here and wait for it to move away."

They did sit there, wide awake, with hearts racing. Allen picked up a butter knife they had, and Bill opened the wine bottle corkscrew they brought along. It seemed like hours, but eventually they stopped hearing the noise. Bill peeped out the door and said, "I don't see anything."

"What about behind us?"

"I can't see behind us."

"Since it's so cold, let's hop in the truck and turn the heater on for a little while and get warm."

Bill thought and said, "Good idea. You go first and unlock the doors."

"I can automatically unlock them. Since you're already there, you go on out and I'll get the doors."

Bill looked back at Allen and said, "If something eats me when I go out there, I'm gonna come back and haunt you every night."

"Shut up and go on out, chicken."

Bill looked left, then right, then he bolted out as Allen tried to unlock the doors to the Ford F-150. But because he was so excited, instead of hitting the "unlock" button on his keys, he accidentally hit the "alarm" button. The lights on the truck starting flashing, the horn started beeping, and people from adjoining campsites were stepping outside to see what was happening.

Allen quickly got the truck to stop beeping and flashing, but a neighboring camper walked over with his flashlight and asked, "Is everything alright here?"

Allen, who was standing at the doorway of the camper said, "Everything's fine, sir. My friend here just got a little excited."

The flashlight man replied, "Okay fellas, I'm right next door if you need anything . . . goodnight."

They decided it might be prudent, safe, and warm to spend the rest of the night inside the Ford F-150. They started the engine and got it nice and toasty inside . . . then reclined the seats all the way back, locked the doors securely, and finally dozed off.

★★★

At the ranger station in the morning, they learned that the noise they heard was probably either an elk or a moose nosing around the campground. Allen asked the ranger, "You sure it wasn't a bear?"

"Well, I'm not a hundred percent sure, but it's pretty unlikely. They don't like to be around us anymore than we like being around them."

"But there are bears out here, right?"

"Yes, sir. Plenty of them. Grizzlies and black bears, but I doubt you'll ever see one—especially in a campground."

Bill could see the wheels spinning in Allen's mind, thinking of all the stories he was going to enhance about being attacked by a grizzly bear in Glacier National Park. The ranger spent a few minutes with them and offered some hot coffee, which was very welcome. He explained a little about the park. He told them that, yes, there were glaciers here now—about thirty of them. Considerably down from the one hundred and fifty that were here in 1910.

Automobile exhaust, greenhouse gases, and other factors were taking a toll on them.

The ranger also told them there were over seven hundred miles of trails throughout the park, with waterfalls and glaciers visible on nearly all of them. Plus, there were seven hundred and sixty-two lakes inside the park's eighteen hundred square miles. The ranger ended his short summary by telling them that the waters from the glaciers and streams inside the park were all headwaters flowing either to the Pacific Ocean, the Gulf of Mexico, or to Hudson Bay.

The boys took the famous "Going-to-the-Sun Road" and were filled with awe and wonder throughout the day. All around them were snow covered mountain peaks, glistening lakes, glaciers, and more wildlife than they could imagine. They stopped on a pull-off to watch a family of mountain goats come down a glaciated peak and walk right past them like the Ford wasn't even there.

Around another curve, they stopped behind two other cars where they saw a bull elk standing in the road blocking traffic. After the first two cars moved on, Bill stopped and they looked at the elk from six or seven feet across the roadway. It was huge. Allen said, "Here, give him this."

He tried to hand Bill some cookies they had, but Bill said, "We're not supposed to feed them anything—you know that."

"A few cookies ain't gonna hurt him . . . give 'em to him."

Bill looked both behind him and in front of the truck, and didn't see any other traffic—especially rangers. Then he rolled the window all the way down to feed the cookies to the elk. As he looked over to Allen to get the cookies from him, the elk had taken two steps and was at the Ford, sticking his massive head inside the window—at least, as much of it that would fit, which wasn't much. Before Bill knew what was happening, the elk's big snout was in his face, and it was drooling slobber all over his lap. Allen quickly reached over with the cookies, and the elk's huge lips gobbled them up, getting slobber all over Allen's hand. As soon as the elk pulled back from the window, Bill took off, screaming, "He slobbered all over me."

Allen started laughing, while drying off his hand and said, "I told you not to feed the wildlife."

They stopped at a rest area where Bill changed clothes. Then they found a restaurant at the welcome center to grab a bite to eat. It was an incredible day for two self-admitted rednecks from North Carolina . . . glaciers, waterfalls, mountain peaks, mountain goats, bear attacks, and a slobbering elk.

33

THE BOYS EXITED THE PARK on the eastern side, which was the boundary of the Blackfoot Indian Reservation. They stopped to get something to drink and went into the gift store run by the Blackfoot tribe. They each bought a colorful blanket handmade by the Blackfeet . . . just in case they got cold again. Bill bought a wood carving of an elk to commemorate his slobbering episode, and Allen bought several small arrowheads that intrigued him.

As they were walking out of the gift store, a fairly young Indian woman was coming in the same door. Allen held it open for her, and when she looked at him, he said, "How."

She stopped momentarily, started to say something, but thought better of it, and kept walking. When they were outside, Bill looked at him and said, "How? What is wrong with your mind? Sometimes I wonder how you put your pants on in the morning."

Allen said, "That's their native language . . . they talk like that."

Bill shook his head and sighed, "Old man . . . "at that point, sensible thought escaped him, so he just said, "Get in the truck before we get scalped."

They found the interstate and drove into the town of Missoula, Montana where they decided to find a Holiday Inn for the night. As they pulled in the parking lot of the Comfort Inn, Allen said, "You know this is the capital of Montana, don't you?"

Bill stopped and thought for a second and replied, "I thought the capital was Butte."

"No. It's Missoula, which is also the hometown of one of Duke's greatest basketball players, Trajan Langdon, the Duke Assassin."

"What?" Bill exclaimed, "Trajan Langdon was from Alaska, you numbskull. And they called him the Alaskan Assassin."

Allen never flinched, "Well, somebody was from Missoula. I remember him making a shot one time to break old Dean's heart."

Bill wasn't sure about that, but didn't want to argue, so he let it go. When they registered at the hotel, the guy at the check-in desk seemed pretty intelligent, so Allen asked him, "Wasn't there someone from Missoula who played basketball at Duke back in the seventies or eighties?"

The guy knew immediately, "Yeah, that was Mike Lewis. He played about ten years in the NBA, too."

Allen was so happy, he was about to burst, "See, I told you. Mike Lewis . . . I remember him well. He broke old Dean's heart one night."

The check-in guy said, "He was pretty famous around here . . . still is, but he lives over in the capital now."

Bill asked, "The capital? Isn't this the capital?"

The check-in guy frowned and said, "No, Helena is the capital."

Allen acted very surprised at this news and blindly asked, "Helena? Is that a real town?"

"Yeah! It's the capital of our state."

Allen was flummoxed and then asked the guy, "Are you sure?"

"Well, it has been for the thirty-seven years I've been alive. But they could've changed it today, and I just haven't heard the news yet."

He handed them the cards for their room, and they walked over to the elevator as they each thought, "Helena?"

After settling in their room, they walked three blocks down the street to a place the check-in guy told them about. The restaurant had huge steaks and ice cold Coors Lights—it was a very nice choice. The meal was so filling, they each begged off dessert, settling instead on an Iron Maiden to sip on. It seemed that Bill was deep in thought, and Allen assumed he was thinking about his ex, Eliza, again. He finally tapped on the table and said, "What's on your mind, Mr. Goode?"

Bill set his drink down and wistfully replied, "I was thinking about those two old girls at the campground, the ones from Sausalito."

This revelation shocked Allen. "You kept saying those two old girls were gay. Now you're wishing you'd jumped their bones?"

"Not that . . . sometimes you just have a one track mind, don't you?"

"Well what then? You're wondering what their camper looked like inside? You wanted to play dominos with them?"

"Shut up! I was just thinking that they're probably lonely, like we are, and were just looking for somebody to spend some time with. That's all. Maybe we should've just spent a little time with them . . . been friends for an evening. Sometimes that goes a long ways."

Allen thought a moment, then added, "Yeah, I'd like to have spent a little time being friends with that dark-headed one alright. I'd teach her the meaning of true and lasting friendship."

"You're a dirty old man with a vivid imagination, aren't you?"

"What do you mean? You're the one who was thinking about them."

Bill took a small sip of his Iron Maiden and replied, "Even if you had taken that dark-headed one to her bedroom, what would you have done? You don't have any Viagra with you . . . at least I hope you don't."

Allen smiled and said, "I'd have figured something out, grandpa. We ain't all prudish like you are."

Bill took the last sip of his drink, rose from the table, and said, "Keep dreaming, old man . . . keep dreaming."

★★★

Yellowstone was all they thought it would be—and more. They made the pilgrimage to Old Faithful and watched the eruption with hundreds of others, wondering "How in the world does it do that?" They stared in awe at the multi-colored pools of hot, boiling water. And, they hiked around a geyser field without causing any damage, or getting hurt.

As they were driving to a separate location, they came upon several cars all stopped in the little two lane road. A herd of buffalo was leisurely moving from one field to another, crossing the road and stopping traffic. The buffalo didn't care about traffic . . . they just wanted some fresh pasturage. They were massive animals, which appeared to weigh over two thousand pounds apiece. Each year some crazy tourists forget these are wild and untamed creatures, and they try to take a close up picture of them . . . or worse yet, a selfie. And, invariably, they either get knocked down, gored, or even killed—it happens every year.

After the herd moved across the roadway, all the other cars moved on, except for Allen. He pulled over and stopped. He started to open the door, and Bill said, "What do you think you're doing?"

"I'm just gonna take a closer look. They're all across the field now. It'll be alright."

"I don't think you should mess around with those buffalo, Allen. You never know what they'll do."

"Them buffalo don't care nothing about two rednecks from North Carolina. Just stay in the truck there and don't get your panties in a wad."

Allen walked across the road, maybe twenty yards away from where the buffalo had stopped to graze. He stood there staring at them, wondering how in the world they got that big by eating only grass. As he was wondering this, a mama buffalo didn't like the fact that Allen was standing a little too close to her newborn calf. She turned toward him and huffed. Allen noticed her and took one step backwards. Bill yelled out the window, "You'd better come on back here, old man."

Allen started to say something in response when the mama buffalo started moving towards him. He quickly turned and ran across the road to where Bill had opened the door for him. He jumped in and shut the door. Unfortunately for the Ford F-150, the buffalo didn't care if the door was shut or not. That mama buffalo wanted a piece of Allen and was going through the door to get to him. She rammed into the side of the Ford F-150, then backed up and shook her head as Allen started the engine. She started to ram the truck again as Allen hit the gas and accelerated as fast as he could. Bad luck for the camper though—she missed the door where Allen was, but did hit the camper full force.

They stopped a mile or two up the road, away from the buffalo, to inspect the damage. It was not pretty. There was a big dent in the door and a puncture wound through the side made by one of the buffalo's horns. There was only a small dent in the camper, but they had noticed a scrapping sound when they were driving. The collision had obviously pushed the side of the camper against one of the wheels.

Leaving the park they made it to a service station where they gassed up and asked the attendant to take a look at the camper. He walked out and looked at the dents, then said, "Messed around with a buffalo, huh?"

Allen, who was standing a little behind Bill, pointed to him and replied to the attendant, "Yeah, made a slight miscalculation. Can you try to pull the metal away from the wheel for us?"

He got some sort of tool that seemed to be a cross between a jack and a lever, and pulled the camper off the wheel enough that it didn't scrape anymore. The boys thanked him, and they all stood there looking at the dent and the puncture hole in the side of the Ford F-150. The attendant then said, "Ain't nothing I can do about that."

34

THEY STOPPED AT A NICE HOLIDAY INN named the Geyser Springs Motel for the night. The little town also had a cowboy bar down the street that served ice cold Coors Lights. After dinner Allen and Bill made their way to the cowboy bar down the street, which oddly enough was named "The Citizen." It was just as they hoped it would be: sawdust on the floor, a mechanical bull riding machine at the rear, and a long bar, with a foot ramp for the cowboys to rest their feet on after a hard day of herding cattle.

However, they didn't see anybody but tourists from New Jersey, Michigan, and Connecticut—no cowboys in sight. They sat at a table next to a family from Sea Girt, New Jersey and Allen immediately started up a conversation. He told them about the journey they were on and about the run-in with the buffalo. The husband acted as if he didn't believe anything Allen had told him, certainly not the story about the buffalo. He asked his teenage son to run outside and look at the Ford F-150 and report back to him. Allen said, "The truck's back at the hotel, but that dent is there . . . trust me."

The man from New Jersey sneered and said, "Sure it is. Just like my son here is going to Harvard next year!" The teenager lowered his head, certainly tired of being verbally abused by his dad. The New Jersey guy laughed and yelled over to the bar, "Hey, what's a guy gotta do to get another drink around here?"

Allen and Bill left the table and went to sit at the bar. The bartender, who didn't appreciate being yelled at from some guy in plaid Bermuda shorts and a tank top, looked back at the New Jersey guy and said to Bill, "I hope you aren't from the same place he is."

They tried to finish their beer in peace, but the New Jersey guy kept berating his son and his wife loudly enough so that everyone in the bar could hear his rude behavior. The bartender asked the boys if they wanted anything else, but they looked at the New Jersey guy and said, "I don't think we could stand another one."

The bartender nodded and leaned in close to them saying, "How would you like to be involved in a little mischief?"

Allen immediately asked, "What?"

"When you guys leave, outside the door, just around the left corner is a portable 'handicapped' sign that we sometimes use. How would you feel about putting it in front of that van from New Jersey while I call my friend on the police force to come by and check things out?"

Allen thought for sure that Bill would nix this idea, but instead, Bill immediately said, "I'll do it. Call your friend right now."

They walked outside and found the sign. Bill picked it up and placed it right in front of the van from New Jersey. They looked in the window at the bartender who gave them a thumbs up sign. It was going to be a good night after all.

The next day, the guys kept going south towards the Grand Tetons and soon crossed the Yellowstone River before arriving in the scenic little town of Jackson Hole, Wyoming. At the bridge over the Yellowstone, Allen slowed down and thought about pulling over. But he changed his mind and kept going. The Grand Tetons appeared to rise dramatically from the surrounding plains and go straight up into the sky to over fourteen thousand feet. They were probably the most photographed mountains in the country.

The boys stopped in Jackson Hole for the evening and, when they got out of the truck at the hotel, a guest in the parking lot walked over to them and asked, "What in the world happened to your door?"

Allen answered, "We were riding through the Bitterroot Mountains and heard this loud commotion—we didn't know what it was. It was like a rumbling noise . . . almost like a freight train. Then, off to the side we saw a big dust cloud rising and saw half the mountain rumbling right at us. Landslide! We had two options: stay there and get covered up by tons of rocks, or floor it and try to race the landslide towards safety."

He looked over at Bill to get his reaction, but Bill only smiled. So Allen continued, "We didn't know if we'd make it or not, but I floored it. And then, we felt the crash into the side here, where a big boulder smashed into us. Then, right when we thought we had made it through, another boulder hit the camper back there."

Allen pointed toward the dent in the camper, and the other tourist exclaimed, "Wow!!"

Allen said, "Yeah, it was a close call, and my friend over there almost wet his pants—in fact, I think they were a little damp. But we made it."

The tourist shook his hand and wished him luck as he walked back to his minivan to tell his wife about Allen's story. Bill walked over to him and said, "You ain't no good at all, boy. You ought to be ashamed of yourself."

Allen laughed and replied, "Since when did you start talking like me and saying 'ain't?' I must be rubbing off on you."

Bill grinned and said, "Let's hope your rock throwing skills don't rub off on me."

They decided to stay in a local hotel for the evening, since they were still in the high country. They bought some burgers and Diet Pepsis and went back to the room to relax, and watch television, and catch up on correspondences and business from home. Allen was reading emails and suddenly said, "Norman died."

Bill looked up at him, but didn't know how to respond. He finally asked, "How?"

"Says here he just went to sleep and never woke up. That came from one of his kids."

They both sat there silently thinking about their friend, Norman. They hadn't been "best friends," but they'd both been good friends with him. Bill asked, "Should we try to go to the funeral?"

"The funeral was today. I hadn't checked my emails in a few days."

They finished everything in quiet reverence and got ready for bed. After they turned the lights off, Allen asked his friend, "What don't you know that you don't know?"

At first, this question seemed silly to Bill. But the more he thought about it, the more thought-provoking it became. Sleep was hard to find as they both silently tried to answer that unanswerable question . . . lying in a bed, in a hotel room in Jackson Hole, Wyoming.

The following morning Allen called both of his kids . . . just to hear their voices. And he made a few other calls while Bill was in the shower. Bill didn't call anyone. They were both thinking about their friend Norman as they sat in a restaurant and had their morning coffee. The moment was broken when an actual cowboy-looking guy came in the restaurant. He had a large cowboy hat on, cowboy boots, denim pants, a cowboy shirt, and a huge belt buckle. Since the only other table of customers in the restaurant was a group of older ladies, the cowboy walked up to Allen and Bill and asked, "Is that your Ford F-150 out there?"

Allen proudly answered, "Yes, sir, it is."

"Did you know there's a big dent in the door?"

Allen thought about giving a smart alec answer, but had a little too much admiration for the cowboy. So he simply said, "Yeah, we got rammed by a buffalo up in Yellowstone."

The cowboy tilted his cowboy hat back a little and said, "No, really . . . what happened to it?"

Allen had given him an opportunity to hear the truth, but the cowboy declined to accept it. So he continued, "We were at a biker bar in Missoula the other night, and it started getting rowdy. We decided to leave and went out to the truck. But three or four Harley riders started harassing us. As we tried to pull out of the parking lot, they all surrounded us on their bikes, circling us like a bunch of buzzards. Well, my friend here started getting a little scared, so I just gunned it, and one of the Harleys rammed into the side of my truck. We took off, and I saw him get up off the ground shaking his fist at me. But we didn't stop 'till we crossed over into Wyoming."

Bill expected the cowboy to laugh at that wild story. Instead, he said, "That is incredible. I've never heard of anything like that happening back in Ohio."

Allen stopped drinking his coffee and asked the cowboy, "You're from Ohio?"

"Yeah, we've been traveling around out here for about eight days now. My wife and her parents are still at the hotel. I just came out to bring back some biscuits and tea for my wife—she don't like coffee."

Simply to keep Allen from any further insanity, Bill quickly asked, "Your wife doesn't like coffee, huh? That's pretty unusual."

"Well, she'd probably drink it, but just between you and me, I think she drinks tea because she thinks it makes her look a little snooty . . . you know, trying to impress people. But if it makes her happy, Lord knows, it's worth it."

Both guys nodded in agreement, and the pseudo-cowboy tipped his hat to them and said, "See you guys later. Have a fantastic day . . . and stay away from those biker bars!"

35

JACKSON HOLE WAS SUCH A BEAUTIFUL AND CHARMING TOWN, the boys decided to stay an extra day and, more specifically, stay out of the Ford F-150. They needed some walking around and relaxing time, instead of driving time. The Grand Teton Mountains could be seen in all their majestic glory from virtually any point in the town. They found an outside café and sat watching the mountains, and the other tourists pass by. They actually saw one car from North Carolina and watched as it pulled in front of a restaurant down the street.

They observed as a man and woman got out, stretched their legs, and started walking in their direction. As they neared, Allen rose from the table to greet them, "Howdy folks, we're from North Carolina, too."

The man seemed disturbed that someone would actually speak to him, his wife stopped to check her text messages. The man looked at Allen and said, "What?"

Allen repeated, "I saw your license plate from North Carolina. That's where we're from, too."

The man said, "We're not from Carolina; that's a rental car. No way in the world I'd live down there with all that heat and humidity."

Then the woman looked up from her cell phone and added, "Plus all the discrimination . . . we'd never live in Carolina. We're from Philadelphia!"

At this moment, Bill, being prudent as he was, knew that if he didn't act first, Allen would. He jumped up from his seat and said, "Sorry to have disturbed you both . . . enjoy your day." He grabbed Allen's arm and pulled him back to his seat as the couple sauntered away. Allen stared them down until they went in a gift shop at the corner.

When he finally regained his composure, Allen said, "There's times like that when I wished we'd won the war."

"Oh, shut up, you old bigot."

"I'm only a bigot against rude, snarly, ugly Yankees—that's all. I like everybody else."

Bill looked over at him and added, "There might be a little truth to that. You do, in fact, treat everybody else equally: you lie to us, you make fun of us, and you treat us all like dogs."

Allen smiled and said, "Exactly . . . I'm fair. I treat everyone the same way."

They walked around a bit, but didn't see anything they really wanted to buy . . . except for a cold Coors Light later that afternoon. As they sat contemplating the sights, Allen said, "Well, I guess we need to decide which direction we want to go from here."

Bill asked, "Since when was it ever a question of 'we?' I thought you were the tour director."

"And you're correct, my octogramarian friend. I did have everything planned out until you ruined it all by insisting we go out of the way to Green Bay, Wisconsin. That messed everything up! But being the gentle, accommodating soul that I am, I'm going to take you to Green Bay so you can bow down in front of the Vince Lombardi shrine and kiss his feet."

Bill stared at him and asked, "What's an octogramarian?"

"It's what you are, old man . . . except uglier and more stubborn."

Bill sluffed that off and said, "Okay, what is the decision WE have to make?"

"Well, we can keep going south into the Rocky Mountains and see what's there. Or, we can keep going east. There's one place I would especially like to visit if it doesn't disembowel you."

Bill took a drink of Coors Light and said, "I've seen enough of the mountains, if you have. What is this other place you want to visit? And please, don't disembowel me. I'm sure that would hurt."

"I would love to visit the Little Big Horn and see the place where Dustin Hoffman slayed Kirk Douglas and won freedom for all Americans."

Little Big Horn was the only part of that statement that made any sense at all to Bill. So he asked, "Where is the Little Big Horn?"

"It's right next to the Big Horn. Didn't you learn anything in college, boy?"

Bill asked, "Do you even know what state the Little Big Horn is in?"

Allen stopped and thought a moment, then said, "It's in the state of fascination and wonderment—right next to the state of astonishment—and that's where we're headed, my un-geographical friend."

Before they went to dinner, Bill Googled the Little Big Horn and learned it was located in eastern Montana. He told Allen, "I guess we're headed back to Montana, Mr. Kite."

"Why? Do you want to go see the capital and visit your friend, Mike Lewis?"

"No. Montana is where the Little Big Horn is, Ponce de Leon."

"Who? Ponce . . . who?

"He was a famous . . . forget it." Bill said, not really knowing if Allen was just messing with him or not.

They thought about getting vegetable plates for dinner, but the pork chops special won them over. Allen said, "We've been driving all over Montana and Wyoming, and I ain't seen no pigs anywhere. Have you?"

Bill thought a moment and replied, "No. That's weird isn't it? We've seen ten million cows, thousands of horses, and even some sheep—but no pigs." Then he added, "We have bacon and ham nearly every day, and sausage and pork chops. But where are the pigs?"

When the waiter brought the plates out to them, Allen asked him, "Where do they keep all the pigs out here? We haven't seen a single one—anywhere."

The waiter knew right away. "Pigs don't like cold weather. And they don't like the rain either. They don't have any hair to keep warm like other animals do, so they have to be kept inside. That's why you never see them."

When he left, Bill asked Allen, "Do you ever see any pigs in North Carolina?"

"Not that I can remember. I've never thought about it though. I just like eatin' 'em, not wondering how they live."

After dinner they went back to the little pub they'd seen earlier and had a Coors Light before bed. Even though ninety-five percent of the customers in the little pub were middle-aged and older, the music playing from the speakers in the pub was one hundred percent rap. One beer's worth of rap was all they could stand. They headed back to the room, but the television in the hotel room only had European soccer showing. So they turned it off and went to bed.

When the lights were off, Allen asked another question, "Bill, how old is old?"

Bill thought about that and was trying to decide how to answer it when Allen asked, "Are you awake?"

"Yeah, I'm awake. OLD is different for everybody. I've known some people who were old at thirty-five, and other people who were young at seventy-five. It depends on the person, not the age."

After a few seconds of silence, Allen said, "I always felt young until Barbara died. Then something changed in me. I don't feel that way anymore."

"Well how DO you feel?"

"I feel lost."

36

BILL WAS A LITTLE CONCERNED about his friend until breakfast, when he started flirting with the waitress whose nametag read, Nancy. She was a woman about thirty-five or thirty-six years old and was not wearing a wedding ring. Nancy had a nice, pretty face, but had gained a little weight around her thighs and hips, as most women do. But on her, it looked good . . . as it does on some women. Allen liked the way she looked. And she knew how to talk to men . . . even old men.

They flirted back and forth as she brought their pancakes and bacon and refilled their coffee. Then Allen said to her, "Nancy, you ought to think about moving to North Carolina where real men live."

 She smiled and replied, "You don't think these cowboys around here are real men?"

Allen winked at her and said, "Honey, there ain't nothing like a southern man."

Nancy smiled and replied, "That's not what Neil Young said."

Bill had no clue what she was referring to, but Allen vaguely remembered that old song. He answered, "I think old Neil was singing about how smart and handsome and hard-working us southern men are."

"Nope," Nancy said, "not at all."

"Well what do you expect from some hippie from California? I bet he ain't never been down south."

"I think he's from Canada, but you're probably right. After meeting you two, I'm sure Neil was mistaken."

When they finished their breakfast, Nancy brought them each a piece of apple pie—on the house. Even though they were full, they ate the pie anyway. As with Farrah back in Spokane, Nancy received the biggest tip she would get all week. As they were leaving, Allen said to her, "If you ever change your mind about moving to North Carolina, be sure to look me up."

Nancy stepped a little closer to him and whispered, "And just what would you do with a woman like me?"

Allen smiled and whispered back, "I'd figure it out, Nancy. Don't you worry about that."

They went back north a little and hit the interstate in Montana heading east, on their way to the Little Big Horn. It was beautiful country to ride through, and the boys were fairly quiet as they took it all in. Just when Bill thought Allen might be napping, he perked up and asked a question, "Bill, what's your favorite childhood memory?"

"Define childhood."

"Mmm, anything before we graduated high school."

Bill thoughtfully replied, "It might be all those times we'd just hang around and goof off together."

"No, I'm talking about one thing . . . one memory that you can distinguish from all the others."

Bill took a couple of minutes and concluded, "It would probably be playing catch with my dad in the back yard. We'd go out there and just throw the ball back and forth. I'd try throwing curves and knuckleballs, and he would always say, 'Great job! That really broke a lot.' It made me feel good. He made me feel good. I never realized it then, like I do now, how hard that must've been for him to come home after working all day and go out in the heat and play catch with me for thirty or forty minutes. But he'd always come out whenever I asked him—every time. He never told me he was too tired, or wanted to watch TV, or anything . . . he always made time for me."

They both let those thoughts sink in for a few minutes as Bill drove on. Eventually, he asked Allen the same question, "What's your favorite memory?"

Allen smiled and sat up in his seat a little, then said, "Remember that old girl, Viola?"

"Who?"

164

"Viola. She lived up near Pilot Mountain, out in the country. You remember her, she's the one . . ."

Bill quickly broke in, "Yeah, yeah . . . I remember her now. Viola is your favorite childhood memory?"

"You better believe it, buddy. She taught me things I never knew existed . . . like what the curves on a woman's body felt like . . . and how smooth the skin was on the inside of a girl's thigh. Viola gave me my initial education into the world of carnal knowledge. Without her, I wouldn't have had the reputation I did with all the girls in Forsyth County."

"I didn't know you had a reputation with the girls in Forsyth County."

"Oh, yeah," Allen said, "ask anybody who was around back then. They'll tell you."

"I was around back then . . . I never heard anything."

Allen replied, "You might have been around, old boy, but you weren't one of the many young ladies who were talking about me and my exploits."

Before Bill could refute that statement, he was distracted and said, "Look out there!"

Allen said, "Where?"

Bill pointed past him out the side window at a group of wild horses running out on the open range. It looked to be about ten or twelve horses of all different colors, just running about fifty yards off the road. They slowed the truck down to get a better look and couldn't see anything chasing the horses. But couldn't understand why they'd be running out in the open like they were either. They must have paralleled the herd for a couple of minutes before the horses then turned off to the right and ran away in a different direction. Allen sighed, "Wow! You don't see that every day. Wonder what they were doing?"

Bill just shook his head and said, "Who knows, they were just horses being horses; doing what God put them on the earth to do. Just being wild and free . . . like us."

They decided to stop for the evening near Billings, Montana. They saw billboards on the interstate for a new and fancy campground, so they thought they'd take advantage of it. The campground was located next to a meandering stream with cottonwood trees lining the banks. Each camp site had its own shelter and fire pit. Plus, there was a small grill in the office that sold wings, burgers and pizza—comfort food for the road.

The boys set up their camper and started walking towards the office to check out the food when they noticed dark clouds starting to gather. When they arrived back at the camper with their food, it started raining a little. Then it started raining hard! Soon, thunder was shaking the earth and lightning bolts were striking all around them. They didn't feel comfortable huddled under their little metal shelter, so they climbed back inside the truck, feeling more secure. It stormed for nearly an hour before the thunder and lightning eased off. The rain, however, continued all evening.

Once the lightning ceased, they got out of the truck and went back to their chairs under the shelter to have a Coors Light and listen to the rain on the metal roof of the shelter. They couldn't decide which was better: the ice cold Coors Light, or the sound of the rain on the shelter. Fortunately, they were able to enjoy both.

When the rain slacked up a little, they noticed the door open on the RV across the dirt road from them. A man stepped out of the RV under his little shelter and waved at the boys. They waved back. Allen yelled over to him, "Would you like a beer?"

The man didn't even answer. He just ran across the road, dodging as many mud puddles as he could. Bill handed him a Coors Light, and the man took a seat on the bricks around the fire pit. He said, "My name's Cleve, thanks for the beer."

Allen and Bill introduced themselves. Then Allen asked Cleve where he was from, "Right over there . . . that's where I'm from."

Bill and Allen didn't understand what in the world Cleve meant. It seemed like he was pointing at his RV. Cleve could sense their confusion so he explained, "The RV is our home now, me and my wife. She's in bed reading, or asleep probably. Her name is Elizabeth."

It was difficult for Allen to comprehend what Cleve just told him, so he asked, "You live in the RV fulltime?"

"Yep. We have been for nearly three years now. We sold our home in Kansas City and just travel around . . . visiting our three kids, seeing the country, staying as long as we like, leaving when we want to."

Bill said, "That is absolutely awesome! How much longer do you think you'll be doing it?"

Cleve took a long drink of his beer and said, "Till one of us dies, I imagine. It'd be too much for one person to do all the driving. But we're in pretty good health, and we love it."

Allen asked, "Do you mostly go visit your kids?"

Cleve explained, "You know, we thought that's what we'd do. Go see them and stay with each of them for several weeks, but it just didn't turn out like that. After a few days, we'd either get tired of them, or they'd get tired of us, and we'd take off. Then it got to the point where we enjoyed just being by ourselves and seeing the country. So now, we don't see the kids very often at all. And when we do, it's only for a day or two as we're passing through."

Bill was simply astounded at Cleve's story and asked him, "Do you go all over the country?"

"Well . . . that was the plan. And we probably will at some point. But it's hard to leave the west—it's just so beautiful. For the last three years, we've gone from Arizona, California, and Nevada in the wintertime; to Oregon, Washington, Montana, Wyoming, Colorado, and Utah in the summers. We never get tired of it, and there's so much to see . . . we love it."

Allen asked, "Your wife like's all the traveling, too?"

"Heck, she loves it more than I do." Cleve laughed, "If we came off the road, she'd leave me!"

37

CLEVE AND HIS WIFE ELIZABETH invited the boys to come over to their RV in the morning for a fresh, hot breakfast. As they sat around drinking coffee and talking about travelling, Bill asked them both what was the most beautiful state they'd been to. Without hesitation, Elizabeth said, "Utah. Without a doubt. There are places in the south and east of that state that will take your breath away." She looked at the boys and asked, "You've been there, right?"

Bill sighed, "No, we didn't make it there. Our tour director must have forgotten that one."

He looked over at Allen, who then added, "But we went all over California—that's a beautiful place, too."

Cleve got a little excited hearing they'd been all over California, so he commented, "We loved the harbor in San Diego and the beaches there, it's just gorgeous."

Bill looked over at Allen and said, "We missed that . . . didn't we, buddy?"

Before Allen could answer, Elizabeth asked, "Didn't you think Joshua Tree National Park was one of the best hidden secrets in the country? We loved going there."

Again, Bill looked over at Allen, and answered, "I think we missed that one, too."

Cleve asked, "What about Death Valley?"

"Nope."

"The Salton Sea?"

Bill said, "Doesn't ring a bell."

Elizabeth asked, "I know you went up to King's Canyon. Everybody goes there."

"Mmm, I don't think so."

Cleve was beside himself, wondering what exactly the boys did see in California. He then said, "Well, you had to go to Yosemite—everybody in the world goes there."

Bill looked at Allen, and they both hung their heads in embarrassment.

Elizabeth tentatively asked, "The wine country?"

They were each ashamed to verbally answer any longer, so they just shook their heads.

After a few seconds of awkward silence, Elizabeth said, "Who wants some French toast?"

Cleve and Elizabeth were on their way to Moab, Utah to spend a few weeks hiking the trails around that mystical place. Bill and Allen set the Ford F-150 towards the Little Big Horn. As they were nearing the exit, Allen asked his friend, "You know what happened here, right?"

"I know a little about it, like most people do. General Custer got killed, and that's basically why it's famous."

Allen said, "To be a college graduate, sometimes you can be so uneducated. You need to know more about your country's history."

"Well why don't you enlighten me, Dr. Riklefs."

Allen looked over and asked, "Who?"

"Dr. Riklefs! He was our history teacher at Appalachian. Lord have mercy, son. Has Alzheimer's already set in on you?"

"I remember him," Allen said, "I just wanted to see if you remembered him. He lectured us that day about how Custer stormed into the Indian village, but didn't realize that Jim Thorpe was there visiting. Jim and Geronimo were cousins and were having a party when old George Armstrong busted in uninvited. Well, they didn't like it, so they chased them back over the Rubicon . . . all except George, who was as hard-headed as a tree stump. He wouldn't leave, so they had to capture him and hold him for ransom."

Bill drove along, shaking his head, then interrupted the story, "They held him for ransom?"

"Yep. They wanted the combination to the vault in Fort Knox, but old George, being the brave American he was, wouldn't tell them. So, they made an example of him, and that's why he's so famous today."

Allen finished his bizarre interpretation of American history as they entered the National Park. The first thing they saw was Custer National Cemetery, which sobered up Allen's story substantially. They stopped and got out of the truck to walk the paths around the two hundred and sixty-eight grave sites in this hallowed ground. Next they stopped at the interpretive center and sat with a group of school children in the small auditorium as a short documentary played.

On the early morning of June, 25, 1876, General Custer and his troops attacked the unsuspecting Indian village, consisting of men, women, and children. Custer fully expected the Indians to make a run for it as they had in the past. What he didn't know was that the Sioux were massed here in celebration. And their two leaders, Crazy Horse and Sitting Bull, along with over two thousand other Sioux had no intention of running from this small band of soldiers.

General Custer brought all the disaster upon himself by being impetuous, foolhardy, and vain. Unfortunately, his recklessness came at a high price . . . the lives of two hundred and sixty-eight of his troops—including two of his brothers, a nephew, and a brother-in-law.

Allen and Bill walked away from the documentary and made it up to one of the small hills overlooking the battlefield. They sat down on the ground and imagined what it must have been like on that fateful morning of June 25, 1876. For the Indians: panic and fear among the women and children as soldiers raided their camp. For the soldiers: panic and fear as they realized the Indians were not running and had them extremely outnumbered, and eventually surrounded.

The boys spent nearly half an hour imagining those sobering events. Finally Bill patted Allen on the arm and said, "Let's go." They toured the small museum and gift shop, but didn't buy a single thing. It just didn't seem right.

38

THEY DIDN'T FEEL LIKE DRIVING any further that day, so they located a campground near the Little Big Horn and decided to spend the night. When they were coming to their camp site, they noticed a van from Warren Wilson College in Asheville, North Carolina. Allen looked at Bill and asked, "Warren Wilson College—you ever hear of that?"

"I've heard of it. It's in the mountains and sort of a quirky type school, I think."

"Quirky?" Allen asked, "What does that mean?"

"That's probably not the right description. They just have a lot of classes not associated with mainline colleges. I don't think their main agenda is business, accounting, and math."

"I wonder what in the world they're doing out here in the middle of nowhere?"

Bill answered, "Probably the same as us: exploring the world and broadening their horizons."

"Broadening your horizons?" Allen asked, "I thought you were just following me around in a camper trying to pick up women."

★★★

As they were setting up their camper, they noticed a group of young people across a field about a hundred yards away from the campground. They were all sitting on the ground, and a man was standing up, gesturing wildly as he walked among them. Bill said, "That must be some sort of class they're all taking, and the guy standing is the professor."

"What kind of class would be out here? Seems crazy to me." Allen said.

About an hour later, the "class" broke up and most of the young people started filtering back to the campground. They passed by Bill and Allen, who were sitting out in their chairs drinking a Diet Pepsi and eating hot

FRIENDS

dogs from the campground office. They looked like any other college students, and most of them spoke as they passed by. A few minutes later a man walked up and saw the North Carolina license plates on the camper and stopped as he asked, "Are you two guys from North Carolina? That's where we're from."

Allen answered, "We sure are. We saw your van from Warren Wilson College. Are you on some sort of field trip?"

"Yeah, I'm taking this group on a tour of sites of oppression throughout American history."

Bill said, "Sites of oppression? What exactly does that mean?"

"Our goal is to make the students aware of social injustice, like here at the Little Big Horn, and inspire them to a life of change and giving and creating a new social order. We want to show them that the current state of economics in our country needs to be changed to help all our citizens, not just the privileged few."

Bill rose from his chair and said, "I would think the first thing you need to teach them is that there is never enough of anything to satisfy all those who want it."

The college guy took a step closer and replied, "Our goal is to change things . . . to inspire diversity . . . to make them think."

Bill asked, "So, I'm assuming you're the teacher of this class?"

"Yes, sir, I am."

"What department are you in?"

"Sociology and Psychology."

"If you're teaching them about diversity, let me ask you this: How many conservatives are there in your sociology department?"

The guy didn't answer. So Bill continued, "Too much of what is called 'education' is little more than an expensive isolation from reality. The welfare state is the oldest con game in the world. First you take people's money away quietly, and then you give some of it back to them flamboyantly."

The teacher then answered, "So you don't think our country owes a decent life to those who can't take care of themselves?"

GARY HOPE

Bill replied, "One of the consequences of such notions as 'entitlements' is that people who have contributed nothing to society feel that society owes them something, apparently just for being nice enough to grace us with their presence."

The college guy said, "That just sounds like pure greed to me."

Bill raised his voice a little and replied, "I have never understood why it is 'greed' to want to keep the money you've earned, but not greed to want to take somebody else's money."

The teacher didn't know how to respond. Or if he did, he chose not to. So without any further discussion, he walked back towards the van and his disciples who were waiting on more words of wisdom from him.

Before Bill sat back down in his chair, Allen popped open a Coors Light and handed it to his friend, saying, "Here you go, buddy. You really learned him a good lesson didn't you?"

Bill took the Coors Light and sat down, saying, "Crazy people! I might even pull for the Tar Heels if they ever play Warren Wilson College."

"I cannot believe you said that."

Bill took a long drink of the beer, looked at Allen, and said, "I had my fingers crossed."

★★★

The following morning, the boys packed up the camper and took off before any of the college students stirred. They found a truck stop not too far away and pulled in to get some coffee and breakfast. After the coffee came, Allen asked, "Well, did you take a nitroglycerin pill last night when I wasn't looking?"

Bill smiled and looked at his friend, and said, "Shut up."

After they ate, Allen said, "I guess we need to make a decision about our next destination. Now don't get mad, but I have to ask you a question."

"Go ahead."

"It seemed that after last night, you may be a little tired and irritable. Maybe you just want to go home. It's okay if you do . . . I understand. Just let me know so I can plan accordingly."

173

Bill moved his coffee cup a little, just to collect his thoughts, then answered, "I'm not tired. In fact, I feel more alive than I have in twelve years. It would suit me if we turned around and went back to see all those places you made us miss in California . . . and Utah!"

Allen smiled at this news, and said, "Sorry, Mr. Goode, but we ain't going back—not now anyways—we got new horizons to broaden and other majestic peaks to conquer. Plus, I promised I'd get you to Green Bay so you could kiss the shrine of your idol. And I'm always a man of my word. So wipe the crumbs off your face, go take your morning constitutional, and let's hit the road, Jack."

Bill did all of those things, then followed his friend out to the truck. As they got settled, he asked Allen, "Where to next, Mr. Kite?"

"I want to go see Mt. Rushmore. Be a shame to be this close to it and not see it. I've always admired the magnificent sculptures of those four famous men: Abraham Lincoln, Benjamin Franklin, Babe Ruth, and General Douglas MacArthur. It would be an honor just to stare up at them."

"Anything you say, old-timer. Lead the way."

39

AS THEY WERE DRIVING ALONG IN SILENCE, Allen asked Bill, "What did you want to be when you were younger?"

"You mean besides a baseball player?"

"Yeah, something realistic."

Bill said, "Well I could strike you out."

Allen smiled and said, "Big deal. Who couldn't?"

"I always thought I'd do something important . . . something that would make a difference."

Allen answered, "You did do something important. You made cigarettes. Just think of all the doctors and nurses and hospitals you've kept busy over the years. They ought to give you some sort of medal or something."

Bill said, "Yep, between us, we've probably filled up half the grave sites in Forsyth County."

"You ever feel guilty about making cigarettes, knowing that they were dangerous and caused cancer?"

Bill thought a moment, then said, "No, sir. People had a choice. They didn't have to smoke. They knew the consequences and chose to smoke anyway. Same way with liquor or driving fast or anything else. You can't blame somebody else for poor decisions that YOU make."

Allen mulled this over in his mind, but didn't respond. Instead he just kept looking at Bill who was driving at the time. Bill could feel the stare and said, "Don't insult the alligator until you've crossed the river."

Allen wasn't exactly sure what that meant, but he continued, "I never wanted to do anything else. I guess I was too busy living life to think of changing careers . . . keeping Barbara happy, raising the kids, working.

Before you know what happened, your life is done. I never thought of anything else."

They stopped for the night at a Best Western Hotel near Mt. Rushmore. As they cruised into the parking lot of the hotel, they noticed cars from everywhere. Allen said, "Over or under fifteen? Loser buys the first beer."

Bill said, "Okay . . . under. There's never as many as you think there are."

They rode around the lot and counted cars from seventeen different states. Once they got to number sixteen, Allen said, "I wonder what time the bar opens?"

It was open when they checked in, so they took the luggage to their room and came back downstairs to relax. They took two open seats at the bar, next to a man sitting by himself. As soon as they ordered, Allen said hello to the man and asked where he was from. The guy said, "Minot."

Allen and Bill didn't respond, because they didn't know where Minot was. The guy understood and explained, "It's in North Dakota, near the Canadian border."

"Wow," Allen said, "I've never met anyone from North Dakota. Do you like it up there?"

"Yeah, what's not to like: cold weather, winter that lasts eight months, dark days, no sunshine, no mountains, no hills, no beaches, no . . . should I continue?"

The boys didn't know what to say. Then the guy put his hand out and said, "Just kidding fellas, it's okay. My name's Mickey. Where are you guys from?"

Allen replied, "North Carolina . . . home of short winters, plenty of sunshine, beautiful mountains, and glorious beaches."

Mickey smiled and said, "I hate you already."

Bill bought all three of them a round of beers, and the boys listened to Mickey's story. He worked in "oil exploration," and his wife and three children were up in the room taking baths and getting ready for bed. He told them his family was here to see Mt. Rushmore . . . education for the kids. He continued, "Every vacation we go somewhere 'educational.' We're either going to have the smartest kids in the world, or kids who hate our guts for boring them to death."

Allen asked, "Mt. Rushmore isn't boring is it?"

"Have you been there before?" Mickey asked.

"No, it'll be our first time. We're looking forward to it."

"Okay . . . well, you'll probably like it then."

Bill asked, "Didn't you like it?"

"It's not that I didn't like it, but . . . all this educational stuff is fine for my wife and the kids. But, don't you ever repeat this to my wife if she comes down here, I'd like to just have some fun. You know? Just have some fun without having to learn anything."

Allen asked, "What kind of fun? What would you like to do?"

"All sorts of things. Go on a cruise . . . the kids would love that. Go to Disneyland. Visit New York and see Yankee Stadium. My dad named me after his idol, Mickey Mantle. You know, stuff like that."

Bill asked, "You don't do those things now?"

"No, sir. Our last vacation was to Springfield, Illinois to visit Lincoln's home place. The year before that we went to the Indian museum in Pierre. Have you ever been to Pierre?"

Allen answered, "No. I don't even know where it is."

Mickey shook his head and said, "Trust me, you don't want to know."

Allen said, "Well, why do you keep going to these places then?"

Mickey said, "Cause I love my wife more than anything in the world. And if that makes her happy, then I'll go to museums and crap like that for the rest of my life."

Allen knew exactly what he meant. Bill knew exactly what he meant. Mickey knew exactly what he meant. The three guys sipped their Coors Light and thought about the women in their lives . . . and the women who used to be in their lives.

After breakfast, they headed straight out to Mt. Rushmore. There were already a few tour buses parked and dozens of other tourists milling around.

The boys got out and walked over to the viewing area, staring up at the faces of the four presidents. Allen said, "Which one is Babe Ruth?"

They stared for a few minutes, then walked down the pathway and stared from a different angle. Bill asked, "Why would anyone want to bring children to this place?"

After a few moments, Allen said, "Why did you bring ME to this place?"

"What? If I remember correctly, Mr. Riklefs, it was you who said you wanted to visit here . . . not me."

Allen replied, "There you go again . . . always circumventing the facts with the truth. All I can say is that Mickey's wife must a dang good looking woman. Let's go."

They stopped for a late lunch at a small town out in the middle of nowhere. Allen asked, "You're in no hurry, right?"

"No, sir, I'm not."

That guy Mickey, from North Dakota, got me thinking."

Bill broke in, "You want to go to Disneyland?"

"I want to go to North Dakota. What do you think about that, grandpa?"

Bill was silent for a moment and then answered, "Okay with me. What exactly will we do in North Dakota?"

"There ain't nothing to do in North Dakota—that's the point! Nobody goes there. If we go there, we'll have gone to a place that nobody's been before. Everybody goes to the Grand Canyon and Las Vegas and stuff like that. Nobody goes to North Dakota. We'll be trailblazers and pioneers— we'll have grand stories to tell our grandchildren. Heck, we'll probably be famous!"

Bill smiled and said, "We're already famous, Mr. Kite. But, lead the way. I can't wait to see what North Dakota looks like."

40

IT HAD STARTED RAINING as the boys drove some back roads up into North Dakota and hit I-94 east into the city of Fargo. They were going to find a nice Holiday Inn in Fargo for the night, but all the exit ramps into the city were closed. They stopped at a gas station to fuel up and find out what was happening. The guy in the store said that the Red River had flooded again and most of the roads in the inner city were under water. He explained that this happened nearly every time they had a big rain . . . nothing to worry about. Apparently, Fargo was built right on the Red River flood plain, and it doesn't take much for it to be under water.

The gas station attendant told them of a nice campground a little north of the city, up I-29. They took the interstate north for about twenty minutes and found a newer looking KOA that was nearly full. The campground employee explained that heavy rains usually brought people out to his campground, which was located on higher ground. The boys couldn't see any higher ground—it all looked the same to them—flat! As they were checking in at the campground office, they looked at the TV behind the desk, which was forecasting the low temperature for the night to be around twenty-eight degrees.

Allen looked at Bill, then asked the clerk, "Is that the temperature for here, tonight?"

The clerk looked at the TV and said, "Yep, that's not too bad though. You'll be alright."

Bill looked at Allen, and Allen and shook his head, "No." They politely declined the open spot for the night and asked the guy where the closest unflooded town was. They went back to the interstate and continued northward to the town of Grand Forks, North Dakota, where they found a nice Holiday Inn. It was actually a Red Roof Inn, but they didn't really care. They just wanted to be warm and dry.

It rained hard all night, which made the boys happy they drove up to Grand Forks instead of staying in the camper. The Red Roof Inn didn't have a bar or much of anything, except a drink machine. So Bill took the Ford F-150 and went to the local McDonalds and brought back dinner. When he walked in the room, Allen was just hanging up the phone. Bill looked at him, but didn't ask anything. Allen saw him look at him, but didn't volunteer anything. They ate their Big Mac's and fries, with an apple pie for dessert and watched an old movie on television about a boy in Los Angeles who fell in love with a girl attending Cal Berkeley. Bill said, "We were there."

"Yes, Mr. Goode, we were there."

When they turned the lights off for the night, it was Bill's turn to ask the nightly serious question, "Allen, what is the biggest lie that you once believed was true?"

Allen paused a moment, then said, "That love would last forever."

The next morning, in the Red Roof Inn lobby, Allen found a brochure for Lake Superior. It charmed him, and they quickly decided that was their next destination. Plus, it was sort of on the way over to Green Bay . . . sort of. They left Grand Forks, North Dakota and started eastward. Much of the landscape they saw was under water; the rest of it should have been under water. At least they could tell their grandchildren and friends that they had indeed visited North Dakota and spent the night there. Not many people could ever say that. Even less would want to say that.

As they were driving across northern Minnesota, Allen said, "After we visit Lake Superior, I also want to go by Marquette University up there and ride through that campus. I always liked old Al McGuire, especially after he beat Dean that one time . . . remember that? They had those uniforms that the shirts didn't tuck in the pants and everybody got upset about it."

Bill waited until he was sure Allen had finished, then asked, "You know Marquette University isn't up at Lake Superior don't you?"

"Yes it is. I saw it on Google when I checked out Lake Superior."

"No," Bill adds, "what you saw was the town of Marquette on Lake Superior. The university is located in Milwaukee; not in the town of Marquette."

Allen immediately fired up Mr. Google, and after a couple of minutes he said, "I knew that. I meant I wanted to see Lake Superior, THEN drive to Milwaukee and see Marquette University. You need to pay better attention to what I'm saying . . . you might learn something, boy."

The drive across northern Minnesota was fairly uneventful. It was a land of forests and lakes, mostly uninhabited from what they could see. They stopped on the outskirts of Duluth when they spotted a nice looking place called the Superior Motor Inn. From the parking lot they did not see the lake, but when they checked into their room on the fourth floor, they could see the vast expanse of Lake Superior.

Even better, the restaurant and bar were located on the top floor with amazing views of downtown Duluth in one direction and Lake Superior in the other direction. The hotel seemed to be buzzing with all sorts of activity, and the boys soon learned that State Farm Insurance was holding a conference at the hotel—that's why it was so full.

After a dinner of fish caught fresh from the lake, the boys retired to the bar for their nightly Iron Maiden before bed. Allen started up a conversation with an insurance agent from Appleton, Wisconsin and asked him if their auto coverage included being rammed by a buffalo. The guy wasn't sure, but told Allen he'd check on it and get back with him. All the talk of premiums and deductions drove the boys back to their room pretty quickly.

After the lights were off, and they each had time to reflect on life and elderliness, Allen asked his nightly question, "Bill, what do you want more of in your life?"

Bill took so long to answer that Allen had to ask if he was still awake. He was, and finally said, "I want more life in my life."

Allen nodded to himself and thought, "Me too, buddy. Me too."

They crossed the border into Wisconsin and drove along the rural shores of Lake Superior until they spotted a State Park located right on the lake with a campground and nice facilities. It was very near the town of Bayfield, Wisconsin. There were several other campers, mostly fishermen or boaters, almost all of them older—no young people that Allen or Bill could see. They set up their camper, which was much smaller than all the others in the campground. However, most of the other people probably hadn't travelled half way around the world in their campers either.

They walked down to the camp headquarters where the offices and grill were located. They decided to get something and take it back to their place and sit out in their chairs and take in the beauty of the lake. As they were waiting on their food order, an attractive woman about sixty years old came out from one of the offices. She had on some sort of State Park uniform with a name tag that identified her as Ellen.

Ellen had gray hair, but it was the color of gray that was natural and attractive . . . the color that a lot of women would aspire to have. She was graceful in a way that led you to believe she'd once been a dancer. She also had a small mole beneath her left eye that drew attention to her brilliant hazel colored eyes. As soon as she came from the office, Allen elbowed Bill and said, "Hey, look at that. I'd let her arrest me anytime."

Bill didn't respond, but he did not take his eyes off Ellen either. As she noticed them, Ellen caught Bill's stare, and her eyes met his eyes for a few seconds. Those few seconds seemed much longer to both Bill and Ellen. She continued on towards the exit and left the building, while the boys continued to stare, hoping she'd come back through the doorway. When their food was ready, Allen asked the guy who that lady ranger was that just left. He answered, "That's Ellen. She's a part-time volunteer here who gives interpretive talks and guides around the lake. She does that every morning at 9:00 if you want to go to it—she's pretty good."

After seeing Ellen, they both definitely wanted to go.

They took their dinner and sat in their camp chairs, staring out at the rolling waters of Lake Superior. After starting a small fire, which was acceptable, they each had a Coors Light for dessert. The sun had set off to their left and had cast a shining glow across the lake—a color the boys had never seen before in nature. As soon as it got dark, it also got cold. They each put on a jacket on and wrapped up in their handmade, Blackfoot Indian blankets. Allen sat there thinking, "What better way to spend an evening: sitting by a beautiful lake, sipping a Coors Light, watching a fire glow in the dark, wrapped up in a handmade Indian blanket, sitting next to your best friend in the world."

Bill sat there, sipping his Coors Light, wrapped up in his handmade Indian blanket, watching the fire glow in the dark, and thinking, "That ranger woman had the most beautiful eyes I've seen in a long time."

As they bundled up in their camper for the night and turned off the lamps, Allen asked his friend, "Bill, have you done anything worth remembering lately?"

Of course, Bill didn't answer. These nightly questions had become the sort of questions that didn't require answers—they only required thought. And Bill thought, "Yes. I did see something today worth remembering."

41

THE BOYS WERE UP EARLY because they were cold, and because they were excited about Ellen's interpretive lecture about Lake Superior at 9:00. When they arrived at the ranger station, Ellen was there waiting with hot coffee for all the guests. The guests included a man and woman from Potawatomi, Wisconsin, two other older women from just across the border in Michigan, and the two boys.

Ellen had a way with her speech and demeanor that held everyone's attention. It was fun listening to her talk, no matter what the subject might have been. She started off by asking what everyone knew about Lake Superior. She got the usual answers: largest of the Great Lakes, good fishing, fairly clean. Then she told them what they didn't know.

She started, "Do any of you realize just how big this lake is?" There was no answer, so she continued, "Lake Superior contains ten percent of all the fresh water on the planet Earth. It also covers about thirty-one thousand, seven hundred square miles, at an average depth of four hundred and eighty three feet." Ellen let those facts sink in as the guests tried to comprehend the numbers.

She continued, "There have been about three hundred and fifty known shipwrecks in Lake Superior. Everyone also agrees, there have probably been at least that many unknown shipwrecks over the years."

Allen raised his hand and asked, "Didn't Barry Manilow sing a song one time about a shipwreck on Lake Superior?"

Ellen smiled and answered, "Close, but it wasn't Barry Manilow. It was Gordon Lightfoot who sang about the Edmund Fitzgerald's sinking."

The man from Potawatomi asked, "Was that wreck special, or he just liked the name, Edmund Fitzgerald?"

Ellen explained, "It was special in that the Edmund Fitzgerald was the largest ship to ever sink in the lake. It was caught in a storm on November 10, 1975, and the entire crew of twenty-nine was lost."

The man asked another question, "How could a big ship like that sink in a lake?"

Ellen explained, "Like I told you before, this lake is huge—almost like an ocean. The night of the wreck there were record hurricane-force winds up to seventy-five miles per hour and waves up to thirty-five feet high. The storm came so quickly that the ship gave out no distress signals before it sank—it happened that fast. The exact cause of the sinking remains unknown even today."

All the guests were thinking "Waves thirty-five feet high?" Except Bill, who was thinking, "She has the most beautiful eyes I've ever seen."

Ellen continued her lecture, "Lake Superior contains as much water as ALL the other Great Lakes COMBINED, plus three extra Lake Erie's!" She let that fact sink in, then added, "There is enough water in Lake Superior to cover all of North and South America with water one foot deep."

One of the two older women asked, "Is the fishing good here?"

"There are seventy-eight different species of fish that call the big lake home. So, yes, the fishing is very good . . . from the shore, or out on a boat."

Then Allen asked, "Does the lake ever freeze? Completely freeze?"

Ellen looked at Allen, but then diverted her gaze to look directly at Bill before speaking, "It very rarely freezes over completely. And when it does, it's just for a few hours. Complete and solid freezing has only happened four times in recorded history—the last time being in 2009."

Ellen fielded several other questions about camping and boating and things of that nature, then said, "If any of you are interested, I'm going to lead a group over to Madeline Island this afternoon for a nature walk. The boat will leave the pier at 1:00."

They all shook hands with Ellen as they left the ranger station. Bill's handshake was just a tad longer than anyone else—because Ellen didn't let go immediately. The boys started walking back towards their camp and Allen said, "I think she likes you, grandpa."

"Oh, shut up." They walked a few more steps, then Bill asked, "You think so?"

"Didn't you see how she kept looking at you and making that googly, cute face?"

"No."

Allen exclaimed, "Well, she did! And you know it. I saw the way you were looking at her, too."

They were almost at their camper and Bill said, "I think I might go on that boat ride over to the island for that nature walk today. You want to go?"

Allen stopped and looked at his friend and said, "Two things: First, me and boats aren't exactly copacetic. And second, I think you might want to take your ranger friend off behind some bushes over on that island."

Allen wasn't exactly sure, but he thought Bill might have blushed at that statement. He certainly didn't dispute it, and he didn't tell Allen to "Shut up." So it was decided that Bill would take the boat ride over to the island for a nature walk, and Allen would rent a fishing pole and see if there were any s-a-l-m-o-n lurking about in Lake Superior.

When Bill reported to the pier at 1:00 for the boat ride to the island, he was surprised to find he was the only person there. He thought he may have the time confused. But then he saw Ellen coming out of the office, walking toward him. She came close to him and said, "Are you ready to go?"

"Where is everybody else?"

She said, "Looks like it's just you and me. Is that okay?"

Inside his body Bill was screaming, "Yes, Yes, Yes, Yes!" But to Ellen, he only said, "Yeah, okay."

The short twelve minute ride over to the island was a little bumpy—Allen would have had trouble with it. Ellen was right in that this lake was huge and had some significant waves. They pulled up to the small pier at Madeline Island, and Ellen secured the boat. Then they started off on their ninety minute nature walk.

Four hours later, Ellen untied the boat, and they started back to the mainland. Allen was waiting at the pier wondering where in the world his friend had been all day . . . until he saw the look on Bill's face. Then he knew where'd he'd been all day. Bill exited the small boat. Then Ellen got off and tied the boat to the pier. Bill said, "Thanks for the tour . . . I really enjoyed it."

Ellen said, "I hope it wasn't too boring for you. Maybe the next tour will be better."

Allen overheard all this mumbo jumbo and was thinking, "Give me a break!"

After Ellen walked towards the offices, Bill said, "How's it going, buddy?"

"How's it going? You've been gone all day, and you ask me 'How's it going?' You better start giving me details NOW! I want to know everything in graphic, lurid detail—do you hear me?"

Bill stared at him with a quizzical look on his face and answered, "What?"

"Bill!!!"

"Nothing. We went on a nature walk. It was very informative."

"Bill . . . cut the crap and tell me what happened."

"Nothing happened. It was a nature walk."

Allen was getting excited now, "You went on a ninety minute nature walk that took five hours! That ain't nothing!"

Bill said, "Five hours?"

"Yes, you've been gone five hours."

Bill looked at his watch and was absolutely, totally surprised. He said, "Wow!"

"Wow, my butt. You'd better start talking now, or we're not gonna be friends anymore."

Bill smiled and quite calmly said, "There's nothing to tell, buddy. We went on a nature walk, and I guess it lasted longer than I thought it would. That's all."

Allen threatened him, coaxed him, bribed him, and cursed him, but that's all Bill would say, "We went on a nature walk."

FRIENDS

They went to the grill for dinner, and Allen was unusually quiet . . . for a while. Then he asked, "Did you kiss her?"

"Nature walk."

"Did you hold her hand?"

"Nature walk."

"You boinked her, didn't you?"

"Nature walk."

"Bill!!!"

Bill wiped his mouth with his napkin and quite slowly said, "Nature walk."

On the way back to the camper Bill said, "There's going to be a picnic tomorrow, a little ways up the coast that I'd like to go to. You don't want to go, do you?"

Allen looked at him and said, "Picnic? On the coast? Well that just sounds dreadful. Of course I want to go, knucklehead. But I won't . . . I'll just go back and make friends with as many salmon as I can tomorrow."

Bill asked, "There's salmon out there?"

Allen snorted, "What do you care, Mr. Nature Walk?"

42

THE NEXT MORNING ALLEN WALKED WITH BILL over to meet Ellen at the offices. When they reached the shore Bill said, "Pick up a rock, buddy, and let's see how you do on a lake." They both found a suitable rock, and Bill said, "I'll go first, if you don't mind." He made a grunting noise and threw his rock out into Lake Superior—not far by Bill standards.

Allen saw where the rock splashed, then threw his rock back on the ground and said, "I ain't taking no sympathy wins. Either you throw it hard, or don't throw it all."

Before Bill could answer, they saw Ellen come out of the office and stop to talk with another ranger. Then Allen said, "You want my advice about what you and her should do today?"

Bill punched his arm and replied, "Get behind me Satan and lead me not into temptation."

Allen said, "Heck with that, I know a shortcut to temptation that you'll love."

They were both giggling as Ellen came up to them. When she saw Allen standing there with Bill, a concerned look came over her until Bill said, "Allen's gonna do a little fishing today. He doesn't really like picnics—right, buddy?"

"Hate 'em. Cold food, mosquitos, bugs, hot beer . . . no, sir. You'll not get me on no picnic."

Allen walked away singing, "Zippity-do-da, Zippity-day, my, oh my, what a beautiful day."

Ellen said, "Is he alright?"

"Nah, he's never alright . . . he's just Allen."

189

Allen rented another fishing pole and sat on the pier with two retired guys from Escanaba. When Allen asked where that was, they answered, "It's over on Lake Michigan, but the fishing sucks over there. So we come up here to catch something good."

Allen told them about "catching" the biggest salmon of the day in Washington and having it mounted especially for him. They were surprised there were salmon four feet long in little creeks like that. It seemed these two fellows were a little more interested in drinking beer than they were in fishing, and they drug Allen right down in the intoxicating hole with them. By early afternoon Allen had passed out in his chair and dropped his fishing pole into the lake.

The two guys left him blissfully unaware of their absence, and he continued snoring until a ranger came out on the pier to check on him since he hadn't moved in over an hour. The ranger shook his shoulder, waking him up, and asked, "Are you okay, sir?"

It took Allen a few seconds to realize where he was, but he answered, "Yes, ossifer, I'm fine. Just doing a little fishing."

The ranger said, "I'm not an officer . . . I just wanted to make sure you were okay."

"Doing great, sir. The fishing is really good here."

The ranger said, "So you're doing a little fishing, huh?"

"Yes, sir. Love it."

The ranger nodded, then looked all around him and asked Allen, "Where's your fishing pole, sir?"

Allen sat up quickly and looked around him. Realizing his pole was gone, he said, "Those two fellas must've taken my pole by mistake."

"Do you want me to try and find those two guys, sir?"

"No, that's okay officer. They'll be back, we're good friends. Thanks for checking on me."

When the ranger left, Allen picked up his empty beer bottles and threw them away. He skulked into the pier office to tell the guy he'd lost his rented fishing pole. The guy said, "Nah, you're okay. It was floating in the water, and somebody saw it and brought it in here. No worries."

Allen decided a short nap in the camper was a good idea at this point in time.

★★★

Late that afternoon when Bill returned and didn't see Allen anywhere, he went to the camper and found him in his underwear, lying on the bed and snoring very loudly. He intentionally made some loud noises, which eventually woke Allen from his slumber. Allen saw him and said, "Hey, old man, I was just catching a nap. Did you have fun?"

"Yeah, it was fun. What did you do all day?"

Allen ignored him and said, "I'm starving. You hungry?"

Bill really wasn't hungry at all, but he said, "Yeah, I could eat. Get dressed, and let's go get something."

They didn't want to go to the trouble of closing up the camper again, so they just walked back down to the camp headquarters to the little grill. As they were looking at the menu, trying to decide whether they wanted a hamburger, hot dog, or fish sandwich, the guy who rented Allen the fishing pole earlier walked in and recognized him. "Just how did you lose that pole anyway, sir?"

Allen looked at Bill and said, "Inside joke. We were telling stories earlier today."

The guy understood and nodded, saying, "Yep, have a good evening, fellas."

Bill got a hamburger and a Coors Light. Allen got two hot dogs and a Diet Pepsi. Once they sat down and were eating, Allen said, "Well, are you going to tell me what happened at the picnic?"

Bill put his hamburger down and replied, "Are you going to tell me what happened with the fishing pole?"

They looked at each other a few seconds, then each took another bite of their meals. No further discussion of these two subjects occurred during dinner. Later, they lit a campfire and sat around looking at the lake and the stars. Bill had another Coors Light, and Allen had another Diet Pepsi. Bill didn't ask why he was drinking a Diet Pepsi . . . he knew.

Allen said, "It sure is peaceful here, isn't it?"

"Yep."

"And beautiful, too."

"Uh huh."

Allen glanced over at his friend and continued, "A man would probably love living up here."

Bill said, "And just why do you think a man would want to live up here?"

"Oh, you know . . . beautiful lake, amazing scenery, peaceful, secluded, hazel eyes."

"Don't go there, Allen. Just don't go there."

"I wouldn't blame you, brother. She's a beauty. And I know you like her."

Bill took a deep breath, then said, "Allen, there is no way in the world she's going to leave Lake Superior. And there's no way in the world I'm leaving North Carolina. That's just the way it is. Let it go."

"But . . ."

"Let it go! Just let it go, please."

★★★

Just as the guys were thinking about going in the camper for the night, they noticed a car coming down the road. It stopped at their place, and Ellen got out of the car. Allen said, "I think it's time for me to turn in . . . I'll see you kids later."

Bill and Ellen walked down the road and were gone for almost two hours. When they returned, Ellen got in her car and drove away. Bill went in the camper, and Allen was still awake, waiting on him. Bill didn't volunteer any information, and Allen didn't ask anything. They turned the lights off and waited. Eventually Bill asked the question of the night, "If you weren't scared, what would you do?"

He wasn't really asking that question for Allen to answer . . . he was asking that question to himself.

43

Bill woke up the next morning and started packing up the camper. Allen asked, "Are we leaving today?"

Bill asked him, "Did you want to stay longer? Is there something you wanted to do?"

"I thought there was something you wanted to do. We can stay as long as you want to stay—until it snows. Then I'm outta here."

Bill never looked up at him and answered, "No, let's go."

They finished packing everything and drove out the exit gate, right by the offices of the park rangers, and Bill never even looked over. They found a roadside diner and stopped for breakfast, which was eaten in complete silence. When they were on the road towards Green Bay, Allen said matter-of-factly, "You know, I've always loved the Dallas Cowboys."

Bill finally smiled and replied, "Bite me."

The mood began to loosen up as they crossed into Wisconsin and saw the mileage signs for Green Bay. Allen said, "Remember that 'Ice Bowl' game between the Packers and the Cowboys?"

Bill only nodded, so Allen continued, "If Sonny Jurgensen would have only passed that ball to Bobby Richardson, we'd have beaten you cheese heads and history would have had a better ending."

Bill smiled again and said, "Maybe . . . but he didn't, did he? Certainly, God was on the side of the good guys that day."

They both smiled, and they each thought, "Okay, we're good again."

They made it into Green Bay too late to do anything except ride by Lambeau Field and stare. They found a hotel named the Packer Lodge and checked in for the night. Everything in the Packer Lodge was Green Bay's colors. All the walls had pictures of the Packer legends throughout the years, with the largest of the pictures being the largest of all the Packers-- Mr. Lombardi himself.

They had dinner in the Lambeau restaurant and then had drinks in the Super Bowl Bar. All the drinks were named after legendary Packer players: The Bart Starr Cosmopolitan, the Brett Favre Gin & Tonic, the Jim Taylor Screwdriver, and on and on it went. Bill ordered a Ray Nitschke Vodka drink, and Allen ordered an Aaron Rodgers Margarita.

The bedspreads on each queen sized bed had a big "G" in the center, and each pillow had a smaller "G" on them. As they were getting ready for bed, Allen said, "I'm not really a Cowboy's fan. I don't want someone sneaking in the room tonight and stabbing me in the back. I love the Packers!"

When the lights were turned off, Allen said, "Bill . . ."

But before he could continue, Bill interrupted him and explained, "It just wasn't meant to be, Allen. I wasn't gonna move, and she wasn't gonna move, and most importantly . . . she wasn't Eliza."

That wasn't what Allen was going to ask, but it ended up being the best answer he could've hoped for.

The next day they took the tour of Lambeau Field and stood out on the field itself, right where Coach Lombardi had once stormed the sidelines. As they were walking back toward the tunnel that ran out of the stadium, Bill said to his friend, "You know, Coach Lombardi was a lot like you."

"Thanks, buddy, I appreciate that. In what respect were you referring to?"

Bill explained, "A reporter once asked one of the black players on the team if Coach Lombardi was prejudiced, and the player answered, 'No, he treats us all the same . . . like dogs!'"

They went in the gift store, and Bill bought a Green Bay Packers hat, a Green Bay Packers tee-shirt, a Green Bay Packers sweatshirt, and a Green Bay Packers calendar with pictures of all the Packer greats. Allen bought a Diet Pepsi.

As they were walking back to the Ford F-150, Bill said, "You know what the difference is between my Green Bay ball cap and your Bear Bryant

Hounds Tooth hat?" Before Allen could answer he explained, "I can actually wear mine out in public."

Their final stop was at the large statue of Coach Lombardi that stood majestically in front of the stadium. There was a vendor there who would take a "professional" picture of you standing with the great man for only ten dollars. And he would put it in a frame for you for twenty dollars. Bill took the twenty dollar deal.

As they were walking away, Allen said, "Bear Bryant won more championships than Lombardi did—that's a fact."

Bill opened the door to the Ford F-150 and replied, "That was college, son. This is the pros."

They took the smaller roads south towards Milwaukee, because they wanted to ride as closely as possible to the shores of Lake Michigan. Along much of the way there were local farmers selling their harvest in roadside stands. The first one they stopped at, Bill said to Allen, "No cherries for you." So they bought a few grapes and a couple of apples, as well as some homemade ice cream. The rain had all cleared out, and it was gorgeous weather as they admired the few places where they could actually see the lake.

It was still early afternoon, but they saw a nice campground located on the lake shore and decided to stop for the evening. This campground didn't have any sort of grill, but the manager told them a food truck would come by in an hour or so for all the campers.

Sure enough a Mexican food truck pulled up at 6:00 pm with burritos, tacos, enchiladas and tostadas. The boys loved it, and each got a bag full to take back to the campsite and sit out by the lake. The sun was actually setting behind them, which kept the glare out of their eyes. But it still cast a glow on the shimmering water. As they finished their meal and were thinking of opening up a Coors Light from the cooler, Allen asked, "You know why it's named Lake Michigan, don't you?"

Bill merely looked over, and Allen began, "When Lewis and Clark first came to this place, they met an Indian tribe who gave them shelter and food for a few days before they continued on up to Alaska. Old Lewis was a bit of a prude, but Clark had a pinch of the devil in him—sort of like you. Anyway, old Clark met an Indian princess named, Mishi. She was a beauty and she and Clark had quite an affair going for those few days."

Allen looked over at Bill, who was apparently ignoring him, and continued, "The final morning, before Lewis and Clark had to leave, Mishi and Clark were in the final moments of . . . well, you know what they were doing. Anyway, just as the princess Mishi said she had to be going, old Clark said, 'No, Mishi—let's do it again. Please, Mishi, again.' Well, at that moment, old prudish Lewis was passing by the tent and overheard all that pleading."

Allen took a sip of Coors Light and continued, "Later, when they were packing up the horses, Lewis asked Clark what all that talk was in the tent— 'Mishi, again.' Well, old Clark was a quick thinker so he said, 'I was just coming up with a name fitting enough for this beautiful lake here—Mishi-again, which means beautiful lake, in Indian language.' Lewis was gullible and believed that story. And the name stuck—Mishi-again. Years later, the white men anglicized that original Indian name to the current name of Michigan. And that, my friend, is the true story of how this place was named."

Bill finally looked over at his friend and said, "Yep. I believe it."

44

AROUND MIDNIGHT, the burritos, and tacos, and enchiladas began extracting their revenge on the white man. Bill and Allen both made several trips to the bathroom during the night. By morning, they were drained—literally and figuratively. Allen said, "We've got to get us something to settle our stomachs—ain't no way we can be driving like this."

Bill agreed, so they packed up the camper, made another trip to the bathroom, and got directions to the closest little town. They found a pharmacy on Main St. and told the pharmacist what the problem was. He recommended a fast acting, terrible tasting medicine. They each drank twice the recommended daily usage right there in the store. Bill said, "Let's sit down somewhere until this stuff works."

They walked out and saw a bench across the street in a little park under some zelcova trees. They noticed an older man sitting on the bench next to them smoking a pipe, so they said hello to him. He took the pipe from his mouth and asked, "What happened to your truck?"

The boys didn't initially understand what he meant. Then he explained, "Your truck . . . how'd you get that big dent in the side? Looks like a bull hit it to me."

Allen said, "A bull? Why would you think that?"

"I've been around cattle all my life. I know what a crazy bull can do. And it looks like a horn pierced the side of it, too. Yep, that ain't from no car wreck."

Allen grinned and said, "You're almost right—it was a buffalo though, not a bull. You're pretty smart, sir."

The old man puffed on his pipe and replied, "Well I ought to be, you don't get to be ninety-six years old by being stupid."

Bill spoke up and said, "My name's Bill; this is Allen. Nice to meet you, sir."

FRIENDS

"Norwood Miles is the name, but you can call me Ralph."

That made absolutely no sense to the boys, but Ralph it was. Allen asked, "Is this your home, Ralph?"

"No, sir. I'd never live here with all these hicks if I didn't have to. My son is making me live with him now—ain't my choice."

Allen asked, "Where are you from then?"

"Up the road about fifteen miles . . . where people have some sense."

Bill said, "You look to be in pretty good health to be ninety-six. You must take good care of yourself."

"Don't do nothing special. It comes from a life of hard work and sensible living."

Allen couldn't help himself and asked, "You been smoking that pipe long?"

"No, only a couple of years. My son made me give up cigarettes. I've been smoking cigarettes since I was eight years old and they ain't never bothered me. You ain't got one on you, have you?"

"No, sir, I don't. But we both used to work for Reynolds Tobacco Company before we retired."

The old man said, "I was a Marlboro man myself, but I got nothing against Camels and Salems."

Bill asked, "How long have you been living with your son?"

"Too long! Three years now since my last wife died. I've had three of 'em. Not at the same time."

All three men sat there thinking about their wives and were all silent for a few minutes. Then Ralph said, "I've seen a lot in my ninety-six years."

He was waiting for an invitation, so Allen gave him one, "Tell us about it."

"I saw old Charles Lindbergh land his plane in a cow pasture the same year he flew across the Atlantic for the first time. That was quite a sight! He was probably the most famous man in the world at that time. Then I saw a President of the United States give a speech right here in this town—right over there." He pointed to the corner.

Bill asked him which President it was, and he thought for a few seconds and said, "I don't rightly remember his name—the fat one! Then I saw

Eddie Mathews and Hank Aaron both come through here in a parade back in '57 when they won it all."

He took another long puff from his pipe and said, "Yeah, boys, I seen a lot."

Then he sort of drifted off, maybe thinking of one his three wives, or the fat President, or maybe even Hank Aaron. But they let him dream and decided to walk around and see if the medicine was working yet.

They stopped at a place that sold ice cream and each boy bought a cup of vanilla to help settle their stomachs. They didn't know if it was the ice cream or the medicine, but after a while they both started feeling better. Walking back down the street, they noticed a man about their age helping old Ralph up from the bench. When the man tried to hold his arm, Ralph swatted it away—yep, he'd seen a lot. The boys felt well enough to get back in the Ford F-150 and continue towards Milwaukee, which they reached just before dark.

Milwaukee seemed to be a clean city, with not much traffic. They drove right into the middle of town and stopped at a big hotel that had valet parking. The attendant assured them the camper would be no problem, so they got their luggage out and checked into the big hotel. When they were at the front desk, Allen asked the clerk, "Marquette University is here, right?"

"Yes, sir. Just a few miles from here."

Bill punched him in the arm and asked, "Didn't you believe me?"

"No."

"Why not?"

"Because of all the times I've messed with you, I just figured you owed me one."

Their room was on the seventh floor, but it was facing downtown . . . not towards Lake Michigan. However, the restaurant and bar on the ninth floor had a panoramic view of downtown and the lake. They weren't a hundred percent sure of their stomachs yet, so they just ordered soup and a glass of wine.

As they sat gazing out across the lake and sipping their wine, they heard a commotion across the bar. Then they saw a pretty red-haired girl, with a short skirt on, quickly walking out of the room. The guy she was with just sat there, staring in the direction she went. He didn't say anything or make an attempt to follow her—he just sat there.

Allen said, "She caught him sneaking around behind her back."

"Nah," Bill added, "If she'd caught him, she wouldn't have come out here to dinner with him. He probably told her he didn't want to get serious right now."

"Trust me, old man," Allen said, "I know women. She caught him doing something he shouldn't have been doing. Pretty, sweet girl like that . . . he did something to her."

They alternated their glances between the lake and the abandoned guy. The lake never moved, but the guy eventually got up and started walking towards the door. He noticed Allen and Bill looking at him, shrugged his shoulders and said, "Call girls . . . watcha gonna do?"

45

THE NEXT MORNING, THE GUYS DROVE OUT to Marquette University, which was only seven or eight minutes from their hotel. It was an urban university and not at all scenic like the campuses of Wake Forest, Duke, or Appalachian State. Allen thought since Marquette's basketball team had colorful, innovative jerseys in the past, that the campus would be innovative and pleasant—it wasn't. As they were leaving Marquette University, they saw an advertisement for Harley-Davidson tours of the factory there. Allen said, "I didn't know Harley-Davidson was here . . . did you?"

"No. I never thought of it. Do you want to go check it out?"

"Yeah, let's see what it looks like. Have you ever been on a motorcycle, Bill?"

"Nope. You?"

"Only once, and it scared the dickens out of me. You remember old Joe Mac, don't you? He talked me into getting on the back of his Triumph one day down at the bowling alley on Stratford. I didn't know any better. So I hopped on that sucker, and he pulled out of the parking lot. It felt like we went from zero to a hundred miles an hour before we got to the stop light . . . and that was only about a hundred yards. When he stopped at the light, I jumped off the back of that thing and ran back to the bowling alley. Old Joe was laughing his tail off at me, but I didn't care. I was just happy to be alive and not to have peed in my pants."

Bill smiled at the story and thought to himself how many times he'd dreamed of buying a big bike and taking off across the country—wild and free—sort of like they were doing now. The Harley place was huge. Milwaukee was the corporate headquarters as well as the main assembly center. They pulled in the lot with the hundreds of other on-lookers and dreamers and started walking around. Soon, a well-built, Harley-mama saleswoman came up to them offering her assistance. "Can I help you guys find anything?"

Allen took one look at her studded vest, low cut leather top, tight-fitting jeans and said, "Yes, ma'am. I'm thinking about getting me a bike and taking off for California on an extended vacation. What do you recommend for a long and exciting journey like that?"

She asked if he had ridden before, Allen lied and assured her he was an experienced rider back in his younger days. They walked around the lot while she pointed out the various styles and accessories available. The only accessory they paid any attention to was the cleavage that was trying spill out of her leather top. She said, "By the way, my name's Lucy. Nice to meet you gentlemen."

Lucy showed them several styles and models, pointing to one in particular that she said would be a good road bike for a long trip to California. She asked Allen if he wanted to take it for a test drive, but since he didn't have a motorcycle license, or the slightest clue how to start it up or drive it, he said, "I've let my license expire, Lucy; but I would have loved to see how it feels out on the road."

Lucy said, "Hop on the back, and I'll take you for a spin so you can get a feel for how it rides."

"Oh, no . . . you don't have to do that, Lucy. It's okay."

"No problem at all, sir. I'll go get the key and be right back."

She went into the offices, and Bill said, "You'd better not get on that thing with her."

"Why not? It'll be fun."

"I'll tell you why not. If the ride itself doesn't give you a heart attack, surely sitting on the back of that thing holding on to her will."

"Oh, hush. Here she comes. Just sit over there and try not to act too old."

Lucy said, "Are you ready, sir?"

"Let's go, Lucy."

Lucy straddled the bike, then told Allen to climb on behind her and hold on to her waist for stability. Allen looked over at Bill and smiled at the thought of holding on to Lucy's waist. They eased out of the parking lot, and everything was simple and easy—just hold on to Lucy's waist—no problem at all with that. Then, after the stop light, Lucy wanted to show Allen the kind of power the bike had. She gunned it and surprised Allen, who was suddenly thrown backwards. In an involuntary reaction, his hands slipped up Lucy's waist to grab two rather accessible handholds—Lucy's breasts. Allen honestly did not realize he had a firm grip on Lucy's boobs. He was just holding on for dear life.

Once they came to a comfortable cruising speed, Lucy gently loosened the grip from Allen's hands and moved them back to her waist. Only then did he realize what he'd been holding on to. He wasn't embarrassed; he rather enjoyed it. He kept his hands in the proper place for the duration of the test drive and was smiling broadly when they pulled back into the lot. Bill walked up to them and asked, "How was it, old-timer?"

Allen was still beaming and answered, "Felt great!"

Allen told Lucy he'd really think about purchasing that bike. He also told her that he appreciated her time and loved the test ride. She smiled, and as she started to turn away, she winked at Allen and said, "I did too."

After the Harley experience, the boys stopped for lunch on the outskirts of Milwaukee and discussed their immediate plans. Bill said, "Anyplace in mind, Mr. Kite?"

"Are you still okay, grandpa?"

"I'm good. I'm in no hurry. Whatever you say is fine with me. How do you feel?"

Allen honestly said, "I'm having so much fun, I'm not sure I ever want to go home."

Bill smiled and nodded, then asked, "Okay . . . well, where to next?"

Allen took another sip of lukewarm coffee, then said, "It seems like two intelligent, college-educated, handsome men like us could figure out where to go."

"You would think so."

Then, a thought came to Allen. "Remember that old boy we met back in some saloon who said his wife was always going on 'educational vacations?' He mentioned that they went to Lincoln's home place once. Wasn't that somewhere in Illinois?"

Bill nodded and answered, "Yeah, Springfield. You want to go there?"

"Well, I don't care anything about going into Chicago since neither of us has a gun. So, yeah . . . let's go down there and see where old Abe came from. Let's see what gave him the inspiration to break away from England and form our own country and write the Declaration of Independence. What do you think?"

"I think you need to write your own version of history. You could call it 'World History, According to Allen.'"

They made it all the way around Chicago without getting shot and decided to stop and spend the night at a campground along the Illinois River. They got a carry-out pizza and a side salad. And they were proud of themselves for eating something green! After seeing all the swift moving rivers of the west, the Illinois River seemed to be in slow motion, or even stagnant. But they still enjoyed watching it move lazily along, listening to the crickets, birds, and squirrels as they kept a little fire going for company.

After trips to the bathroom, taking all their pills, and changing clothes, they crawled into their beds and turned off the light. Before long, Allen decided to ask the nightly question, "Bill, back up there at Lake Superior . . . "

Before he got another word out, Bill said, "Nature walk! Now shut up and go to sleep."

"Bill . . ."

"Goodnight, Mr. Kite."

"Goodnight, Mr. Goode. But you ain't no fun at all."

46

IT WAS A LITTLE CHILLY THE NEXT MORNING, and as Bill rose from his warm bed, he told Allen, "I'm a little stiff this morning. Hope I get to feeling better." He got dressed and said, "I'm going down to the bathroom. I'll be right back."

Allen had already been to the bathrooms, but finished what he was doing and quickly went outside next to the river. He picked up four or five rocks and threw them as hard as he could into the water. Then he went back to the camper and waited for Bill. When Bill arrived, he said, "Well, I guess you're probably too stiff and sore to be throwing a rock this morning, aren't you, old man?"

"Let's go. I'm not that old, yet."

They went to the banks of the river, and Bill said, "Let's throw one or two to loosen up with before we have the contest."

"No, no, no, no, no, old-timer. This is a one-time deal. We both slept in the same camper. We're both the same age, so everything is equal here. Just pick you a good one and take one throw out there over the river—one throw only."

Bill looked fiercely at Allen and said, "You sure are weird." He found a nice, dark rock and looked out over the lazy river. As Bill threw his rock, he simultaneously yelled, "Ouch! That hurt."

They both noticed Bill's rock landed just in front of a half-submerged branch in the water . . . not nearly up to Bill's usual standard. Allen was excited; he knew it was time for him to now claim the title of World's Best Rock Thrower. He had already picked out a shiny, light-colored rock which he planned to claim his crown with. He looked over at Bill, who was expressionless, but expecting the worst. Allen looked out past the half-submerged branch to where he was aiming. As he put his left foot forward in the throwing motion, his foot slipped a little. It seemed as if he almost tried to stop the throwing motion, but he couldn't. His arm came forward, half trying to balance himself from falling down, and half throwing the rock.

His light-colored rock landed considerably short of the half-submerged branch. Allen immediately said, "I slipped . . . let me get another rock."

"No, no, no, no, no . . . One throw, and one throw only."

Bill turned around and started walking back to the camper as Allen yelled out to him, "Bill!"

"Nature walk, buddy. Nature walk."

Springfield wasn't too far away, and they arrived at Lincoln's home before lunch. They stopped at Honest Abe's Grill and had a Lincoln Burger before touring the grounds. It was very educational. Not much fun, but it was educational. They went over to Oak Ridge Cemetery to visit the actual vault that held President Lincoln's remains. They stood there in reverence with dozens of other tourists, some of whom were crying. Allen leaned close to Bill and said in a low, solemn voice, "It's hard to believe I'm actually standing here at the grave of the man who dropped the first atomic bomb."

Bill said, "You ought to be ashamed of yourself. He was probably the greatest of all the Presidents."

"If he's so great, why is his picture on the five dollar bill and not on the hundred dollar bill? Answer me that, Mr. College Graduate."

Before Bill could formulate an answer, Allen continued, "It's not because he wasn't great; it's because somebody in Washington, who owned an electric company, figured they owed a debt to the man who invented electricity—President Benjamin Franklin. That's why old Ben's picture is on the hundred dollar bill, and not Abe's." Bill just silently shook his head . . . it wasn't worth the argument.

They went in the gift shop, but didn't buy anything except a Diet Pepsi. As they climbed back in the Ford F-150, Bill asked, "Well?"

Allen answered, "It was very educational."

They decided to get a hotel room in Springfield because they had no idea where they were going next. First, they gassed up the Ford F-150 and

206

bought a map of the United States to study over drinks later that evening. They saw a nice Italian restaurant, and decided to have some spaghetti for a change. It was excellent, as was the salad and wine. The owner came by their table to ask how the meal was and to make small talk. He asked where they were from and where they were going. They could answer the first question, but not the second one.

When they asked him for suggestions, he told them to make sure they visited the Lincoln home place—he said they'd love it. They asked him if there were any other interesting places nearby. He looked towards the ceiling for a moment, then volunteered, "Yes, there's a working farm near Macomb. And over at Hannibal, there's supposed to be the largest haystack in the world. You might want to check those out."

They thanked him for the information and decided to have a drink in the hotel bar while looking at the map for better ideas. Allen ordered an Iron Maiden, and Bill got a Coors Light as they spread the map out in front of them. Their eyes immediately went over to the California coast and Monterey. Bill said, "That sure was fun over there, wasn't it?"

Allen nodded, then added, "It would have been more fun if you'd have allowed us to visit those two old girls in Sausalito."

"You mean the two gay girls who were on their way to Texas?"

Allen said, "See how you are? Always taking a potentially good time and turning it into something depressing. I don't know how I put up with you."

Bill added, "I'll tell you how . . . because nobody else would go with you and put up with all your nonsense, that's how."

"Maybe . . . but I'd still like to have had an evening alone with that dark-headed one."

They pulled their attention back to the map and located Springfield, their present location. Then they found the town of Hannibal that the restaurant guy had mentioned. Allen said, "Hannibal's in Missouri. I didn't realize we were that close to Missouri."

Bill then remembered, "Oh, yeah, that was Mark Twain's home town."

"No, professor . . . Hannibal was where Harry Truman was from."

FRIENDS

Bill set his beer down and said, "I think Alzheimer's is winning. Harry Truman was from Independence, Missouri, knucklehead. Samuel Clemens was from Hannibal."

Allen stared at his friend, then asked, "Are you sure?"

Bill answered, "Of course I'm sure. Any high school kid knows that."

Allen nodded and said, "Okay, then it's settled. We're going to St. Louis and climb the archway to heaven, or whatever it was that Jimi Hendrix sang about."

Bill shook his head, thinking, "Is he just messing with me, or not?"

47

AFTER SPENDING THE NIGHT OUTSIDE OF ST. LOUIS, the boys went to the parking lot of the famous "Archway to the West." They stood in the lot staring up at this incredible structure. Bill asked, "How in the world did they build that?"

Allen answered, "It wasn't near as hard as when the Israelites built the pyramids. They didn't have any equipment at all. The only thing they used was slave labor from China."

Bill ignored him and said, "Are you ready to go to the top?"

"Top of what?"

"Top of the arch."

Incredulously, Allen asked, "And how are you going to get up there?"

"We ride the elevator, Mr. Riklefs. What century were you born in?"

Allen was still staring at the top of the arch and answered, "Same century as you, just a more handsome one."

"Well let's go get in line then."

Bill took a couple of steps, but Allen never moved. Bill asked, "You coming?"

"Are you sure that's safe?"

"Well they've been doing it for fifty years . . . I guess it's safe. What's wrong?"

Allen sort of mumbled, "I'm not too sure about this."

"What do you mean? Don't you want to go?"

Allen mumbled again, "My stomach's a little queasy. Why don't you go on up, and I'll wait here for you."

Bill was certain there were other factors besides a "queasy stomach" keeping his friend from riding the elevator, but he let it go and said, "Okay, grandpa . . . I'll be back shortly."

Bill rode to the top and enjoyed the amazing view of the river and the city. Allen bought a Diet Pepsi and sat on a bench watching a group of school kids throwing a Frisbee around. After Bill returned, they started walking back to the Ford F-150, and Allen said, "I'm glad we came here, that was fun."

"It was fun sitting on a bench, drinking a soda?" Bill asked.

"You have your fun and I'll have mine, and I'll be in Scotland afore ye."

The boys had earlier picked up a brochure at the hotel for tours of the Budweiser Brewery plant and decided they would do that before leaving St. Louis. Bill was driving out to the brewery, which was located right on the banks of the Mississippi River. Allen was Googling Budweiser, then looked over at Bill and said, "Did you know that Budweiser is not owned by Americans?"

"Yeah, I remember reading about that."

"That ain't right. I mean I don't drink Buds, but still . . . it ain't right."

They drove in silence for a few minutes more, then Allen said, "Bill, how many chucks could a woodchuck chuck, if a woodchuck could chuck wood?"

He was staring at Bill, waiting for a response. But Bill ignored him, so he answered, "Says here in Google that a woodchuck could chuck about seventy chucks of wood on a good day—more, if he had the wind behind his back."

Bill tried his best not to laugh, but he couldn't help himself.

The Budweiser tour was amazing! The warehouse was huge, and the brewery itself was state of the art. Still, it wasn't American owned, and Allen didn't like it. The tour ended in the sampling room, and everyone in the tour group could taste free Buds. They each sampled a few varieties—some they'd never heard of—then Bill asked Allen, "What's your favorite three?"

Allen set his empty glass down and said, "Coors, Coors Light, and free Coors."

★★★

After the brewery tour, the boys started driving north out of St. Louis. They chose north because they'd already been across the river to the west . . . north because they'd already been south into Mississippi . . . and, north because they didn't really want to go home yet to the east. Before it got too late, they came across a nice campground on the Mississippi River. They got a bucket of KFC and had their cooler full of Diet Pepsis and Coors Lights. They set up their camp chairs around a little fire they built and watched the mighty river flow by as they each ate dinner next to their best friend in the world.

As they started on their second, and last, Coors Light of the evening, Allen asked, "Where does all the water come from? It never stops; it never runs out; it just keeps on flowing."

He didn't expect an answer from Bill . . . and he didn't get one. They sat there in silence until the fire started to burn out, then Allen asked his friend, "What are you thinking about?"

"Eliza. What are you thinking about?"

"Barbara."

48

THEY STOPPED FOR BREAKFAST at an IHOP and brought the United States map in with them. They opened it up, and almost reflectively, both of their gazes were drawn to the California coast again. They looked at the map and sipped coffee, then Allen asked, "Are you one hundred percent certain that wasn't the house OJ lived in?"

Bill didn't answer, but he did smile. Then Allen said, "There's still one thing I don't understand, Bill."

Bill knew he shouldn't ask, but he did, "What?"

"Why wasn't there any snow on Snowhill Drive?"

Bill picked up another packet of sugar and threw it at Allen. Then they both started laughing.

They finally diverted their attention to the eastern half of the map and sat there staring at it. Just so they could look at it together, Allen came around the booth and sat next to Bill so they could both see the map right side up. As they were studying the possibilities, a middle-age man and his wife walked by and paused, looking at the two guys sitting next to each other in a booth at IHOP. Allen saw the two staring at them, then looked at Bill and said, "Would you like some more coffee, darling?"

The man and woman huffed away, and Bill elbowed him in the side and said, "Get back on your side, you pervert."

They didn't really see anything on the map that excited them as much as Monterey, Sausalito, the Grand Tetons, and Yellowstone had. But they finally decided it might be nice to visit the Rock and Roll Hall of Fame in Cleveland—not visit Cleveland—just the Rock and Roll Hall of Fame.

They drove northward up through Indiana, and just as they entered Ohio, they decided to stop at a KOA that had several restaurants nearby. It was getting cooler now, but they both had their Blackfoot Indian blankets. And Bill had his Green Bay Packer sweatshirt. There was a family diner near the entrance, and they had a nice vegetable plate dinner—which they were both proud of.

After they set up the camper, Bill went to the showers first, and Allen gathered a few small twigs and broken limbs for the fire they were going to build in the grill. When Allen had showered, they set up the chairs and started the little fire just as it started getting dark. They each had a Coors Light and sat there staring at the fire . . . and thinking. After an unusually long period of silence, Bill leaned forward to stir the fire. He looked over at Allen, who was wiping tears from his eyes.

"Are you okay?

At first, Allen didn't answer. Then he simply said, "Yeah, I'm fine."

By that tone, Bill knew he wasn't "fine." They sat a few more minutes in silence, which was totally out of character for Allen. Then Bill asked, "What's going on old-timer? You thinking about Barbara?"

Silence again. Then after a few minutes Allen answered, "Not really. Well, yeah, a little. Thinking more about me, and what I'm gonna do now. Thinking about this trip. Thinking about how I'd rather be in this camper than to go back home to that empty house and be alone. Thinking about how an old, lonely man is supposed to survive like that. And I don't have answers to any of those questions."

Bill let the moment settle a little, then said, "You know everything's going to be alright, don't you?"

Allen looked over at him and replied, "No, I don't know that, Bill. In fact, I have serious questions that it'll ever be alright."

Bill said, "Well, if you don't trust me, then trust in the Lord. He wouldn't lie to you."

Allen looked at him, but didn't say anything. So Bill continued, "The Lord promised us—He promised us, Allen—that even in our old age, that even when we turned gray, He would carry us. He said He made us, and He will carry us, and He will save us. That means you and me and everyone who believes in Him. You have to believe that, buddy. He wouldn't lie to us."

Allen nodded, then asked, "He said even when we turn gray?"

"In Isaiah, yes."

"And when we turned old? You're sure he said those things?"

Bill looked directly in Allen's eyes and answered, "Yes. It's the absolute truth."

Allen leaned back in his chair, and said, "Okay. Then I believe it; but I'm still not ready to go home."

Bill added, "Good, cause there's another place I thought of that I'd love to see before this old Ford gives out on us."

Allen looked over, and before he could ask where, Bill said, "Niagara Falls, if it doesn't upset your plans too much."

Allen smiled, took the last drink of his Coors Light and answered, "For you, Mr. Goode, I'd go to Kalamazoo and back."

There were times when it felt great to have a best friend who knew how to be a best friend.

49

SURPRISINGLY, CLEVELAND WAS VERY NICE. It had a bad reputation, but the boys enjoyed the city. They spent an entire day at the Rock and Roll Hall of Fame standing in awe of some of the exhibits, and wondering how some of the other exhibits got in the front door. They had lunch in one of the restaurants and watched a well-endowed, young lady play Led Zeppelin songs on an acoustic guitar.

They stopped the longest at the Elvis exhibit. Bill said, "Eliza and I went to see him in Greensboro a few months before he died. He was a little overweight, but man . . . he was still Elvis. There'll never be another like him."

Allen looked at him and replied, "You go see Hendrix without me; now I hear you went to see Elvis without me! What else have you done without me? I think my feelings are hurt."

"We were going to invite you, but I found out you had tickets to go see KC and the Sunshine Band that night. And I knew you'd never miss that."

They ended up in the gift shop where Bill bought a tee shirt with a picture of the Eagles' Desperado album cover on it. Allen bought a Linda Ronstadt tee shirt, which he immediately changed into on a trip to the restroom.

They decided to find a hotel for the night and start for Niagara Falls in the morning. They found a Kempton hotel downtown that had a nice view of Lake Erie. At the check-in counter, the young lady asked if they'd be needing one king-sized bed, or two queens. Allen looked at Bill and quickly answered, "Which would you prefer, darling?"

Bill elbowed him rather stiffly and told the young lady that two queen-sized beds would be appropriate. They went to the lounge, which had a fantastic view of the lake. Each of them had a Coors Light as they sat staring out the window. Allen finally spoke up, "Remember what that ranger, Ellen, told us? That Lake Superior was so big that it could hold all the Great Lakes combined, plus three additional Lake Erie's? Looking out there, it seems hard to believe, doesn't it?"

Upon hearing the mention of Ellen's name, Bill's mind drifted off. He didn't hear anything Allen said after that. Then it dawned on Allen why Bill's mind was apparently preoccupied. He hadn't meant to bring up the memory of Ellen again; but it was too late now. After a few quiet moments, Allen asked, "You thinking about her . . . the ranger, Ellen?"

Bill smiled and answered, "No . . . I was thinking about Eliza."

"What brought that on?"

Bill smiled again and said, "I never stop thinking about her, Allen."

They each had an Iron Maiden as they watched the sun set and the lights start twinkling, reflecting off Lake Erie . . . which could easily fit at least four times inside Lake Superior.

The next day they drove along the contours of Lake Erie, taking their time and stopping for snacks and viewing scenes of the lake when available. They came into the town of Dunkirk, New York late that afternoon and decided to stay in the tidy, little town. Dunkirk was located right on the lake, and there was a hotel that had great views up and down the coastline. It wasn't a Holiday Inn, but it was nice.

After they checked in, they decided to walk down the streets of Dunkirk and find a restaurant. As they were walking, Allen asked, "You know this place is named after the original Dunkirk, don't you?"

Bill answered, "And just how would you know that?"

"Because I went to college, son, and actually paid attention in class instead of looking at girl's legs like you did."

Bill said, "Right."

"Dunkirk," Allen continued, "was a great English port and industrial center . . . "

"Whoa," Bill interrupted, "Dunkirk is in France, Mr. Riklefs, not England."

Allen never missed a step and continued, "If you'd stop interrupting me, I could finish the story . . . Dunkirk was a great port and industrial center that was copied by the French on their coast. Dunkirk is the French name, and

Liverpool is the English name of the port they copied. Now can I continue?"

He didn't wait for Bill's response, "Dunkirk is where the famous Battle of Bull Run took place during World War II . . . where General Grant turned the tide of the war when he drove the Russians into the sea. Some of General Grant's officers later immigrated over here and named this place after the battlefield of that same name in France. That's why it's named, Dunkirk."

Bill said, "It amazes me you can remember all those facts of history so vividly and clearly."

Allen smiled and said, "You're right, Mr. Goode, I am truly amazing."

They found a nice restaurant that specialized in fish caught fresh from the lake. Their waiter was the son of the restaurant's owner. After the boys placed their orders, Allen asked him, "This town was named after the original Dunkirk, in France, wasn't it?"

He sort of held his breath as the waiter answered, "Yes, it was. It was settled in the early eighteen hundreds, and the name was taken from the home of where several immigrants came from in France."

When he left, Bill said, "That's not exactly the same story you told me earlier."

"He's a waiter! He ain't no college graduate like me. He ain't got no concept of history like I do."

"Well, Mr. Kite, I totally agree with that."

The fish was very good, but they wished they'd ordered Coors Lights or Diet Pepsis with their meal instead of the waiter's suggestion of a dry, bland-tasting white wine. Allen drank most of his water; then poured his white wine in the water glass when no one was looking. After dinner, they went to the bar area, which was built out over the lake and had glass windows on three sides. It must've been a slow night in Dunkirk, because there was only one other guy in the bar . . . and he was a man older than either Allen or Bill.

When they were halfway through their first Coors Light, the older man went to the bar and waved at the boys. Of course, Allen spoke and introduced himself, then invited the man over to their table. On closer inspection, he didn't really seem to be that much older than they were—maybe a couple of years. He seemed in good health and had a full head of white hair. He told the boys his name was David, and that he owned a retirement home here on the lake, near Dunkirk.

He said he actually lived in California, but was spending more and more time here, as he got older. Bill asked him what he did in California, and he said he was in the entertainment business. He asked them about their trip, where they were from, where they were going, and all the things you'd normally ask when meeting someone new. Bill and Allen had one more Coors Light, while David had two more mixed drinks and was becoming more and more animated describing life in Los Angeles.

He started telling them stories of being on Johnny Carson's boat with a bunch of naked women and partying with Dean Martin in Las Vegas—nobody could drink like Dean, he said. He told of accidentally making Frank Sinatra mad one night and being scared some goon was going to come to his room and make him "disappear." The boys sipped their Coors Lights and continued to listen to the old guy tell story after story about life in Hollywood. The boys let the old man talk all he wanted to, they didn't want to spoil his evening.

After one more mixed drink, David said he'd better call a cab and be going. They all shook hands, and he left the bar in a rather wobbly state. After he'd gone, the barman came to see if they wanted another round; but they were done. Allen said, "Is that older guy who just left a regular here? He was telling us some wild stories. Have you heard it all before?"

"Oh, that was David Steinberg, the comedian. He has a summer home here. He still lives in L.A."

Bill asked, "You mean the same David Steinberg that used to be on TV all the time?"

"Yeah, he's pretty famous."

Bill looked at Allen, who looked at the waiter; neither of them knew what to say. They walked out to the front of the hotel, but didn't see David Steinberg anywhere. Allen looked around the empty hotel lobby, then looked back at Bill and said, "Dang!"

50

THEY MADE IT TO NIAGARA FALLS the next day and were unprepared for the sight before them. Words escaped their descriptions as they stared in wonder at the waters from the Niagara River falling over the cliff. Since they didn't have their passports they couldn't go over to the Canadian side, which they'd heard was more scenic. But then again, it was difficult to understand how that could be. They did, however, take a boat ride on the lake that nearly went under the falls . . . close enough that everyone on board got thoroughly soaked—even with raincoats.

For hours they walked around the falls, mesmerized at the view from all angles. They hadn't planned on staying, but couldn't make themselves leave either. They checked into one of the many hotels located on the lake shore that had views of the falls. Even from inside the hotel lobby, they could still hear the roar from the water falling over the edge.

Over dinner that evening, Bill asked Allen which of the rivers they'd seen on their trip that had impressed him the most: The Mississippi, the Colorado, the Columbia, the Snake, the Yellowstone, or the Niagara?

Without hesitation, Allen answered, "None of those. My favorite was that little stream in Oregon where I caught the biggest salmon that was ever caught in the history of that stream. That, my old friend, is a memory better than all those rivers put together."

Bill just smiled and nodded. He didn't want to ruin his friend's memory by telling him the stream was actually in Washington, not Oregon. Nor did he want to remind him that he didn't actually "catch" that salmon—it jumped out of the water and landed at his feet. So, he just smiled and nodded—that's what friends do for each other.

The following morning, Bill stepped out of the shower and went back into the bedroom because he'd forgotten his toothbrush. As he walked unexpectedly into the room, he saw Allen on the phone again. Allen hung up quickly and started whistling an old Eagles' tune. Again, Bill didn't ask . . . he figured it was none of his business. If Allen wanted him to know, he'd tell him soon enough.

After breakfast, they once again pulled out the map of the United States and stared at it. This time their stares gravitated to different areas of the map. Allen's eyes went to the coast of Oregon, where he thought he had caught the biggest salmon ever. Bill's eyes went to shores of Lake Superior where he recalled a nature walk that would never be forgotten.

Only when the waitress came to check on them were their dreams interrupted. Their focus came back to the present, and the question was asked: "What's next?"

Bill looked at New York City and pointed to it. Allen curled his upper lip and said, "New York City? You cannot be serious."

"What's wrong with New York?"

Allen snarled, "Besides about ten million people, terrible traffic, pollution, and terrorists . . . I'm sure it's a fine place."

Bill said, "Terrorists? Where did that come from?"

"Well, you know there's probably some left over, hiding out, waiting for two rednecks from North Carolina to show up so they can bomb us."

Bill said, "Well, terrorists could be in North Carolina, too."

"Ain't no way! Sam Ervin and Jesse Helms made sure we're safe . . . that our American way of life is secure, and the Nazis, Communists, and ISISists are all locked up."

Bill asked, "Are you sure you're drinking regular coffee and not decaf?"

Allen smacked the table with his hand and exclaimed, "Death before decaf!"

They argued about New York City for a few minutes longer, then Allen said, "Okay, there's only one way to settle this. We'll have a contest. If you win, we go into that bastion of crowds, and Yankees, and terrorists; but if I win, we don't go. Fair enough?"

"Fair enough. But you know I'll out throw you, old man." Bill explained.

"That's not the contest I had in mind, Mr. Goode. We're going to have a fair, unbiased, scientific contest that will decide this question."

Bill looked at him and asked, "Scientific?"

"Yes, sir. Are you ready?"

"The anticipation is killing me."

They were at a table next to one of the windows, and it was sprinkling outside. Raindrops were on the windows streaking down, as raindrops do. Allen said, "Pick you a raindrop, and I'll pick me one, and we'll see which one gets to the bottom of the window first."

Bill said, "Raindrops? That's your scientific approach?"

Allen explained, "It's all natural, and you can't cheat me like you do at rock throwing."

"Okay, are you ready?"

Bill picked one, and Allen picked another one several inches away. They watched as the raindrops would slide down the window a few inches, then stop. Then slide down again, and stop. The boys were rooting for their raindrops and cheering for gravity to increase on their side of the window pane. The waiter and other customers in the restaurant all thought these two older guys had completely lost their minds.

Finally, Allen's raindrop made a mad dash for the bottom and beat Bill's raindrop by about two inches. They would not be going to New York City! As they left the restaurant, Allen put his arm around Bill's shoulder to console him, saying, "I'm sorry old timer, but truth, justice, and the American way of life has won—you can't argue with that."

Bill didn't really care one way or the other. He and Eliza had been to New York several times during their marriage. He probably didn't need to relive those memories anyway. However, the question remained, "Where to next?"

They sat in the truck and looked at the map again. They came to an agreement that neither of them really wanted to venture into any big cities. So, they quickly excluded Philadelphia, Boston, and, of course, New York. Bill was looking at the coast and saw a little town in Connecticut by the name of Mystic. He asked Allen, "Have you ever heard of this place, Mystic?"

"Nope, but it sounds mystical. Do you wanna go?"

"As long as you act your age, don't insult anyone, treat others with compassion and respect—yes, I'd like to go."

Allen looked over at Bill as though he was speaking Mandarin Chinese.

Then Bill added, "Or, just be yourself."

Allen exclaimed, "Now you're talking, grandpa. Here we go, over the rainbow, and whatever these Yankees can throw at us."

51

MYSTIC WAS A SMALL TOWN of over four thousand people with the largest maritime museum in the country. A huge, multi-masted sailing vessel sat in the harbor reminding everyone of life on the seas during the eighteenth century. The Mystic River emptied into the little bay where the museum was, with the small town gathered around the shoreline. It was also home to a very large aquarium—not as big as the one in Monterey—but nice.

The boys didn't realize it until they were there, but Mystic was also the setting for the Julia Roberts' film, Mystic Pizza. Allen remembered her from the movie and said, "I was always secretly in love with her. She had great legs."

Bill asked, "I thought you were secretly in love with Linda Ronstadt?"

"Oh, no! My love for Linda was no secret. Everybody knew that. Barbara knew if Linda came calling for me, I was gone! Julia was my secret. I didn't ever want Linda, or Barbara, to find out about Julia."

So, like all the other tourists, they had to stand in line and order a pizza from Mystic Pizza—just so they could say they did. It wasn't as good as Vincenzo's or Little Italy back home, but it was okay. They toured the museum and visited the aquarium where they housed two beluga whales in large tanks. They rested at a coffee shop in the center of town and sat outside to watch all the other tourists watching them.

Soon, a man and woman on vacation from Florida came and sat next to them. They introduced themselves as Tom and Earline Cope from Port St. Lucie. Allen told them all about the adventure they'd been on and the beautiful places they had visited as they travelled across the United States. The man asked them what adventures they experienced when they visited Florida. Allen sheepishly said, "We didn't actually have a chance to go to Florida."

The man asked, "But you were in Georgia, right?"

"Yeah, we did go into Georgia, but we were on a tight schedule."

Tom and Earline didn't actually believe that story and directed their conversations back to each other, instead of to Bill and Allen. After a minute or two, Earline blurted out, "Just what have you got against . . ."

Tom interrupted her and said, "We need to be going, dear . . . good day, gentlemen."

As they were leaving, they passed behind the boy's table and Earline said something that sounded like, "Sluts!" But neither Bill nor Allen could be sure. When they were gone, Allen said, "I'm glad we didn't go to Florida. Nothing but displaced Yankees down there anyway."

"Shut up and drink your coffee, grandpa."

All the hotel rooms in Mystic were booked for the night, so the boys had to find a campground outside of town. The closest open space near the bathrooms was next to a group of college students from their alma mater, Appalachian State University. There were thirteen of them, counting the professor and chaperone. The group was from the Geography Department, touring urban areas of the northeast. They came to Mystic from New York and were on their way to Boston.

Allen and Bill introduced themselves to the professor, who was foreign, and neither of the guys could understand him when he said his name. It sounded like he said, "Oly Gade," but they were completely unsure and didn't want to ask him more than twice to repeat himself.

The Geography students were all well-mannered, and the professor was very respectful . . . not at all like the other college teacher they met from Warren Wilson College. The boys tried to remember someone they knew from back in their days at Appalachian that the professor knew now. But they never could find a common acquaintance.

Allen and Bill watched as the college students set up their tents and started to prepare their dinner. They overheard one long-haired guy ask, "Peanut butter and jelly, or peanut butter and banana tonight?"

Bill and Allen came up with a plan. They walked back to the camp offices where the small grill sold burgers and pizza, and they bought eight large pizzas and brought them back to the college students. Needless to say, Allen and Bill were the heroes of the evening. All the students came by to thank them and shake their hands. Later that evening, as Bill and Allen were finishing the last of their second Coors Lights, they smelled the unmistakable aroma of cannabis coming from the college area tents.

Allen said, "Go over there and see if they'll give us a toke."

"Old man," Bill sighed, "Even if they would give us a toke, it'd probably kill us, or at the very least, give us a heart attack."

Allen said, "But just think of the headlines: 'Two old men killed by doobies on the Mystic River.' We'd be famous, son."

"Alright, Mr. Doobie, let's pee and go to bed."

When the lights were turned off and all was quiet, Allen asked his friend, "Bill, where will you be five years from now?"

There weren't many things Bill was afraid of . . . but he was afraid to answer that.

Surprisingly, the group of college students was gone when Allen and Bill got up in the morning. However, they found a plastic bag on top of the Ford F-150 that had two ASU tee shirts in it. The boys proudly changed into their shirts and starting packing up the camper. When everything was finished, Bill smoothed his tee shirt out and said, "That sure was nice of those kids."

He looked at Allen, who was adjusting his Bear Bryant hat on the dash board. Allen looked back at him and replied, "I'd have rather had a doobie."

★★★

The doobie brothers stopped at McDonald's to have breakfast and study the map again. Their decisions were getting easier and easier to make: They weren't going into New York City; they weren't going north into Boston or Canada; and they weren't going back west. Allen looked closely at the map and said, "I've got it, old timer . . . West Point. It's right there on the Hudson River and we're going that way anyhow."

Bill said, "Great idea! I've always wanted to visit that place."

Allen excitedly commented, "You know, I almost went to West Point."

"You what?"

"I almost went there. It was my second choice after Appalachian."

Bill stopped and said, "You know you have to be first in your class to go there, and have a SAT of about fourteen hundred, and have the recommendation from a Senator—you know all that, right?"

"Of course I know all that. That's why I said I ALMOST went there."

Driving the road that parallels the Hudson River was a treat. It was a gorgeous drive. The road itself was probably a few hundred feet above the river, which allowed them fantastic views of the river and surrounding countryside. At one point on the drive, the elevation changed, and they rose about four hundred feet above the river. They came to a pull-off, and stopped to stare up and down the Hudson River. Magnificent!

Allen went to the side of the cliff and picked up a rock, and said, "Let's go old man, if you think you still can."

Bill followed him and picked up his own rock. Bill threw his rock out towards the river, but the cliff was so steep and sheer, they never could see where the rock landed. Then Allen threw his rock, which also landed down the cliff out of their sight. Then Allen held both his arms up in the air and said, "Finally, the good guys win and justice prevails."

Bill said, "What makes you think you won?"

Allen happily replied, "What makes you think I didn't?"

52

WEST POINT MILITARY ACADEMY WAS IMPRESSIVE. Bill and Allen were overwhelmed with awe and pride at everything they saw. The only way to see the facility was through guided tours from the Visitor's Center in the village of Highland Falls. They took a tour with a group of seniors from Binghamton, New York and thoroughly enjoyed every minute of it. They went into the museum, adjacent to the Visitor's Center, and were overpowered and impressed at the various displays.

Allen's favorites at the museum were the pistols owned by George Washington and the sword owned by Napoleon when he surrendered at Waterloo. Bill was fascinated by the gold-plated pistol owned by Adolph Hitler. Outside the museum Allen and Bill watched as a group of cadets marched by in formation, and the boys saluted them as they passed by—an odd thing to do, since neither of them was ever in the army.

They each bought a US Army tee shirt in the gift shop, and Allen also bought a West Point hat to wear back in Winston-Salem in place of his Bear Bryant hound's tooth hat. Their visit was more than they had hoped it would be, and it made them proud to be Americans. As they were walking back to the Ford F-150, Allen said, "Yeah, I wish I'd have gone there now." Bill bumped him off the sidewalk and kept on walking.

They drove back over to the Hudson River expressway and saw a Holiday Inn, but decided to stay at the All-American Lodge instead—it seemed appropriate. After dinner, they each took a Coors Light with them back to the room. Each guy had several items of business to take care of on the computer. After attending to all that, they sat in front of the television, but not really watching anything. Then Allen asked the question they had both been avoiding, "It seems as though we're headed back to North Carolina . . . is that right?"

Bill drank the last of his Coors Light, threw the can in the trash, then looked at Allen and answered, "I guess we should. I probably need to take care of some stuff in person, just like you probably do as well."

Allen drank the last of his Coors Light and tried to throw his can in the trash—but missed. They both stared at the can lying on the floor until Bill finally said, "Are you going to pick that up?"

"Let the maid get it. Job security."

They both stared at the can on the floor . . . then at each other. Finally, Allen picked it up and dropped it in the trash. After showering and getting in bed, they turned the lights off and contemplated going home. They each needed to go home. They each had business to take care of back home. But, neither of them wanted to go back home.

Eventually, to take his mind off going home, Bill asked, "If you could ask one person, dead or alive, who has lived in the last hundred years, one question—who would that person be, and what would you ask?"

After a few moments of silence, Bill said, "You aren't going to sleep till you answer that question."

"I'm thinking. Give me a minute."

It actually took Allen several minutes to come up with his answer, but eventually he said, "I think I'd ask President Harry Truman what exactly was going through his mind when he had to make the decision to drop the first atomic bomb in history. He had to be overwhelmed with the enormity of it, and he had to know the consequences—not just of that bomb, but what it would mean for all humanity, forever and ever."

They both silently thought of that truth and also thought about President Truman. Then Allen asked, "And what's your question?"

Bill said, "I'd ask Eliza, 'Why?'"

They both wanted to go to sleep. They both needed to go to sleep. But, neither of them could actually go to sleep. When it became evident, due to the tossing and turning, that they were both still awake, Allen spoke, "You know, back there at the Grand Canyon when I walked down the trail that day . . . I almost kept walking."

Bill asked, "What do you mean?"

"I almost kept walking all the way to the bottom . . . and I was just going to stay there."

Bill knew what he meant: Allen missed Barbara so much that he thought about joining her in heaven. He then told Allen, "Well, I'm glad you turned around and came back."

"I had no choice."

Bill asked, "What do you mean?"

"If I stayed down there, what would you have done? You'd have been lost. You wouldn't know where to go and what to see. You'd probably have to call someone from the church to come get you . . . I just couldn't put you through all that."

"Yes," Bill commented, "you are very considerate. Thank you."

Just when it seemed that sleep would finally overcome them, Allen suddenly asked again, "Bill, since we're almost home now, what . . ."

Bill interrupted and answered the question he knew was coming, "Nature walk—now go to sleep!"

After a fitful night of tossing and turning, they sat in the restaurant the next morning sipping coffee while looking outside the window at a steady rainfall. Bill eventually broke the solitude and said, "I guess if we drove straight through we could probably be home by tonight."

Allen set his cup down and said, "By God, I'm still in charge of this here adventure. I'll decide when we go home, and when we don't go home. In fact, there's something else I want to see before I have to boot you out of my car."

Bill answered, "It's not a car, and it's not yours. But, when the Ford place sees that big dent in the side—it might be yours."

"I ain't worried about no dent. I got the full coverage . . . one hundred percent. Ain't no buffalo dent gonna scare me."

Bill smiled and said, "Well that's good to know. Now, are you going to tell me what this other place is that you want to visit?"

"Washington, DC, my friend. I've always wanted to go to the top of the Washington Monument, but I've never done it."

Bill added, "I've been up there. It's a good view, but I sort of thought you didn't like heights . . . after the arch in St. Louis."

"I ain't scared of no arch. And I ain't scared of no Washington Monument either. How big is the elevator?"

"It's not big at all, but it's big enough."

"Well," Allen answered, "you can't scare me off. That's where we're going. Now go on to the bathroom and do your business while I fire up the car and get it ready."

53

THEY TOOK THE INTERSTATE DOWN THROUGH NEW YORK, Pennsylvania, and into Maryland, and only had to stop once for gas and a visit the bathroom. It rained the entire day, making driving a chore. Both guys were tired and decided to stop early at a Holiday Inn. Yes, a Holiday Inn. It was a nice one, too . . . a big restaurant and a nice bar. The young lady behind the counter asked, "Will you be needing . . ."

But before she could finish that question, Bill broke in and said, "No. We'll be needing two beds."

She smiled politely and finished, "I knew that, sir. I was asking if you needed a wakeup call in the morning."

"Oh, I'm sorry, miss. No, we'll be okay."

She handed them the room cards, and Allen said, "C'mon dear, you can hop in the shower first."

After dinner they went to the bar to sit, relax, and do nothing. They accomplished all those in addition to having a couple of Coors Lights. Allen asked, "Of all the places we've been on this trip, pick one that you'd like to go to again."

Without hesitation, Bill answered, "Monterey. I loved that place. What about you?"

"You know, I want to say Yellowstone. But when I think of Monterey, it's just hard to imagine anything better. But if I could find the address of those two old girls in Sausalito, that's where I'd pick."

Bill smiled and said, "Yeah, you keep on dreaming, grandpa."

Allen replied, "Well, I could have me a nature walk too, and I wouldn't tell you a doggone thing about it, either."

"Trust me, old man, I wouldn't WANT to know about it."

They reminisced about other places from their epic journey: San Antonio, Truth or Consequences, the Grand Canyon, Sedona, Los Angeles and OJ's house, San Francisco, Eureka, Seattle, Spokane, the Grand Tetons, the Little Big Horn, and of course, Lake Superior.

After the stories ended and the lies subsided, it was quiet for a moment or two and Allen said, "I'd trade every bit of it for one more day with Barbara."

Bill didn't want to speak, but he felt exactly the same way as he thought of Eliza.

After a fantastic Holiday Inn breakfast, the boys headed for Washington, DC. They didn't get far. The traffic going into the city was worse than anything Los Angeles could imagine. Traffic was at a complete standstill, and they weren't even close to the city yet. After nearly thirty minutes of slowly inching forward, Allen asked, "Is the top of the Washington Monument worth this crap?"

Bill, who was driving, answered, "No. But I'll keep driving if you want to go. Totally up to you."

Allen pointed to an exit sign up ahead and said, "Get off this constipated freeway, and let's go home."

They felt fortunate when some people kindly let them move over to the exit lane. Or, maybe, they saw the big dent in the truck door and the camper and figured these two guys just don't care. After taking the exit, Bill could tell Allen was a little disappointed. He said, "We can go back, old-timer, we've got all day."

"No, it's not worth it. I'm not even sure I would've taken that elevator to the top anyway. I just sort of admire old George and wanted to pay homage to him."

Bill was surprised and asked, "Really?"

"Yeah, he was a great man . . . really great. He'd have been a heck of a football coach."

Bill said, "Well let's go to Mount Vernon then. That's where he lived; he didn't live in that monument."

Allen perked up and asked, "Is it close to here?"

Bill had no idea, but he answered, "Yeah, it's real close. We're going!" That's what friends do for each other.

Allen immediately perked up and set the GPS for Mount Vernon, then started whistling an old Beatles' tune about a meter maid named Rita.

It actually wasn't that far away. They took the exit for Mount Vernon and stopped at a local deli to get something to eat first. Bill had a roast beef sandwich and chips, and Allen ordered a pastrami on rye, but was too excited to eat much of it. The rain had stopped, and the sun was trying to break through when they arrived. Mount Vernon itself was located on the banks of the Potomac River. George's father had picked out a gorgeous spot for his home, and had built the house himself in 1734.

After the death of his half-brother in 1752, George Washington returned to take over residence of Mount Vernon. Over the years, he expanded it to twenty-one rooms. He died in the master bedroom chamber on Dec. 14, 1799.

The boys toured the grounds and saw the distillery that Washington had opened. The distillery had produced over eleven thousand gallons of rye whiskey and other products the year Washington died. They also saw the fishery he had operated, which caught over one million shad and herring from the river in one year. They toured the lush gardens, the slave memorial, and the tombs, where George and Martha Washington are buried.

After a Diet Pepsi in the gift shop, they went inside the mansion and toured the house, which has been restored to what it looked like in 1799. They ended up in the bedroom where President Washington had died on that December night. When the tour group had all assembled, an older lady began the story of the President's death:

"On Thursday, December 12, 1799, George Washington was out on horseback supervising the farming activities from late morning until three in the afternoon. The weather shifted from light snow to hail, and then to rain. When he returned home, it was suggested that he change out of his wet riding clothes before dinner. But, Washington, known for his punctuality, chose to remain in his damp attire rather than be late.

The following morning he had a sore throat and, despite feeling unwell, he went out to inspect an area of trees to be felled. Throughout the day, it was noticed by everyone that his voice became increasingly more hoarse. That evening he was unable to read aloud the newspaper, as was his custom.

After retiring for the night, he woke up about two in the morning with a terrible pain, and Martha sent for help. His friends came and found him having difficulty breathing. He was bled, which was the custom of the day. Then the family doctor arrived and extracted another half-pint of blood. Washington favored this treatment over the objections of his wife. He was given a mixture of molasses, butter, and vinegar to soothe his throat, but instead of helping him, he started to convulse and nearly suffocated.

As the morning progressed, he did not feel any better. Another doctor was sent for, and he arrived, and bled Washington again. At eleven, a third physician arrived and administered an enema and bled him for the fourth time. It was later reported that a total of thirty-two ounces of blood was extracted during this last bleeding alone.

Despite the care of three physicians, his condition worsened, and at four thirty in the afternoon he asked his wife to bring him his will to look over. At five that afternoon he sat up in bed, got dressed, and walked to his chair. He returned to bed within thirty minutes. He thanked all the doctors for their care, and at ten o'clock that night he requested to be 'decently buried' but 'not in less than three days.'

Between ten and eleven that night, December, 14, 1799, George Washington passed away. According to his wishes, he was not buried for three days. During this time his body lay in a mahogany casket in the large room downstairs. The greatest American of them all was dead at sixty-seven years old."

When she finished, no one moved or spoke. Not until she walked out of the room did anyone stir. Allen and Bill were spellbound by the story and found it hard to continue the tour. They made their way outside and found a bench to sit on and reflect on the life of George Washington—the greatest of them all.

They followed most of the crowd into the gift store and walked the aisles. Bill bought a Mount Vernon coffee cup. Allen bought a coffee cup as well along with a framed picture of General Washington crossing the Delaware River.

On their way back to the Ford F-150, Bill said, "He made over eleven thousand gallons of whiskey here, and caught over a million fish in one year. Can you believe that?"

Allen stopped and looked back at Mount Vernon one last time, and replied, "I bet he never caught a five foot salmon."

Bill laughed and said, "Boy, you ain't no good at all . . . none!"

54

THEY GOT BACK ON THE ROAD and found I-81 south. They drove until they reached the outskirts of Roanoke, Virginia and they stopped at a Residence Inn, because it looked to be the biggest and nicest of those around the interchange. They both knew this would be their last night on the road, and they wanted a nice place. Again, a man of middle-eastern descent was behind the counter and greeted them with, "Good evening, gentlemen. How can I help you?" He spoke better English than they did—well, at least better than Allen did.

The boys were happy and sad; tired, yet exhilarated; lonesome, and yet happy to be with their best friend in the world. After a steak dinner, they retired to the bar and listened to a man playing old show tunes on the piano. After sitting down, Allen said, "Let's get drunk."

"So, you want to get sick and puke all over yourself, then wake up in the morning with a terrible headache? Yeah, that sounds like a lot of fun!"

Allen said, "I don't know why I brought you on this epic adventure. You're nothing but a party pooper."

Bill grinned and replied, "Well, better to be a party pooper than a cherry pooper."

They both laughed at that memory, then ordered Iron Maidens in honor of their last night on the road. Next it was time for a retrospective reminiscence of the trip. It wasn't planned; it just happened when Allen asked, "Who was the prettiest girl you saw on the whole trip?"

Bill answered, "You know who it was . . . Farrah." The young lady from Spokane had certainly left a lasting impression on the boys.

Bill's turn, "Best hotel we stayed at?"

"Duh! Seven Garter's Inn."

Bill corrected him, "Seven Gable's Inn?"

"You know what I mean. Best campground?"

"The one in California where we watched the sun set into the ocean. Not counting the naked guy."

Allen asked, "Not the one at Lake Superior?"

Bill said, firmly, "California. Weirdest moment of the trip?"

Allen remembered the old guy with the shotgun and said, "That old weirdo in Washington who tried to shoot us."

They argued for a few minutes if that was actually in Washington or Idaho, but they couldn't remember. Then Allen asked, "Most fun day, not counting the nature walk, of course."

Bill had to think about that. Finally he said, "They were all fun. But I really liked the day we went to the hot springs, and then I beat you throwing a rock over the Rio Grande River. Or it could've been the day you slipped in the mud and fell into the Columbia River. Or, maybe even the day the buffalo chased you down."

Allen stopped him and said, "Okay, okay, I get your drift."

They finished another Iron Maiden and retold a few more stories. Then when there was a lull in the moment, Allen asked, "You know what would've made it all better?"

"Yeah. I know, buddy. I know."

They went to their room, without getting drunk, and started getting ready for bed. Bill had just stepped out of the shower when he heard Allen's voice coming from the bedroom. He clearly heard him say, "Tomorrow." But he couldn't make out anything else. Coming out of the bathroom he asked, "Who were you talking to?"

"Ain't none of your nosy business who I was talking to."

"I heard you say something about 'tomorrow,' and since I'll still be with you tomorrow, I figure it is my business."

Allen answered, "Well, if you must know, Mr. Nosy pants, I was arranging my evening with a young lady who has been missing me and can't wait for my return."

Bill said, "If you're going to lie about it, just forget it then."

"Alright." Allen said, "It's forgotten."

After the lights were out, for the last time, Allen asked, "What advice would you give yourself four years ago?"

Bill thought about that, and finally said, "Enjoy the heck out of life, and quit worrying so much."

"Good answer." Allen said. Then a few moments later he added, "I would tell myself to spend every single, solitary minute I could with Barbara."

And with that, the boys went to sleep on the road for the last time on their epic adventure.

They left in the morning, going down I-81 until they merged with I-77 south into North Carolina. Soon after crossing the state line, they took U.S. 421 south towards Winston-Salem. It was a familiar road they'd each been on plenty of times, but they saw it differently now. They saw everything differently now.

Elkin, Jonesville, East Bend, Yadkinville . . . the closer they got to home, the more trepidation crept in. As they were near Yadkinville, Allen yelled out, "Stop! Turn this monster around and let's do it all over again!"

If Bill had thought for one millisecond that Allen was serious, he would have indeed turned that monster around. But they both knew they had things to take care of, things they had to do, things they didn't want to do, and empty houses they didn't want to see.

55

As THEY APPROACHED WINSTON-SALEM and Forsyth County, Allen once again screamed out, "Stop this monster right now! I want my revenge!"

Bill knew the Yadkin River was just ahead. He pulled over to the side, just in front of the bridge. They each got out, and Allen said, "Find you a good one, old man. You're gonna need it. This is double or nothing for the whole trip."

Bill was looking for a suitable throwing rock and asked, "How could it be double or nothing when I've beaten you about a hundred times in a row?"

"Quit being so picky, and just get your rock and let's go."

They each held their rock and looked out over the Yadkin with it's muddy looking waters. Then Allen turned to Bill and quite seriously said, "If you LET me win this last time, I'll never forgive you. If you beat me fair and square, then fine. But if I think you've let me win, just so my feelings won't get hurt, I'll never speak to you again."

Bill looked back into his eyes and solemnly said, "Promise?"

"Bill! I ain't joking. You'd better give it your best shot. You understand me?"

"Don't worry, old man. I'd never LET you beat me in a hundred years. You know that."

Allen nodded and said, "Well, you could've at least considered it!"

"Not going to happen, Mr. Kite."

Allen reared back and threw his rock as hard as he could. It almost felt like his shoulder came out of the socket he threw so hard. His rock landed just over a large boulder in the river channel. He smiled, knowing he could never throw that well again.

Bill took his rock and bounced it in his hand a few times, looking out at the boulder where Allen's rock had landed. Allen said, "Throw it, old-timer, don't just bounce it in your hand all day."

Bill took his rock and reared back to throw; and as he did, he let the rock fall back into his palm, instead of out toward his fingertips, where he could grip it better. He knew a palm throw would take off at least twenty or twenty-five percent from his distance. Then he threw as hard as he could, which elicited a small grunt from him. Allen could tell from Bill's arm motion and the grunt that he had indeed thrown his rock as hard as he could.

They both watched Bill's rock fly out over the water and splash down . . . just short of the boulder in the river channel. When Allen was certain that what he'd just seen wasn't an optical illusion, he started jumping up and down and high-fiving Bill. Several cars passing over the bridge slowed down to gaze at the sight of an old man jumping in the air and high-fiving another old man. It was quite a sight!

Allen was smiling so broadly and so hard that he developed a cramp in his jaw. But it was worth it. Double or nothing had finally paid off, and he was the rock throwing champion of the world. He went over to the driver's side and said, "Winner drives across the finish line! Hop in, buddy."

Bill got in the passenger's side and buckled his seat belt for their drive across the Yadkin . . . and eventually home. He loved the pure joy he saw on his friend's face as they crossed into the Winston-Salem city limits.

That's what best friends do for each other.

After taking the exit for Silas Creek Parkway, they made their way to Bill's neighborhood so Allen could drop him off at his house. When Allen pulled up to 215 S. Cross Street, they noticed a car in the driveway with South Carolina license plates. Bill asked, "Who in the world is in my driveway?"

Allen turned the motor off, and they both noticed a woman sitting in the porch swing, gently rocking back and forth. Bill again asked, "Who is that?"

Allen looked over at him and said, "Why don't you go up there and see who it is."

Bill put his glasses on and looked again at the woman in the porch swing, then he looked back at Allen and asked, "Is that Eliza? Is that who you've been calling?"

Allen looked at the lady and said, "It's been twelve years since I've seen her, but it sure looks like Eliza."

Bill looked back at the porch again and asked, "What's she doing here?"

"Why don't you get your lazy butt out of my Ford F-150 and go up there and ask her."

So he did. He walked up on the porch and sat next to the woman he'd dreamed of for twelve long years. Allen cranked up the Ford and slowly drove down the street. He'd bring all Bill's stuff back to him later. Now, his friend was a little too busy with life . . . and love.

Allen turned the corner on the way to his lonely house, but he had the unmistakable feeling that only comes by being a friend to your best friend.

To the world you may be one person; but to one person you may be the world.

I hate my editor.

She's cruel and mean.

She doesn't understand me.

She makes me re-write stuff.

She hates commas, unless I don't use one, then she loves commas.

"But, Gary . . . didn't your sister edit this book?"

Oh . . . I love my editor. She's smart and pretty and good and she's my sister

Elizabeth Anne Hope

If you have one good friend in your lifetime, you're lucky. If you have two good friends, you're more than lucky. If you have five . . . you're blessed.

CPSIA information can be obtained
at www.ICGtesting.com
Printed in the USA
BVHW07s0737250518

517269BV00009B/161/P